You Will Grow Into Them

Malcolm Devlin

Influx Press
London

Published by Influx Press
Mainyard Studios
58B Alexandra Road
Enfield, EN3 7EH
www.influxpress.com / @InfluxPress

First published by Unsung Stories, London, UK, 2016.
Published by Influx Press, London, UK, 2024.
© Malcolm Devlin, 2016, 2024

The right of Malcolm Devlin to be identified as the author of this work has been asserted in accordance with section 77 of the Copyright, Designs and Patents Act 1988.

This book is in copyright. Subject to statutory exception and to provisions of relevant collective licensing agreements, no reproduction of any part may take place without the written permission of Influx Press.

This edition 2024
Printed and bound in the UK by TJ Books
Paperback ISBN: 9781914391156
Ebook ISBN: 9781914391163

Cover design: Luke Bird
Text design: Vince Haig

This book is sold subject to the condition that it shall not, by way of trade or otherwise, be lent, re-sold, hired out, or otherwise circulated without the publisher's prior consent in any form of binding or cover other than that in which it is published and without a similar condition including this condition being imposed on the subsequent purchaser.

For Mum and Dad

Contents

Introduction by Angela Slatter	1
Passion Play	7
Two Brothers	34
Breadcrumbs	55
Her First Harvest	81
We All Need Somewhere to Hide	102
Dogsbody	130
Songs Like They Used to Play	174
The Last Meal He Ate Before She Killed Him	232
The Bridge	259
The End of Hope Street	266
Acknowledgements	311

Perilously Elegant

Angela Slatter

Someone far wiser than me once said that if you've got any sense at all, you're not here to read the Introduction; that you've already gone straight for the stories; that, maybe, you'll come back to read it later. Wherever you sit on that spectrum, I'll try to make it worth your while.

So, what's a short story? If we're considering a short story collection, it makes sense (to me at least) to think about the nature of the building blocks that make it up. Murakami calls them 'soft shadows I have set out in the world, faint footprints I have left'. Gaiman says it's 'the ultimate close-up magic trick'. For Bacigalupi they're 'hand grenades of ideas', and for King a short story is 'a kiss in the dark from a stranger'.

All of these things are true. But perhaps all of these things are also lies. Or maybe half-truths because every writer is different. Every writer takes the form and makes it their own. We like to think – always before we've started to write one – that the short story will bend to our will. They never do. That they'll be quick to create because they're short. They seldom are.

So, what's a short story?

Well, a story that's short.

A facetious answer, yes. Still, I could just leave it at that, but it would be too flippant and it would definitely be dismissive, and the short story doesn't deserve that because it requires so much skill to get right. It takes, as David Henry Thoreau said, 'a long while to make it short'. It should have a single affect, according to Poe. For me, it should deal with crisis, choice and consequence. It should feel rich and complex but may well look achingly, annoyingly simple. That's the giveaway that it wasn't simple at all. It most certainly was not easy. And it's ending should leave you with the sense that somewhere, somehow, the story's still going on – you're just not there anymore. That's a lot of shoulds.

Perhaps one thing is certain: the short story is a matter of angles. Its shape will depend on the perspective you've chosen, the slender facet of life and time you're examining, trying to show to the reader; calling to them with 'Look here!' before you open Pandora's Box. The tale will live and die by all the things you bring to it, and all the things you leave out but imply.

Brevity is key. The trick is to flense out all the details except the ones that hit hardest at the readers' cultural capital, shared experiences – the half-remembered things that live in the back brain – and set off a series of depth charges, a lighting of beacons, triggering recognitions – or something we think we recognise. It's a sleight of hand to make readers think what you want them to think. It's the impressionist painting that makes sense only from a particular distance or corner of the gallery, but when you're done feels like an expressionist did a break-and-enter in your heart; the emotional devastation seemingly much larger than expected.

For the relatively brief time they take to read, the very best ones will haunt you for the rest of your life. Sending a cloud over a summer's day sun. Waking you in the cold hours with an echo. Making you smile though you don't quite know why. Sometimes, they feel like memories you're not sure you own.

Malcolm Devlin's stories are like that.

In 2017, way back in the Light Ages – i.e. before the Plague Years – I read the original edition of this collection to do a cover quote. It went something like this: '*You Will Grow Into Them* is filled with stories that are deceptively simple and perilously elegant. They look like fairy tales, but aren't really – in fact, they are best described as a precise alchemy of language. Perfectly pitched, thoroughly disquieting. *You Will Grow Into Them* is like a light in the darkness that might lead you home or lure you from the path. Malcolm Devlin is one of our finest voices.'

It's comfort to all of us to know that after a re-reading I haven't changed my opinion.

Which brings me to another consideration: It's all well and good to produce a tale or two, but after having written a bunch of short stories? A bouquet of them? A murder of them? A herd? Well, then you've got to construct a collection, and when I say 'contruct', I mean yes, 'construct'. That's not an easy task either. As with cooking, you don't just dump in whatever you've got in the pantry, unmeasured, untasted and untried. You weigh the stories, their subjects, their emotions, their impacts, their joys and their violence. How they rest on the mind, how they ring or sing in the ear. You assess the themes and the characters, what they might say to each other as well as the reader. You keep some back for a rainy day.

A more apt comparison might be designing a rollercoaster ride: planning and plotting the highs and the lows, the sideways swerves, the crawling ascents, the stomach-dropping descents, the bone-jarring stops. What effect will this story have when it's sat next to this one? Or this one? Will they be good neighbours or start a turf war over the placement of the privet hedge? Putting together a short story collection is an art in itself, and it's a pleasure to feel that *You Will Grow Into Them* achieved the right balance.

Devlin's stories engage with and transform ancient and modern tales, giving them an unexpected spin. The crosshatch man in 'Passion Play' stalks religion and the terrain of urban legend; leavened with warnings against leaving the path it shifts you from the real to irreal. 'Two Brothers' explores a loss of identity, the ghosts of old selves and toxic masculinity via a lens that's almost Hansel and Gretelish. In 'Breadcrumbs' the world is morphed into something fantastical and possibly even more threatening, a place where threads of Rapunzel and Sleeping Beauty meet, and folk become both less and more themselves – which sometimes requires feathers and fur and thorns. There are cursed inheritances and inherited curses, stolen skins, unexpected escapes and unemployed werewolves, mushroom cotillions and war hero widows, and a street where no hope can be found.

A debut collection's a showcase of what the writer can do when they're starting out. It's a very tangible and public mud map of where the mind and pen have roamed in the early days, putting a pin in things and saying 'Here. Now. This is what I've been thinking about for better or worse.' It says 'This is where I started. This is where I've got to so far.' It can be as simple as surprised cry from the writer: 'OMG, look at all these stories I've got lying around!' And it should definitely say 'Keep watching. Whether anyone likes it or not, I'll keep going.'

Later stories and collections will track the writer's journey across a career. You can see new obsessions and interests, interrogations and angers. You can see the writer's skills and gifts mature. You can see them changing their mind about things, getting more mellow or (hopefully) raging and rebelling still and refusing to go gentle into a good night or a bad one. With luck, a writer will be sensible enough not to want to rewrite their early stories – what's the point of a do-over? It won't show how you've gotten better, how you've grown as a writer – because that's one of the great joys in reading an author's work across time, seeing how they've changed. Writers shouldn't remain the same or they get stagnant, stunted, boring. They lose their bravery and their daring – a writer who never fails is a writer who never tries something new. But a debut collection says 'Wake up. I start here.'

One of the things I love about Devlin's stories is that they reach – you can see them putting forth tendrils and creeping outwards to new ideas and forms and expression. They're all united by themes of transformation, isolation, and the inexorable wheel of the universe that keeps moving whether we want it to or not. Change isn't death (although a lack of it is), it's simply adaptation. One thing becomes another and the sooner you accept it the easier the transition will be. Stories (and writers) should always be growing, changing things, casting the shadows of what will come next: newer stories, bigger stories, stranger stories whose reach exceeds their grasp – perilously elegant stories you will grow into.

Dr Angela Slatter
Brisbane, AUSTRALIA
2 May 2024

Angela "A.G." Slatter is the award-winning author of, among other things, the gothic fantasy novels *All the Murmuring Bones*, *The Path of Thorns*, and *The Briar Book of the Dead* (Titan Books), twelve short story collections, three novellas, and a Hellboy Universe collaboration with Mike Mignola, *Castle Full of Blackbirds*.

angelaslatter.com

Passion Play

Cathy McCullough's mother fastens the chain around my neck and turns me by the shoulders. It's a small cross, unadorned, and she puts her hand on my chest, covering it with her palm. Her hand feels warm, like it's been balled in a fist too long.

'She would have wanted you to have it,' she says.

She looks at me and I wonder what she sees. I don't look like Cathy, not really. Her hair is redder and mine is browner. I'm a little taller, and the idea that we might look similar didn't cross my mind until her old class photo started doing the rounds. We all look the same in those photos, but on any other day you'd never confuse us if you knew us both.

Mrs McCullough is looking at me like she doesn't know Cathy anymore. She's looking at me as if she'd take anything of her she can get.

'She loved you so very much,' she says, and then she holds me tight.

Maybe she didn't know Cathy at all.

I stand stiff and awkward in her arms. I can see my own mum is watching us from the other side of the street. She's watching Mrs McCullough holding me with the same expression Cathy would use if she knew I was being given her crucifix.

Mum marches forward to intervene. Gentle but firm, she pries Cathy's mother off me. She does this with one of those carefully pitched smiles she sometimes uses when she wants to change the subject.

'They want to start now,' she says. She reaches out and touches me on the shoulder. She's already given me the '*you-don't-have-to-do-this*' speech. She'd do it again if Cathy's mum wasn't there.

Instead, she says: 'Be careful.' And she leads Mrs McCullough away. Cathy's mother folds up against her chest and I don't hear her crying until she reaches the other side of the street.

Because Cathy McCullough has gone missing. Because Cathy McCullough went to find the cross-hatch man.

I didn't volunteer to be Cathy.

The police came to the school, and from the classroom I could see them parked out in the playground, two of them: a man and a woman, who was so tall and beautiful even Mr Newland, the headmaster, stared at her wide-eyed like he was a kid.

I saw him nodding at something she was explaining and then he looked round and met my eyes like he knew I was watching. I panicked, thinking he'd caught me not paying attention in class and I turned to stare at the French verbs Mrs Parkhirst was writing on the board. When I risked a glance back out of the window all three of them were looking at me.

They called me out of class a little while after. In Mr Newland's office, they told me they wanted to stage a reconstruction for the press. They wanted to retrace Cathy's last known movements, which they'd patched together from witness reports.

They needed someone to be Cathy, they told me. It wasn't a question. They just sat there waiting for me to volunteer.

The policewoman's name was Veronica.

'You should think about this carefully,' she said. 'There'll be a lot of people, a lot of photographers. Everyone will be looking at you and it's a very serious, very difficult thing.'

The other policeman was a little plump and a little bald. He cleared his throat.

'Did you know Cathy McCullough?' he said.

Mr Newland answered for me. 'They're best friends.'

I didn't correct him. It used to be true.

Cathy and I were born within three weeks of each other and we were always in each other's houses as we grew up.

But I've never wanted to be her before. We were too close for that; I knew the worst of her as well as the best. Even when I would hide in my room because I got mad with Mum, I might have looked out the window to see if I could see a light on at Cathy's, but I don't think I ever seriously thought she was having a better time.

At least my parents are still together. True, Dad can be a complete jerk at times, always on Mum's side because he never has an opinion of his own, but Cathy's dad had run away when she was twelve. Some of the kids in school said her mum was a drunk and it was true that Mrs McCullough was usually pink cheeked and friendly when I went to visit, and yes, she'd sometimes go to bed at strange hours. But maybe she just got tired. People get tired. If I lived with Cathy, I'd get tired too.

There were a lot of witnesses to see Cathy McCullough leave St William's Secondary School on Tuesday, February 16th.

Cathy had been one of seventeen students who had attended Miss Buckley's after-school drama club. At five o'clock in the evening, she waved at Leela Allen and Katie Cox, whom she would normally have taken the bus with. Instead of going home, she walked in the opposite direction, sidling through the bicycle bars where Barracks Road becomes Barracks Lane.

The day she went missing, Cathy was wearing a pink Superdry raincoat over her school uniform, with a grey Zara messenger bag slung over her shoulder. I know this because that's what I'm wearing now. I keep catching the reflection of myself in the windows of the admin block and in the corner of my eye. The reflected me isn't me at all.

Veronica is briefing the photographers and journalists. There aren't as many of them as I was expecting. Most are from the local news but I don't recognise any of them. I count only four or five photographers when I was expecting a crowd like you see on TV when a famous singer gets out of a limo. They're watching me, waiting for me to turn around, because it's the back of me they want people to recognise. The me that's walking away from them.

Mum has got rid of Mrs McCullough so she can spend more time looking worried about me. She brushes a stray hair behind my ear.

'I thought you said they wanted to start now,' I say.

'You don't have to do this,' she says.

I smile at her and I wish that Simon was there instead.

Mum kisses me on the forehead and there's a click-flash from the direction of the photographers that makes stick-man shadows appear at our feet and then vanish again. I duck away from Mum, embarrassed, but the photographers aren't looking at us; one of them is looking at his camera and frowning. He's only taking a test shot, I tell myself, but I wonder what he sees.

'Be careful,' Mum says again.

Veronica claps her hands and the crowd's attention snaps into focus. She comes up to me and asks if I'm ready. She barely waits for a response before she's talking to the crowd like it's a congregation. She talks to them about Cathy. She calls her a 'little girl' which doesn't seem the right way to describe someone who's fifteen.

Mum touches me gently on the arm, then drifts away to join the waiting mob. I try to find Mrs McCullough among the faces but she's gone; maybe someone has taken her home. I hope someone has taken her home.

Veronica smiles.

'When you're ready,' she says.

I turn towards the bicycle bars and, behind me, the cameras begin to pop and click and flash. They see Cathy, they do not see me at all.

At around five minutes past five, Sam Clooney and his brother David were having a kick-about on the top pitch when they saw the girl in the pink coat walking confidently through the trees along Barracks Lane. Sam, the younger of the two brothers, was nervous about getting home before it got 'properly dark'. He remembered thinking the girl must be very brave walking through the trees alone where there weren't any street lights.

'She wasn't walking like it was getting dark,' he said.

The crowd thins out as the path steers away from the playing fields and into the trees. There are two policemen clearing the way ahead of me; hi-vis jackets and walkie-talkies. Veronica introduced us but I've forgotten their names. I name them PC Left and PC Right, and it sounds so childish, I find myself smiling stupidly, which isn't like Cathy at all. PC Left is young, black and sort-of handsome. He wears small square glasses and tells me he has a sister my age. PC Right is a bit older and has a thin ginger beard. He won't meet my eyes.

The others are somewhere behind me: the crowd and the photographers and the people from the newspapers. I can hear them rather than see them. I know my mum is with them, and Veronica too. Veronica said I should lead everyone, but I feel like I'm being herded.

There is movement in the trees just ahead and I almost stop in surprise. PC Left ducks off the path to investigate but reappears only moments later empty-handed. I see him talking to PC Right, then murmuring something into his walkie-talkie. It's probably nothing, just a bird or maybe a squirrel. I risk a glance to the side as I walk past and see only trees and the tangled knots of blackberry brambles. Cathy said she's seen deer on this path before but I don't know if I believe her; it sounds too much like a fairy tale to be true.

The noise wasn't Simon, then. Of course it wouldn't be Simon. When a fifteen-year old girl goes missing, her family gets prayers and her boyfriend gets questioned. Even if he has an alibi – and Simon does have an alibi – he's still not welcome. I've already heard people asking why he wasn't there for her. They don't know Simon at all; he's the least threatening person you'd ever meet. If he and Cathy ran into trouble together, she'd be the one rescuing him. Sometimes I think that's why she liked him so much, she liked the idea of having someone to save.

Simon moved to town a few years back; his dad was an engineer who was trying to settle the family after a few military contracts sent them around the world. I don't think Simon's ever been in any place as long as he's been here and sometimes you can see it makes him twitch just thinking about it. He's skinny and lanky and kind of cute in a don't-look-at-me sort of way. Restless, Cathy would describe him.

They've been together for around six months, maybe a bit longer. Well, they had been. I'd hang out with them sometimes. I'd go round to Cathy's and find them together. It was sweet. They never let me feel like I was intruding and after a while it felt like he'd always been there.

Cathy never really told Simon about the cross-hatch man. I mentioned it to him once and he just nodded, like he hadn't been told enough to be interested.

'So,' he said, 'it's like some local ghost story?'

'Something like that,' I said. At first I liked the idea Cathy was keeping it a secret from him, but the more I thought about it, the more disappointed I felt that she hadn't told him. As if it was something she had grown out of; something she thought wasn't important enough to share.

At nearly twenty minutes past five, driving instructor Charlie Brandt was sitting in the passenger seat of his Vauxhall Corsa waiting for his student, Tiffany Lowry, to pull out into the traffic on Hollow Way. They had been practising parallel parking in the lay-by opposite the ironmonger's shop and Tiffany had already lost a hubcap to the kerb.

Charlie reassured her no one had seen anything and it was none of their business if they had. Tiffany was teetering on the edge of tears, and when the girl in the pink coat walked past – the trailing zipper of her shoulder bag striking the car window like a gunshot – she tipped over completely.

From Barracks Lane, Hollow Way is a one-sided street. To the left, a large hedge hides a driving range which nobody uses. On the other side, there's a row of run-down shops which I can't imagine anyone going into. After those, there's a stretch of terraced houses which continue all the way up to The Corner House pub.

I'm surprised to see a small crowd has formed on the pavement opposite. I didn't think Cathy was that popular but maybe people think they'll have a chance to be on TV. They might be lucky: there's an outside broadcast van from the local TV station parked next to The China Girl takeaway. Its giant satellite dish makes it look overbalanced and a bit ridiculous. It looks like a giant wok bolted to the top of the van.

As I pass, there's a burst of static from inside the van. I glance backwards and see a guy in a baseball cap disappearing inside. The sound makes me look closer at the crowd, half-convinced I might see someone amongst them who shouldn't be there. There is no one of course, just a line of everyday figures looking like they're waiting for a bus.

Cathy and I first saw the cross-hatch man on a school trip to the church of St Michael on the Mount, nearly a year ago. St Michael's is a small church teetering on the edge of the Lye Valley Nature Reserve which cuts around behind it. As a school trip, it covered a number of bases: it was a church (Religious Studies) and it dated back to the eleventh century (History). It was also close to the school, so it was cheap to get to (Mathematics).

It was raining when we arrived but Sister Assumptia, who was usually angry and always short, had no patience for complaints. She corralled us inside and instructed us to appreciate the place. The threat that we would go to Hell if we didn't was left unsaid.

Cathy glowered at her. She wasn't the sort to bend to school-sanctioned dogma without a fight. While I was happy to get swept along by the surface rhythm of the various rituals of my family and peer group – school service on Wednesday, church on Sunday, the tick-tock-tick of my mother's monthly rosary – Cathy was looking for something more tangible. The cross she wore had been given to her by her grandmother and her attachment to it was more sentimental than spiritual.

'Besides which,' she told me, 'it's a disguise.'

We fanned out, wandering around the nave and transept and trying to find something interesting to justify our being there. The trouble being that there wasn't really anything there at all. The big rose window above the door might have looked pretty with the sun behind it, but it was dormant on such a dull day. The rest of the church was dull too, built in an age where function was valued above form, it was all square corners and stark empty walls.

Mostly empty. The exceptions were the Stations of the Cross, a series of small paintings spaced neatly around the transept. Cathy described them as a Catholic comic where Jesus takes fourteen panels to die. We'd seen them before of course; we went over them at school every Lent, and more than once we'd been made to draw versions of them ourselves.

Some sets included an additional fifteenth panel, which showed Jesus' resurrection from the dead, but the versions in St Michael's were strictly traditional, and ended with Jesus' body being laid in the tomb. Individually framed, they took place against dark, gloomy backgrounds so the scenes looked as though they'd been spotlit with a torch.

The images were the usual. Jesus is condemned to death, Jesus receives his cross, meets Mary, is crucified and so on. I lost interest pretty quick – there's only so many times you can look at pictures of people suffering before everything starts to feel numb – but Cathy was looking from one to the next with a genuine interest which surprised me.

She beckoned me over.

'Who do you think that is?' she said.

She pointed to the picture. It was the third in the series where Jesus falls for the first time.

'That's Jesus,' I said. 'You might have heard of him. Son of God, that sort of thing.'

'No, idiot, this one.'

She jabbed her finger at the painting and I looked closer. Not Jesus, but something just behind him. A figure was there, barely distinguishable from the shadows. I shrugged.

'A Roman solider, maybe?' I said.

Impatient, she shook her head.

'He's in this one too, look.'

She led me to the next painting, Jesus meets his mother. I didn't spot him at first, but Cathy was right; the same figure, partially swallowed by the darker shades which surrounded it.

Cathy was skipping ahead.

'And here.'

Simon of Cyrene helped Jesus carry the cross. In the background, the dark figure watched, broad-shouldered and tall. Now I could see him, he unbalanced the scene; he did not look painted on, he looked like he had been scored into the surface of the canvas. A series of criss-crossed lines which appeared to catch the light only if you looked at it from the right angle.

Cathy reached out and touched the glass like she was capable of feeling the texture beneath it.

The cross-hatch man was in every picture in the church. Cathy looked at me and there was something in her eyes I had never seen before.

Outside number six, Dene Road, Janet Armstrong was trying to turn into her driveway when a schoolgirl in a pink coat walked briskly in front of her garage door and out in front of her car. It looked as though she had just cut through the garden.

Janet worked as a dentist's assistant in Kidlington and had endured a stressful day. She slammed on the brakes and leaned heavily on the horn. The girl ignored her. She cut directly through the flower bed and continued on her way.

It was six o'clock.

Dene Road is a long trawl of grey-rendered semis, mostly ex-councils, most blind to Cathy on the evening she came this way. Today, the windows are lit and I glance through them as I pass. I see the flicker of televisions and games consoles; people stretched out on sofas, oblivious to the outside world.

Cathy would find all this attention funny: all these foolish people wasting their time for her benefit. A part of me imagines it's all a prank; I picture her sitting waiting for us, waiting so she can jump out and yell, 'Surprise!'

The rest of me is not that naive.

And besides, if she really was there waiting for me, she'd ask me about what happened with Simon. This time, I'm not sure how I'd answer her.

Sister Assumptia liked her Catholic art. She showed us slides of gory paintings depicting saints being bloodily dismembered. John the Baptist's head on a plate, Saint Sebastian pierced with arrows, Saint Bartholomew being skinned alive and Jesus himself of course, blood pouring down his face, a fey hand indicating the gaping wound in his side.

'No one is too young to learn how the saints suffered on our behalf,' Sister Assumptia said.

'I bet you she's a convert,' Cathy said to me one day. 'Mum says the converts are always the worst.'

I hadn't considered that was possible. I was still at an age where the idea that nuns came into existence fully formed was a realistic possibility. Even my Aunt Susan, my father's youngest sister, was a little alien to me. She was in the Benedictine order and I had never seen more of her than the circle of her face, looking out from those black and white robes.

We kept thinking about the cross-hatch man. When we were instructed to draw pictures at school, we'd find a place to fit him somewhere in the background. It was a tiny act of rebellion, a silly but satisfying secret which set us off in hysterics when one of our pictures was put on display with its shadowy stowaway. We weren't always subtle about it, and eventually Sister Assumptia noticed and took us to task. She wagged her finger and threatened us with severe heavenly retribution, because Mr Newland had warned her our crime wasn't serious enough to warrant a detention.

We would imagine stories which explained who the cross-hatch man was.

In one, he was a rich landowner who had so much influence and power he commissioned the sequence of paintings and had a portrait of himself added to each of them, so people would think he had witnessed the crucifixion in person. When some terrible, unspeakable crimes of his past were uncovered, his presence was systematically scratched out by an angry mob.

In another version, we imagined the cross-hatch man as an alien intelligence sent to earth to observe crucial historical events. He also witnessed the rise of Hitler, the assassination of John F. Kennedy, and the fall of the Roman Empire.

If all else failed, we'd grasp at wider explanations. It was a demon, a ghost, an angel. It was God Himself, come to earth to witness the death of his son.

'The Devil cuts him out,' I said, 'jealous of His image. He claws and claws at the beauty of the paintings until He's gone.'

Cathy shook her head.

'He's there for the people who watched,' she said. 'The people who saw everything, and who didn't do a thing.'

Outside number 15, Coverley Road, Ahsan Omer had just arrived back from bringing his two sons home from five-a-side football practice. The boys were arguing about a contentious penalty when they stopped mid-sentence. When Mr Omer asked what had happened, they told him how the girl in the pink coat had smiled at them as she walked past.

They stared after her retreating figure, but when Mr Omer looked down the road he saw no one at all.

There are a bunch of girls on the corner of Coverley Road and I recognise the one at the front with one of those plunging feelings in the gut, the sort you get when you've just fallen off something and you don't know how you're going to land.

Siobhan Breton, big and ginger, with a face that looks like it's been struck with a shovel. She's there with about five of her friends, clustered together and looking as mean as only a bunch of fifteen-year-old girls can.

Cathy used to be more of a target than I was. Cathy had weaknesses: the fact her dad wasn't there any more, the fact her mum always was. They were licences to pass judgement, and Siobhan and her friends would judge anyone if they had the right ammunition. If some of the insults and attacks they threw at Cathy were based on nothing more than hearsay, others were aimed more accurately than even they knew.

PC Left and PC Right are some way ahead of me, the crowd behind have become so quiet, I wonder if they're still there at all. Today I am not supposed to be alone, but the distance of everyone seems to have grown around me as Siobhan and her friends lurk like lions waiting in an arena. I look down at my feet as I pass.

They don't say anything but they stare at me with a bitter resentment which superheats the air around them. I don't breathe until I can feel their eyes on my back.

I'll suffer repercussions for this later in the week. But then I wonder if they're seeing me or Cathy and I wonder what they'd do if they just saw me on my own. But today, they do nothing, they just watch me, watch Cathy come forward down the road and I can feel the malice boiling up in them.

It's a real, physical thing. And I've felt it before.

The last time we went to the church of St Michael on the Mount was a mistake. It had been Cathy's idea.

She was over at my place where we were pretending to help each other with homework, but we were distracting each other instead with music, magazines and video clips on the internet.

Cathy was in no mood to go home. Her father had turned up on their doorstep and, rather than her mum sending him away again like Cathy demanded, she'd invited him back inside. Cathy refused to talk to him, she refused to be in the same room as him, but her mum was caught in some make-believe that he'd never been away.

'There's something about those pictures which isn't right to me,' Cathy said.

'No shit,' I said.

She punched me on the arm.

'I don't mean the obvious, I mean we're missing something else. I want to look at them more closely.'

I was only half listening. I was distracted by something I had found online. Some animal video. Something fluffy doing something cute.

'Seriously though,' I said, 'who cares?'

'I do. I want to know just how weird it is. I want to know who painted them, maybe see if they've done this before. They might have something written on the back, some label we could look up.'

We had both been back to the church to make sure we hadn't fooled ourselves and on the second visit, the priest had been there, dressed in civvies and going about his business. He had asked us if he could help us with anything but we were too embarrassed to even raise the question – it just sounded too silly to share with others. We had left no wiser, and I'd assumed we were both content the figure in the paintings was nothing more than an engine for our imaginations with no real relevance to the outside world.

'So what?' I said. 'You going to talk to the priest? Ask him to take a look?'

'He's already said no,' Cathy said. 'I went back yesterday. Said they were antiques. They look like prints to me.'

I shut down the laptop and looked up at her, surprised by how hurt I was she had gone back without me.

'Well,' I said. 'Shame.'

I realised then, how Cathy's interest outweighed my own. I was content with the day-to-day trappings of the catechism, fed to me by my mother, the school or the priest at St William's when we went on Sundays. Cathy was interested in none of that. For her, the cross-hatch man was the more worthy mystery, one which she might even be able to solve. I don't think I understood why, but it was something she thought she might be capable of believing in.

'I'm not going back there on my own,' she said. 'You're staying over at mine this evening. I've already asked your mum.'

She didn't really tell me much else until later. She told me to bring a coat, a torch and shoes I could run in. I don't think anyone would believe me if I told them I didn't imagine what she had in mind.

Millie Bernard was cleaning the window of her semi-detached house on Glebeland Road when the girl in the pink coat walked through her lounge. Mrs Bernard was waiting for University Challenge to begin on BBC Two. Her husband, Derek, was watching the end of Pointless with a notepad on his lap so he could play along.

The girl walked in the main door and out through the kitchen. She did not look up or pay any attention to them as she passed.

Derek did not see her in the house at all. He only saw her on the television, walking through the set of the quiz show; head down, headphones in.

It was nearly half-past seven.

At the end of Glebeland Road, I can make out the square shape of the church of St Michael on the Mount marked against the fading blue of the sky. My route will not take me inside, but passing by is enough to make my stomach knot.

At the moment, it feels as though PC Left and PC Right are very far away. I want to glance back to confirm I'm not as alone as I feel. Instead, I slow until I can almost hear the voices of the people following me. They don't sound like voices, they sound discordant and broken. A whisper of white noise like a radio caught between stations.

The church looked different at night. The yellow Cotswold stone walls which glowed warm in the sunlight were grey and stark under the moon, everything looked sharper, more severe.

I let Cathy lead me around the side. I was still wide-eyed she had suggested something so extreme and that I had not refused her. The path was narrow, the fence on one side bordering the edge of the nature reserve. Behind it, I could see nothing but a mass of shadows dropping away into the valley; the dark grasping plants clustered at the foot of the fence, reaching through the wire.

Behind the church was a small yard, mostly empty except for a few wheelie bins. Cathy unhooked her bag and searched through it.

'Hold the torch steady,' she said.

The last time she had been in the church, she had seen the priest fastening the door at the back with a simple hook-and-eye latch. The door was locked from the inside but it did not quite close snug to the frame.

She found a penknife from her bag and unfolded the blade.

'Dad gave it me,' she said, seeing my reaction. 'Or at least, I say "gave"...'

She slipped the blade through the gap between the door and its frame, and snicked the hook free from its latch.

'We're breaking into a church,' I whispered, understanding only as I spoke how useless a statement it was. My mind was stitching together words with weighty meanings: desecration, blasphemy, sacrilege, but at that moment I could pronounce none of them.

Cathy put a finger to her lips and scowled. She pushed the door open.

The church was not completely dark. The full moon hung behind the rose window, and the way the moonlight refracted through the glass made it look as though a net of grey shapes had been thrown across the transept.

I stood there like an idiot, and Cathy pushed past. She worked swiftly, picking one of the pictures at random. She took it in both hands and unhooked it, setting it down on the pew beside her. She looked up at me.

'Torch,' she said.

'Sorry.'

I joined her, aiming the light at the picture so she could work. The frame was held in place with a number of metal shards, wedged into the woodwork. Using her penknife, Cathy started folding them back one-by-one to release the backing board.

I looked around, conscious I had my back to an awful lot of the room. There were only two ways in that I could see: the door we had used and the heavy looking main door which was bolted shut.

The church's emptiness made it feel larger. There was something unnerving about the silence of the rows of unoccupied pews, each with their neat little stacks of hymn books and embroidered hassocks.

'Hold this,' Cathy said. She was struggling to remove the backing board without warping the frame. I planted my hand on it, then snatched it away again.

'Ow!'

'Mind those metal bits,' Cathy said. 'They're sharp. And don't bleed on it. Some idiot might mistake it for a miracle.'

She pried the backing off and teased the painting out carefully. It looked like it was painted on a thin wooden board. Perhaps they were antique after all.

'Light,' she said.

I redirected the torch as she turned it over. Without the glass, and under the scrutiny of the torchlight, the painting seemed starker and crueller. Simon of Cyrene bearing the weight of the cross looked as if he was in agony, while the face of Jesus watched him with a heartbreaking and impotent compassion.

And behind them was the cross-hatch man. Cathy hesitated a moment before tracing her finger over the paint. She frowned.

'It's all the same,' she said. 'It's painted on like this. It's not scratched in at all. Here, try.'

There was a texture to the surface of the painting, but it was subtle and my fingers were too cold to make any judgement.

'Jesus, you freak,' Cathy said, 'I told you not to bleed on the thing.'

She batted my hand away and I realised then I had left a smear of blood across the face of the cross-hatch man. I stuttered an apology but Cathy ignored me. She spat on her fingers to clean the painting, then turned it over to check the back.

'Nothing here,' she said. 'No name, no sticker or anything.'

She swore and started putting the painting back in the frame. Around us, the dark gathered. I heard something outside: an owl, I think. An owl and the teasing of the wind in the nearby trees. I have honestly never wanted to be somewhere else as much in my life.

'We should go,' I said. 'We should go now.'

'Not yet.' Cathy shook her head. She was looking around the church. I couldn't understand why she wasn't in more of a hurry; her patience was infuriating.

She hung the picture back where she found it, taking a step back to inspect it and make sure it was straight.

'I want to check another one,' she said. 'One of them must have the artist's name on it.'

'You've got to be kidding me,' I said but she was already pulling another picture off the wall. She shot me an irritable look.

'Keep the torch steady.'

I felt it before I saw anything. A fringe of absolute darkness glowering at the edge of my vision. A weight of something gathering behind me, a faint smell like woodsmoke and meat on the turn.

Cathy didn't seem to have noticed. She was working on the second picture with such an intensity everything else was blind to her. I felt isolated, nauseatingly aware I was on the wrong end of the cone of torchlight. I turned to face the empty church.

Behind me, the darkness clotted and became malevolent. I heard a deep discordant note which filled me and scraped at my skull. It grew fat and thick around me. It edged closer, pulsing in violent spasms, burning up the air between us.

I must have said something, I must have made some noise of distress because the next thing I knew, Cathy was holding me and staring at me and saying my name.

'What is it?' she said. She looked back at the door, commandeering the torch and sweeping it through the darkness like a broom. The church was empty and Cathy was looking at me like I needed taking care of. Right then I resented that above all else; I felt like an idiot.

'What is it?' Cathy said again. 'What did you see?'

I shook my head.

'Nothing,' I said. 'I let myself get freaked out, that's all.'

'Do you want to go home?'

Of course I wanted to go home. I wanted to be in my room, in my bed. I wanted so desperately for this whole thing to have never happened. But I wasn't going to let her know that, so I dug up some stupid smile from somewhere and tried it on.

'Only when you're ready,' I said.

A couple of hundred yards up the road from the church of St Michael on the Mount, a small wooden gateway leads into the Lye Valley Nature Reserve. The valley is a shallow gorge, curving around and down behind the church, following the shape of Glebeland Road. During the day, you can read a board at its entrance which will tell you that the plant species growing in the valley are thought to have been there since they colonised the area following the retreat of the last ice age, some ten thousand years ago.

On the morning of Wednesday, February 18th, a pink Superdry raincoat was found discarded near the entrance to the valley. Farther along the path lay a grey shoulder bag, its contents scattered and damp from the evening's rain.

I didn't tell Cathy about what I had seen until the day before she went missing. Even as we had left the church, even as we had fled down the passageway beside it, even as we had taken off down the road, I was already working back and forth over what I had seen and slowly but surely scratching it out, rationalising it and making it safe.

By the time I got home, I think I believed I could explain everything I had seen; I'd only allowed myself to get scared, I told myself, and I had let my imagination fill in the gaps between the darkness.

So I was far too embarrassed to mention it to Cathy. But then maybe there was another reason for my silence: perhaps I had seen what Cathy so desperately wanted to believe in, and deep down, I don't think I wanted to share it with her.

Shortly after the night in the church, Cathy's father left again. He wrote Cathy a note saying he loved her more than anything else in the world and that he would see her one day soon. The note was written in Cathy's mother's handwriting. Her mother moved from the wine to the whisky and even I couldn't pretend it wasn't happening any more. Over the past few months, we drifted apart because Cathy had become harder and harder to find. She missed classes at school and she had excuses when I turned up on her doorstep. Her phone went straight to voicemail and she didn't answer her messages. We spoke only briefly on-and-off. She was disappointed we hadn't found anything in the church, but at the time, I didn't appreciate how much. I didn't appreciate how the not-knowing was killing her.

I assumed she just needed time, so I hung back, waiting for her to know I was there for her.

That was how the thing happened with Simon. Because she wasn't talking to him either. We found each other because we were the closest each of us could get to her. We talked about her, we missed her together.

I don't think either of us meant to hurt her. I don't think either of us thought anything would happen. I don't think either of us thought it would last.

The last time I saw Cathy was at school the day before she disappeared. She stopped me after chemistry and asked where I had been the previous evening when neither Simon or I had answered our phones. She looked tense, white-lipped, bracing herself for a betrayal.

I lied to her. I told her an old, outdated truth, unearthed and scrubbed clean like it was new.

'I went to the church,' I said. 'I saw the cross-hatch man.'

And because it wasn't entirely untrue, it all came back to me. I described the church as it had felt to me. I described the darkness, the noise, the terror I had felt. And as she interrogated me further I did not need to lie again. The tears I cried? The fear I relived? They were real and she believed me completely. There was that look in her eye. The promise of something tangible she could bottle and take home.

'I want to see,' she said.
'You don't,' I said. 'You really don't.'

At the gate to the valley, PC Left and PC Right stop and turn around, flanking the gates like a pair of bouncers. They both stare past me as if I'm no longer there and even PC Left has turned cold and android. This is where the show ends. I put my hands on the small wooden gate and the cameras behind me go crazy. The flashes cut through the night, opening fragments of daylight beneath it.

I see my shadow jittering ahead of me in sudden bursts of light, already eager to keep going, to take the overgrown path deeper into the ancient valley.

I see the brambled hedges on both sides, a dark and uneven way descending into something chaotic. Up to the side, I see lights on in the church and wonder if anyone was there the night Cathy disappeared.

And when I look back at the path, I see Cathy standing there. Caught by the edges of the camera flashes which are meant for me. Meant for me-as-her. Meant for her after all.

She is wearing her coat and her bag; she stands tall and she looks at me in that way she always did. A wry smile, a raised eyebrow. An expression that says, 'Can you believe this shit?'

Then the cameras stop and darkness takes her again. I hear voices chattering behind me and there is a faint smell like woodsmoke and rot. I don't know why I open the gate. I don't know why I lunge forward into the blackness. But I do know I scream her name so loud I barely hear the voices rise behind me. All I know is that I must see her; I must speak to her. I have to make her understand.

I can't see where I'm going. I trip, I stumble, I persevere. Blind, I press forward, my hands outstretched, snatching at nettles and brambles.

Maybe a cloud passes from the moon, maybe my eyes have just adjusted to the darkness but I see her then. I see her turning away from me and walking farther into the valley, I see a shadow eclipse her and she disappears.

I say her name again, but she does not wait. Patches of moonlight mark her as she passes, a confident shape flitting in and out of the world. I hurry to catch up with her and my urgency cuts me a path.

The way twists downward curving to the left, overgrown on both sides with fronds and brambles and the shadowy shapes of leaves and tendrils. The valley reaches up around me like The Red Sea; parted and poised to drown the unfaithful.

'Cathy,' I say. 'Cathy.'

It's an apology, a question, an explanation all rolled up into one word.

There is a movement ahead. Shadow passing over shadow. Without thinking, I leave the path and plunge after it, into the snatching undergrowth, picking my way towards the steep bank, branches and saplings buckling before me. I glance up to see the jagged outline of the church far above. Stark against the velvet sky, its lit windows burn like beacons.

Ahead of me, there is a crack in the rocky bank; a hole in the earth and stone, hidden by the years of untended growth and decay. An aperture in the shape of a broken star, just wide enough for someone small to squeeze into. Inside it is dark. It is cold and properly, absolutely dark.

My resolve falters and I stop. I stare at the hole like it might stare back.

'Cathy,' I say. A prayer.

This time, there is a response. A rising hiss of white-noise feedback which resonates and echoes against the rock and the scrub.

My eyes, which I thought were adjusting to the darkness, are undoing themselves. The opening in the bank ahead of me is becoming harder to see.

It isn't my eyes. It's the darkness. The darkness is growing around me like thickening smoke. It spills from the gap in the rock and it surrounds me. There is a weight to it, slow and dense like molasses, a rich sweet smell of smoke and canker. It presses around me, cold and patient. I feel a shock of nausea rising inside me.

The crack in the rock fades into the blackness, but before it is gone completely, something inside it *shifts*. A dark convulsion, somewhere darker still.

I step back and something takes my right hand.

It is cold like clay, strong and rough like knotted bramble. Shocked, repulsed, I try to free myself but I am tugged back by something strong and jagged, which cuts through my skin with a sharp and vivid pain. It digs into me with a thousand barbs as I try to wrench myself away. I feel a warm breath on my neck.

The sound of static rises to a shriek. An empty numbness fills me, robbing me of my senses one by one until there is nothing left but that terrible sound and the knowledge that I am not alone.

It is there beside me. *It holds my hand*.

Someone behind me speaks. A name, not Cathy's but mine. Like a glimmer of light falling on something long forgotten.

Passion Play

There is a hand on my shoulder; wide shafts of torchlight cut open the night and a voice, calm and reassuring, murmurs in my ear. Like that, my hand is free, the sound of feedback is gone, its echo rings in my ears but the world rights itself, bobbing back into normality.

And I feel movement as I am drawn back. There is a flash of light and for a moment the valley is full of people. There's Veronica, there's my mother, there's PC Right and PC Left. I am passed from one to the other; I am carried back, back to the little wooden gate. I am carried out to the lightning flicker of the press photographers, to the empty faces of the crowd, cross-hatched by the shadows of the halogen-bright trees. Faces that have witnessed everything and seen nothing at all.

Two Brothers

The day before William found the boy in the woods, a carriage arrived at Birchlands House.

While Miss Frith was writing names on the blackboard – *d'Artagnan, Louis, Philippe, Aramis* – William slipped out of his chair. He ran to the window of the schoolroom in time to see his father step from the carriage onto the gravel drive, which the night's snow had painted a thin and even white.

'Father's home,' William said. Not to his governess who had joined him at the window, but to himself, as though spoken words might corroborate what his eyes doubted.

In previous years, before Stephen had left for the school, their father's visits to the house had been rare. He spent most of his time at his club in Mayfair, and visited the house only on occasional holidays or when the shooting season looked promising. He had not been home when Stephen had left for Greyhurst, nor had he returned during the subsequent four months, when William had been alone.

But now, the day before Stephen was due back for the winter holiday, the boys' father had come home. There was something about his arrival which felt wrong to William in a way he could not articulate.

He ran to the door of the schoolroom and let himself out.

Behind him, Miss Frith's voice rose to a wavering point.

'Wait until you're called, William.'

He ignored her. His father was a cold, unreachable figure and William disliked being in his presence. He had no intention of running to meet him, but he was curious to know what had brought him home. He edged part way down the stairs until he could linger behind the uprights of the banisters, remaining mostly hidden from the hall below.

His father crossed the scarlet tiles beneath him, beckoning for his man to follow. Briggs was a stocky fellow, buttoned tight in his uniform as though it would burst off him if he exhaled without care. He carried a heavy valise in each hand and William saw there was a long-shaped package wrapped in grey cloth and slung over his shoulder. Briggs sensed William was watching. He glanced up to pinpoint him with dark eyes, and William shrank deeper into the shadows. Briggs turned away but remained a moment longer in the hall to exchange a few quiet words with Jessie, the maid. When he turned again, William could just about make out the dark wooden stock of a shotgun wrapped neatly inside the package on his back.

His father didn't call for him that night, and William was content to be sent to bed early. He lay in his room, staring at the ceiling where shadows flickered from the ivy which fringed his window.

If Briggs had brought a gun, his father was expecting guests. He'd been known to host modest shooting parties in the fields and woodland to the north of the property. At this time of year, pheasants or partridges were likely game, but in the past few months William hadn't seen much activity around the gamekeeper's cottages, the presence of which usually served as a reliable warning that a hunt was planned. On such occasions, the boys' freedoms about the house and its grounds would be curtailed. They would be expected to stay out of sight and out of earshot until all the guests had left.

Restless, William rolled over in his bed. If a shooting party was to happen, then it struck him as unjust. It meant Stephen would return to be ignored by father, to be shut up in the school room with William. It was not the welcome home he deserved.

Stephen was a year older than William, but the way the two had grown up together, they may as well have been twins. Their mother had died when William had been six and, since then, the boys had been raised by the staff and Miss Frith, a slender, intense woman, who had shrank and shrivelled as the boys had grown older and stronger.

With their father absent, the boys were left to their own devices, free to explore every inch of the grounds of Birchlands and to make them their own. The house was an austere, angular building, hemmed in by an uneven mosaic of lawns and formal gardens, linked with a network of die-straight gravel pathways which the boys' imaginations refashioned into Roman roads, the Battle of Waterloo or elephant trails across the Alps.

Their father's one stipulation was that the brothers were forbidden from mixing with the children in the nearby village and it was a point on which the village children at least seemed content to respect.

With no one else, the brothers became close allies, and if Stephen had not been told he was due to attend Greyhurst, they might have believed themselves inseparable.

The day before he'd left, Stephen had worn his brave face and it was a poor fit. His eyes were raw from where he'd scratched out the tears he didn't want the staff to see.

'If it were down to me,' he said to William, 'I wouldn't go at all.'

It had not been down to Stephen. Greyhurst was not just a school, Greyhurst was a family duty. William would be sent there the following year, just as their father had attended when he'd been their age, and their grandfather before him. There were photographs in the house which showed their father, their grandfather, their uncles and great-uncles, looking sober in Greyhurst uniforms. There were long panoramic pictures of significant school years, regiments of pale-faced boys standing to attention. The family coat of arms, they were told, was embroidered on one of the score of pendants which decked the school's main hall. The brothers' future there had never been in doubt, let alone questioned.

With Stephen gone, the days had ground by with little incident. William was ill-equipped for being alone. He had rattled around the house in search of distraction, wandering the grounds listlessly. He even came close to breaking his father's rule and considered crossing the southern field to reach the village, where the voices of the playing children rang like siren song, carried across the farmlands by the leading wind. Such courage was harder to muster with Stephen no longer by his side and the sound of the distant, raucous play left him only with a keener awareness of his isolation.

The days had dragged, and as they mounted up behind him, the anticipation of Stephen's return had grown into something unmanageable. But with the anticipation, there was the bud of something competitive which had yet to bloom. He knew his brother would not have been idle over the past four months. He would come home full of stories about Greyhurst, his teachers, and his new friends, but William had nothing to say in return. He'd done almost nothing since Stephen had been away. Certainly nothing new; nothing that Stephen might find interesting, let alone be jealous of.

For the remaining weeks, this understanding galvanised William. He set about finding diversions for himself, if only so he would have something to tell Stephen about, to prove how he could cope on his own.

He took walks around the gardens, finding the longest path which did not cross itself; he asked the gardener, Mr Granville, for a patch of earth to work with and they had planted potatoes together in neat little rows. So that he might look brave, he slipped out before supper one evening and threw his uncle's leather-bound King James, spinning and flapping like a startled jackdaw, until it landed behind the crenellation over the south portico. So he might look agile, he clambered the vine, hand-over-hand, at the side of the door to retrieve it again.

At night, he would lie in bed imagining what more he could have done while left alone in the house, and by the time his father arrived at Birchlands that afternoon, he'd fashioned a complex mythology of stories and anecdotes which never happened. It was a stockpile of cultivated lies to feed Stephen over the course of the holiday. He would ration them and use them to counter whatever true stories Stephen told, and in this way, Stephen would never know that William had been lonely at all.

The following morning, Jessie woke William early and busied herself spreading his freshly pressed Sunday suit across the dresser.

'Your father wants you to breakfast with him,' she said. Ushering him up and out of bed, clucking over him with an impatient frown. Jessie was from the village, young and inexperienced but keen and inexpensive. She had a round freckled face fringed with stubborn ginger curls that refused to stay pinned out of sight beneath her headscarf.

William had asked her once about the children in the village, and now she would talk about little else. She told him about how they played in the snow. They would wrap up warm, and gather amongst it, drawn to it like moths.

'The whole lawn out there is untouched,' she said, nodding at the window. 'If we was in the village, we wouldn't let all that lovely snow go to waste now. We'd have made a man of it, tall as you. Taller.'

'I was saving it for Stephen,' William said. It felt like a foolish reason when he said it out loud. He didn't look up at her. He imagined she didn't know what it was like to be left to play alone.

His father and Miss Frith were in the breakfast room when he arrived. Miss Frith looked pale, sitting upright and silent, more discomforted by his father than William was. His father was reading the newspaper and although he glanced up when his youngest son came in, he didn't say a word. William took his place at the table and waited.

A breakfast of toasted bread and cold sliced meat had been laid and the three ate in silence. The newspaper held his father's attention. He ate around it, refolding it with great expansive flaps, which whomped and cracked like a fire under a clear flue.

When he was done, he folded the paper and set it aside. He looked at William directly.

'Your brother, Stephen, is due to return today on the 2.12 train,' he said. 'I propose we meet him at the station.'

It wasn't a question but his eyes held William as though he were expecting an answer. Thoughts tumbled over each other in William's head but none lingered long enough to make any sense. His father didn't talk to him, his father didn't talk to Stephen. And yet—

'Yes,' William said. 'Of course.'

The train station rang with conflicting noise and industry. For all the steam and smoke, the winter had taken a claim on it. The glass of the roof was muted by a mottled layer of snow and a barbed wind cut across the platforms picking at the coats of the porters.

The cold made William retreat inside himself as they waited. He pulled his coat tight about him and ducked his head as far as he could beneath his raised collar. On any other occasion, Miss Frith would have subjected him to a stern lecture about the importance of posture, but the cold had got to her too. She had nearly disappeared into her heavy coat and her sensible shoes, and her breath came out in short little puffs which lingered about her like a veil.

Only William's father seemed unaffected. His own posture was good, the sort of thing Miss Frith would approve of with a curt nod and a pursed-lipped smile. He stood straight-backed and patient; his features, those solid, dependable lines and contours you often saw on the marble busts of well-bred Englishmen. He looked across the platform with a quiet confidence and a sense of expectancy which William thought misplaced. If anyone should be looking forward to Stephen's return, it should be the brother who had missed him so desperately and not the father who had barely acknowledged him for the first twelve years of his life.

When the train arrived, it appeared vast and monstrous to William's eyes, a black hole of iron and noise screaming as it slowed its speed. It hawked gouts of steam across the platform, making murky grey ghosts of the disembarking passengers and railwaymen alike.

Stephen emerged from the hubbub surrounding him with the newly acquired air of one who understood his place in the world. He looked taller, more confident, unintimidated by the bitter cold.

He smiled when he saw them waiting for him. It was not the lopsided grin which William remembered but a thin smile he didn't recognise, and it was not directed at him personally. When William turned, he saw the same smile reflected on his father's face. It was a cold expression, colder than the snow and the wind, and it was then William understood that while his brother had come home, he would remain alone.

The carriage brought them all back to the house, but during the journey, William found it hard to say anything to his brother. He tried to put it down to their father's presence but even once they were left alone back at the house, Stephen seemed distant. He regarded William's invitation to play with no more than a polite amusement. His attitude had cooled to something a little aloof, a little indifferent and William's plans for the afternoon were dismissed before they could be described.

'I don't think so,' Stephen had said. 'Besides, father and I are busy this afternoon.'

It was only later that William discovered their father had invited Stephen to join him on an afternoon shooting expedition.

On seeing his face, Stephen had laughed.

'Nothing too grand,' he said. 'Not yet. Father bought me a twelve-bore and thought I might try it on some rabbits or magpies. Something to practise on before a real hunt.'

But it did sound too grand to William, it sounded far too adult to consider. The father he knew would never invite him on such a trip, he would never buy him a shotgun of his own. William had never wanted such a thing until that moment. It surprised him: a jealousy which made his hands curl into impotent fists. He retreated to his room, hoping his temper might cool, but he could hear Stephen's voice in the garden outside as he passed underneath his window. He didn't hear what he was saying or who he was speaking to, but there was excitement and enthusiasm there which William felt desperately excluded from.

He lay on his bed and put his hands to his ears.

He waited until they were far gone before he got up again. Maybe he could run away. Maybe he could go for a walk. The house felt inexplicably crowded and he yearned for the quiet he had become accustomed to. He pulled on his coat and boots, and ran downstairs.

As he passed the library, he was startled by the movement of someone inside. He saw immediately that it was Miss Frith, but she seemed unaware of him standing, watching her from the doorway. It was her posture which was strange to him. She faced the shelves, her back turned to him, arms outstretched and her hands were poised on the spines of the books. Her head was dipped and she simply stood there; silent and still except for a small convulsion of her shoulders as though she was expelling a sudden chill. For a moment, William thought she might be crying.

He edged away slowly and cut through the staff wing to the rear door.

The snow had not fallen with any great volume or consistency that winter, but a good inch had settled during the night, covering the front lawn evenly from corner to corner. Now that Stephen was home, its appeal had thawed and the snow remained pure and undisturbed through neglect rather than deliberation.

The far end of the lawn bordered a ragged copse where the boys had once played together. The trees had shed their leaves and the bare branches were spiked like fish bones. The season had diminished them following a decadent summer and now they were a mass of stark grey verticals, fading into a pale damp haze. Between them, the snow lay more thinly, with only disparate patches of white glistening amongst the layer of yellow-green mosses, made vivid by the winter.

A narrow trail led deeper into the trees. It followed the line of the culvert which marked the edge of the family's land but William followed it without paying attention. He'd walked this route so often, he needed no path to lead the way.

When they'd been younger, William and Stephen would play together in the culvert, lining their tin soldiers along its edge. Stephen's would always be the British, leaving William with either the French or the Boers, but William had never objected. He gave his French soldiers voices as they keeled over in the mud: screams and wails; falsetto 'mon dieus' which made his brother bend double with laughter.

They had played lengthy campaigns in those days. Neither had much of an eye for military strategy and when the charge was sounded, numbers on both sides would fall until only two remained standing, one on each side. The end game would stretch on and on. The two survivors would take off around the grounds, fencing, flying, ducking, weaving. They would scale trees and rocks. They would fall and miraculously recover, and only when the brothers would tire of the game would history prevail and Napoleon would fall to Wellington. The summer days stretched long and as the dusk began to gather, they would search through the mud for their fallen redcoats, gathering them in fistfuls and carrying them home.

William caught sight of something in the snow which snapped him back to the present. Alone at the edge of the path, there was the print of a bare human foot, toes clearly defined in the crisp, compacted snow left behind.

William stooped low to examine the find, then looked about him, searching for movement amongst the trees. But he could make no further sense of it than the fact it existed, pointing away from the house, deeper into the copse.

Now, for the first time, he looked at the track he'd been blindly following and saw he wasn't the first to walk it since the snow had fallen. A trail ran along it both ways, up to the border of the woods, and then back again; twin furrows etched in the snow, each erasing and confusing the other. The feet which made them had dragged in both directions, and the way the snow had softened in the vague afternoon sun gave no evidence that the same feet had left the print as well.

William kicked through the undergrowth until he uncovered a stick heavy enough to intimidate and light enough to wield. He struck it solidly a few times, scattering the dusting of snow it had acquired and – satisfied it was not rotten through – he hefted it in both hands like a club.

With that, William was on a hunt of his own. He didn't need his father. He certainly didn't need Stephen. He'd been patiently learning to occupy his time over the past four months and he was damned if he would allow himself to appear as upset and betrayed as he felt.

The tracks led doggedly along the edge of the culvert, detouring briefly only when the low wall which ran along the other side became exposed to the surrounding farmland. As William neared the southernmost boundary of the copse, he held his club out before him.

In the summer of the previous year, the boys had eavesdropped on the groundsmen's conversations about news of the peasant uprising against the Tsar in Russia. The boys had built a fortress at the far end of the culvert as the backdrop for an ill-considered attempt to re-enact the drama. They had not really understood what was happening or why, but both had agreed it sounded exciting. Even when their game had been discovered, and they each had received a sound thrashing for their troubles, they also agreed it had been worth it.

In the intervening year, the fortress had been slowly reclaimed by the untended woodland as though the peasants had breached its defences after all. The rot had set in, but its shape had weathered better than William had anticipated.

'Fortress' was a generous term for such a ramshackle construction: low woven walls plastered with wet mud and leaves, a poorly knitted grass roof and foundations augmented with piles of stones they had stolen from the culvert walls.

William could see the remains ahead of him. The stones had mostly toppled into piles, and the grass roof was gone entirely, but two of the woven walls still remained, propped against each other like a narrow tent. Cords of ivy climbed up through them, knitting them to the ground and lending them the air of something more permanent. They were not the walls the boys had built over a year ago, but walls which had been born out of them.

And behind them, a shadow moved. The shadow of a figure, shredded through the twisted leaves.

Despite himself, William took a sharp intake of breath – a fine huntsman he would make, giving himself away like that. The figure froze at the sound. Its reply was a low, animal-like whimper.

Emboldened by what he took to be a display of weakness, William advanced.

'Come out,' he said. 'You can't hide in there. I can see you.'

Closer, the figure appeared to be trying to prevent itself from moving, but the task was beyond it. It shivered uncontrollably in the cold, and the walls of the fortress shivered with it.

William slowed. This was no adversary. It was something far too wretched to fight back. Some hermit, maybe, or one of the children from the village who had become lost.

William lowered his branch and reached for the fortress wall with his hand.

'I won't hurt you,' he said and immediately regretted how it sounded like a weakness of his own.

But the figure didn't move as he pulled the wall aside. The mat of vines and branches gave easily, folding downwards to reveal what was hidden behind it as though it were concealed by nothing more substantial than a thin curtain.

It was a boy, or at the very least, the remains of one. He cowered in the ditch, shivering with the cold and his hands were held high, his forearms crossed, covering his face. His clothes were ragged and filthy. His feet were bare, the flesh shredded with angry sores. He stank as though he'd been living in a latrine. William gagged with revulsion and took a step back in shock.

Startled by the sudden movement, the boy lowered his arms and looked up with wide, terrified eyes which William knew all too well.

It was Stephen. It was unmistakably Stephen. And it was not the Stephen who had returned, but the Stephen who had gone away. The fear and anger which had haunted his eyes on the day before he left for Greyhurst were still there; they had grown over the months, become wilder, an expression of wordless horror carved onto ruined features.

William barely managed a breath. It was impossible, but it was too real to be anything other than true. And so, when he said Stephen's name, it was not a question.

Stephen's head bobbed up and down, the motion jerky and mechanical. Sounds came out but they were disconnected and senseless. William stared at the boy, his thoughts a confused clutter of conflicting possibilities. He took another step backwards, dropping the branch in the path.

'Wait,' Stephen managed. It was a tortured syllable. It sounded as though it had been coughed up from somewhere dark and hollow. William waited, but although it was clear Stephen was desperately trying to say something else, no more words came, only tears and further splintering breaths.

William looked back down the path as though there might be something, someone there capable of advising him. But he was alone with only the uniform ranks of pale winter trees standing silent and impassive around him, awaiting his command.

He knew he had to do something. He had to get the boy somewhere warm, somewhere safe.

This understanding granted him resolve and he stumbled down the side of the culvert, his feet sinking into the brackish mud and loam which clogged its length. He tried to ignore the shock of cold as the black ditchwater crept up around his shoes.

Closer to, he could see Stephen was in a worse state than he'd first thought. His clothes were torn and mottled with grime. His skin was sallow, the whites of his eyes looked like red cracks in crusted yellow cream. A weak hand reached out and when it touched William's, the coldness of it came as a blow. William withdrew. He felt the chill more strongly himself, it burnt the tips of his ears and fingers; it gathered, heavy at his chest. For a selfish moment, he half-believed Stephen's touch had infected him.

'Please,' Stephen said.

William swallowed hard, cementing a decision which had already been made. He stepped forward, crouching low. He held his breath tight and hated himself for it. The thinness and sharpness of his brother's shoulders appalled him and he felt Stephen spasm at his touch.

'Can you stand?'

Stephen didn't respond. His eyes were closed, his gaunt face tight with pain. William tugged at him, feeling the body give around the bones as though the two were barely connected. He found himself surprised by the weight of him. But it was a dead weight, like something pinned in the mud. Stephen's eyes opened wide and unfocused, staring upwards at the wavering treetops circling above. His mouth opened wider still, a wordless, soundless exclamation which made William let go and stagger backwards.

'I'm sorry,' he said. It didn't seem enough. 'I'll get help.'

It was cowardly, but the alternative seemed far worse, and he would be faster alone. He shrugged out of his coat and pressed it around his brother's skeletal shoulders.

'I'll come back soon,' William promised, impatient not to waste any more time. 'I'll bring back help, I promise I will.'

Stephen's eyes found him again, they stared at him, feral and unblinking. He stammered something which didn't quite make sense and William backed away further, feeling wretched as he did so.

'I'll be as fast as I can,' he said. He clambered up the bank of the culvert and ran.

It was as much as he'd planned. He knew he could not deal with this on his own. For Stephen's sake, it wouldn't be fair if he tried. He needed someone else. He needed someone like Briggs. Briggs could carry him, he thought. His father would get Briggs to help. He ran on, the tender, lifeless branches whipping at his face, snatching at his feet.

He broke out of the copse and into the garden. He didn't even stop for breath and ran headlong across the lawn, leaving a scuffed and slipshod trail through the perfect snow he'd been saving. He rounded the corner of the east wing and immediately collided with someone coming from the other direction. The surprise, rather than the impact, sent him sailing into a heap on the icy path.

Disorientated and shocked, panic overwhelmed reason and he yelled out.

A hand reached down and dragged him back to his feet.

'Watch where you're going, old man,' Stephen said, more irritable than angry. He looked every inch the country gentlemen, all the way down to the pair of mournful looking rabbits strung together, hanging at his side.

William stared at him while Stephen patted the snow from his shoulders, applying his attention to the more stubborn muddy marks which streaked his shirt.

'Heavens, you look like you've been in the wars,' Stephen said. 'Does Frith know you're out without your coat? She'll give us both hell if she finds out.'

The thought appeared to remind him of something that amused him and for a moment, his smile was genuine, unrehearsed.

'You're not still spending time in that ditch?' he said. *'Mon dieu.* I need to have words with Frith about the accent she's been teaching you. Yaxley, the French master at Greyhurst said I had it all wrong. Makes us sound like peasants, he said.'

William said nothing. Having already seen and recognised the Stephen in the woods, he imagined the impostor – because this Stephen must surely be the wrong one – would be obviously monstrous in comparison. But both Stephens looked the same. The brother standing before him looked normal and reasonable. He looked healthier. His cheeks were pink with the smart of the cold, his eyes lit with a flat amusement. If he was alien to William, he was only made that way by experiences over the past few months which William had no part in.

'Something's got you in a bother,' Stephen said, studying him. 'What is it?'

William remained silent, and for his efforts he felt his brother's hand tighten around his shoulder.

'Don't be childish,' Stephen said. 'What is it? What have you done?'

There was something in Stephen's tone which was familiar enough to make William doubt himself entirely.

'There's a boy in the woods,' he said. 'He's hurt.'

It only sounded like a betrayal once he'd said it out loud. His throat felt sharp and sore as though something inside of him had torn loose.

Stephen stared at him.

'A boy?' he said. 'Show me.'

'No. Where's father? We should get Briggs and—'

'Don't be foolish; show me where the boy is.'

For the second time that afternoon, William found himself backing away from his brother. But this time, he couldn't have explained why. Maybe he'd got it all wrong. He remembered the smile Stephen and their father had shared at the station. Would it make any difference if he insisted on speaking to his father alone? The outcome would be the same, he would only waste more time and the boy in the woods, whoever he was, didn't have time to squander.

Nevertheless, it was with considerable reluctance that William led the way back into the copse. The path he'd followed was still there, its clarity muddied by his own trail which criss-crossed it. He scuffed his feet as he walked, obscuring it further. He hoped looking petulant would distract Stephen from what he was doing.

For his part, Stephen remained quiet. He'd left his brace of rabbits hanging over a low branch at the garden-end of the copse and walked behind William, his footsteps precise and silent.

William tried to hide his nerves with noise. He started talking to cover himself and found he could not stop. Everything which had been building up within him for the past four months, everything he'd wanted to tell Stephen when he returned, it all came spilling out, uncontrolled.

Here were his precious anecdotes, polished and perfected. Here were his facts reimagined into fables. Tales of exploration and adventure that had never happened; gossip from the village he had never heard; friends he had never been permitted to make.

Here were the stories he'd practised to himself in the hours and days he'd spent alone. He had been saving them, just as he'd been saving the freshly fallen snow on the lawn, but now Stephen was finally here, he cast them about him as they walked, his voice loud and clear to carry them further. They were no longer stories, no longer boasts or lies. They were distractions, they were warnings, they were lost to the mud and the snow.

The culvert was empty when they reached it, and while the disturbed snow could have been made by any creature in panic, there was nothing to suggest it had been made by anything so specific as the boy William had seen.

Stephen picked his way around the remains, turning over a ruined fortress wall with his toe. He glanced back at William.

'Liar.' He said it with half a smile as though he was still capable of playing along. 'I might have known you'd make a scene.'

He looked out to the edge of the copse where the adjoining field of grey fallow grass stretched upwards to the curve of the hillside.

Already he was tiring of the game. He turned on his heel and marched back the way they had come. When William didn't follow him immediately, Stephen stopped and looked back.

'Father's calling,' he said.

William shook his head stubbornly. He'd not heard anything, but he followed anyway as he always did.

That evening, William's father did something he'd never done before. He came to visit his youngest son in his bedroom. Still wearing his hunting clothes, he brought the smell of smoke and sulphur into the narrow room on the second floor.

At first, neither of them spoke a word. William had already been in bed, and at the sound of the door opening, he'd swung out from under the covers to sit on the edge of the frame. A stripe of shadow hid his father's face, but William felt his eyes on him. Sharp and unwavering, they trapped him where he sat.

His father cleared his throat.

'You must be patient with your brother,' he said. 'Stephen is experiencing new things, a world away from this life you've both become used to. You need time. You both need time.'

He turned to go and for a moment, William saw Stephen was waiting in the hallway outside. He too was dressed in his outdoor clothes. There was a lantern at his feet and something tall propped by his side which glinted brief and dull grey in the shaft of moonlight that fell through the window. William recognised the wooden stock he had seen the day before, wrapped in cloth and hanging across Briggs' back.

His father turned back to William, blocking the view; his watch chain glinted in the hallway light like the flash of a smile.

'You mustn't be jealous of him,' he said. 'Next year you'll be at Greyhurst yourself. Next year, you'll understand.'

He pulled the door to, and it was open barely a crack when he spoke again.

'Next year, William,' he said, 'it'll be you.'

He closed the door. Somewhere outside, a dog barked. And once again, William was alone.

Breadcrumbs

Ellie is alone in her bedroom on the fifteenth floor. She sits crossed-legged on her bed, a brightly illustrated book in her lap that has been passed down from her mother, from her grandmother. Its cover has faded with age, its spine is creased and broken, but the pages are still vivid, their stories preserved. Her hands rest upon the illustration of a beautiful white cat, its head bowed and docile before a prince with a sword.

Ellie has read it so often, on any other day, she would recite from it by heart.

But not today. Today, her parents have grounded her. Today, she's angry.

Let's say they've gone to a ball. Mum, Dad, Louis, they've gone to a big charity number in some enormous villa out on the coast. It would be a grand affair and simply everyone will be there. If Ellie were to turn on the television right now, one of the entertainment networks would almost certainly be covering it.

Ellie doesn't turn on the TV. She never wanted to go to the wretched thing in the first place. She has no one to go with anyway. Who goes to a ball with only their parents? But now she's been denied the opportunity to hate it first hand, it hurts that she was not allowed to go; it's not the sort of hurt to draw blood but it will bruise and, cultivated with the right kind of resentment, this bruise will last.

For her own amusement, she composes vengeful fantasies, relishing the excesses her imagination refuses to censor.

Witness this:

Her father, she feeds to a wolf in drag. He is swallowed whole, his hands and face press desperately against the elastic of the animal's belly. The wolf relaxes; he reads a paperback while he waits for the struggling to subside. Maybe her father will suffocate in there? Maybe he'll be digested piece by piece. Either way, it proves to be a slow process, but the wolf for one is content to wait.

Her mother is set upon by charcoal-coloured carrion birds. They fluster around her face and her hands flap weakly in return. The birds overwhelm her, their heads jab at her, swift and sharp. Pluck! Pluck! Mother's mouth is a wide O; her palms cover her eyes to stem tears that run red, then black, then blacker still.

And little Louis? Louis reaches for an apple from a chest made of iron. As he peers inside, the heavy lid wavers in a current of air. It falls with a clang and a snap and, perfectly headless, Louis sits back in surprise. Ellie scoops up his remains and pops him in the pot she's prepared on the stove. She cooks him on low through the best part of the day, until the meat, such as it is, falls tender from the bone.

Backtrack, backtrack. Maybe that's too much, even for her. Let's say this instead: Louis is dressed up in some preposterous little tuxedo he insisted their parents had made for him; a suit that makes him appear too old, too small, too novel. He joins them like their very own sideshow act, trotting along behind Papa, trying to mimic the cadence of his walk.

Louis. *Louis.* Ghastly little beast.

That, if nothing else, is true.

She imagines the three of them at the ball without her and,

because she is not there, it must be a gaudy, tasteless thing; not her scene at all. She pictures her family entering the ballroom at the top of a sweeping staircase, their names are announced and the revellers, who are already circling the dance floor, turn to stare. Conversation dims in the cavernous hall; the guests lower their masks and gawp at the new arrivals. *Is it really them? Are they really here?* No one wonders where Ellie might be. No one knows she even exists.

As Ellie bounds off the bed, the book slips from the sheets and lands tented on the floor. She ignores it and crashes through her bedroom, crossing the hall towards the front door.

If this were a network TV show, a boy would climb through her window and they'd kiss and the credits would roll and that would be a nice way to end things. Being a network TV show, the boy would be dark-eyed and square-jawed and have perfect skin, none of which would be bad things at all.

No one climbs through her window; the apartment is far too high up for that. Maybe she'd get a window cleaner if she was lucky, but a prince? Sometimes life could be so goddamn unfair.

In her story, the white cat is a cursed princess who asks the prince to cut off her head and her tail with his sword. This is how the curse is lifted; this is how she becomes the beautiful woman she always was; this is how they fall in love and get married.

If this were a network TV show, the audience would complain if the hero took a sword to the cat. Audiences today had no faith in real magic. The boy would be arrested even if the princess did turn out to be beautiful. Cats are more important than princesses, so why change at all?

The apartment is enormous today. Acres of marble, miles of crushed velvet. If she cannot go to the ball, then let the apartment become palatial instead. Maybe it's not on the fifteenth floor after all. Let's say it's a penthouse, a penthouse with views over the glittering majesty of the central district. It is a castle on top of a tower of rock.

Ellie opens the door and leaves it wide. She ducks down the hall to number 1513 and hammers on the door. Jan opens it. He's wearing a vest and drying his hands on a towel. He gives her a look which she absolutely doesn't deserve.

'Hey, El,' he says. 'Thought you said you wanted to be alone?'

She had said that. For all of half an hour, the book had seemed like a good idea. But it's difficult to be alone in her flat, what with the maid – yes, the maid, why not? – pottering about in the kitchen, singing some horrible song from wherever the hell it is she comes from.

'I am the least loved member of my family,' Ellie declares. 'I'm probably adopted. I'm an unloved stepchild of a wicked, wicked queen. I'm probably one of her charity projects.'

Jan looks at her.

'Very Dickensian,' he says. 'You know that means you'll probably end up marrying your brother?'

'Jan! *Gross.*'

'It's a Victorian thing. They thought it was a happy ending.'

'Jan, cut it out.'

She stares at him, saucer-eyed and pouting.

Jan holds firm, but only so he can prove he's doing her a favour when he finally relents.

'Alright, come on in, then.' He looks past her. 'You left your door open,' he says.

'The maid can get it.'

'Maid?' Jan shakes his head. 'Jesus, Ellie.'

Jan's apartment is smaller than hers. It's less tidy too, worn around the edges and cluttered with teetering stacks of books and paperwork which can find no room in the clogged bookcases or the overflowing desk. Ellie makes herself comfortable on the sofa.

'They hate me,' she says. 'The treat me like a servant. They wouldn't even let me go to their silly ball.'

Jan sits beside her.

'They've gone to visit your aunt,' he says. 'She's in hospital. She had a fall, remember?'

Fall. Ball. Whatever.

Ellie shoots him a look. She shouldn't have to explain something so obvious. Jan shakes his head.

'Coffee,' he says. It's not a question, it's an excuse. He gets up and disappears into the kitchen.

Klee comes in from the bedroom. He's wearing a kimono and has the paper folded to the crossword. He doesn't acknowledge Ellie as he sits in the armchair and puts his feet on the coffee table.

'We babysitting?' Klee says to Jan when he comes back in. He doesn't look up from his paper; his pen totters above it. Ellie doesn't waste a look on him; he wouldn't see it after all.

'We're keeping an eye out,' Jan says. 'Accounts are conflicting, but according to princess here, mom and pop are at some charity ball and the maid is being too loud and ethnic.' He arranges coffee mugs on the table, shoving Klee's feet off as he does so.

Klee scowls.

'I sympathise,' he says. 'These days, you simply can't get the staff.'

'Well we could use some help with all the shit you leave behind,' Jan says. 'What's the going rate for make-believe maids these days?'

'An imagination would be a start.' Klee writes something furious into his crossword.

'I'm too old to have a babysitter,' Ellie says. She's nearly fifteen after all; it sounds plenty old enough to her.

'And yet here you are.' Klee reaches for the nearest mug and smiles at her; a well-oiled expression, it comes to him with ease, but it lacks sincerity.

Ellie looks away and imagines something better.

The coffee relaxes her; she has always been contrary. She sits back on Jan and Klee's sofa and lets it give around her. Her fictions shed from her like stubborn orange peel. They flake off in pieces; they leave a residue so she can almost still believe.

Lou is at his friend's place, somewhere across town. He wouldn't be seen dead in a tux. He's a baseball cap and T-shirt sort of kid and defiantly so. Mum and Dad are visiting Auntie B who took a tumble down the stairs. Claudia, Auntie B's twelve-year-old Jack Russell, had a stroke on the unlit landing. The poor mutt fell in a lump at the top of the stairs, solidifying into a trip hazard that sent Auntie B cartwheeling down to the lobby when she was walking about the house shouting the animal's name.

Mum and Dad worry about Auntie B. Auntie B is sad and lonely and needs people to worry about her or she might forget she exists at all. Once upon a time, she had been married, but there was no happy ending there: Uncle Bill went on to have a family with someone else but he was equally miserable. Auntie B remained alone, and now her dog was dead and she was in hospital with a broken who-knows-what.

Dad told Ellie how Auntie B lay at the foot of the stairs screaming, not because her back was folding up in a way it wasn't supposed to, but because when she had fallen, she had kicked Claudia loose from where she had lain, and made her roll down the stairs to meet Auntie B at the bottom. They lay there, nose-to-nose, and Auntie B couldn't move an inch.

Ellie shouldn't have laughed. She knew that at the time.

Don't laugh, she'd told herself, but she could feel it brewing up inside her, making her face red and hot as she tried to keep it down. The image was like something from a cartoon and she couldn't keep her amusement to herself. It demanded to be shared. Her laugh came out as a bark and it kept coming, leaving her breathless.

Ellie still remembers the look her mother gave her after that. It was the sort of look she might have given to a stranger she'd found in her home. In that moment, it was as though Ellie was no part of her. She was no longer her daughter, just a penance she didn't deserve. Her mother didn't say anything. She just turned her back and walked away.

In her room, Ellie had listened to her parents arguing over whose fault she was. The walls in the place were so thin she heard everything they said.

'Always with the fucking stories.' Her dad's voice sounded as though it had been folded up into an accusation and hurled across the room. He only used language like that when he thought he and her mother were alone.

'I'm right here,' Ellie said to the wall, but she spoke quietly, as though by not being overheard, any curse which had been placed upon her might lose its grip and drift away.

Because Ellie was worried about Auntie B too. She really was, because if Auntie B could one day find her way through the woods to a happy ending, then perhaps she could leave a trail for others to follow.

In the lounge in flat 1513, Jan nudges her awake.

'Hey kid,' he says. 'It's getting late. You sleeping here, or at home?'

Ellie blinks at him.

'Are they back yet?'

Klee is in the doorway. Jan looks to him for an answer.

'Not yet,' Klee says.

Flat 1512 feels bigger now she's alone. Not palatial, but the rooms she must fight to dominate on a normal day feel too stretched, too spacious now she has the whole place to herself.

Maybe it's the same size as Jan's flat after all. Jan's is different enough, its rooms are flipped tip-over-tail which makes it makes it hard to judge.

The heat of her anger has dissipated and the absence of everyone else makes her shiver. She wonders if her family are coming home at all. She imagines them in the wood, following the breadcrumbs Auntie B left behind, picking them up as they go so Ellie can't follow. She feels her eyes sting and her throat prickle.

Looking for distraction, she stands at the window in the sitting room and stares out at the world beneath her. She's always preferred the view at night. The estate looks so bleak in the daytime, but now, the grey concrete of the surrounding tower blocks is consumed by the encroaching dark and only the lights remain. Dot-to-dot clues which her imagination mis-draws to denote superstructures coiling up into the night. The lights of the traffic on the distant bypass? Those aren't cars grounded on the road, they're flying machines on an express route, looping the loop at the intersection. She cocks her head and watches them fly.

In the flat next door, Mrs Kiesmoski's radio is still playing that godawful music. A chorus of very determined men singing about something very important to them. She can almost hear them punching the air in time with the drum and the brass. Ellie considers hammering on the partition but Mrs Kiesmoski would only turn the volume up. Ellie's mum complained once. Well-mannered, in that way of hers, she dressed it up as an excuse: 'I'm waiting for a phone call and I won't hear it ring...' Mrs Kiesmoski told her it was all she had of home, so mum could kindly fuck off. And that's exactly what Ellie's mum did. She fucked off, but oh-so-politely. She backed out of Mrs Kiesmoski's flat making little apologetic noises. Ellie's mum really wasn't one to make a scene.

Ellie goes back to the room she shares with her brother. His bed is still in the mess he left it in that morning and she wonders how long it should go undisturbed before she might consider it a monument. But her appetite for revenge has dulled and the morbidity of the thought is distasteful to her.

She rescues her book from the floor and curls up on her bed with it. She teases it open with her thumb, enough for the smell of oxidised paper to promise something familiar, something magical, but she feels heavy and tired. Even though the little white cat tilts its head and winks at her from the pages, she lets the book fall shut again and tries closing her eyes as well.

When she was small, she would tell herself stories at night because she thought it would make her dream. She thought of it like getting a car to start on a cold morning. She would give the story a push and then, at some point, her subconscious imagination would kick into gear and take her for a ride which would last her through the night. But it didn't work like that. She'd get too involved in her own narratives and they'd keep her awake as she tried to figure out how her stories would end.

As she lies on the bed, something inside of her flutters; something light and beautiful growing and stretching deep in the marrow of her. Ellie feels its eagerness, its impatience, but she ignores it and fills herself with blank and empty thoughts. She does not tell herself a story to help her sleep.

At first the urgent knock on the front door sounds like part of a dream she wasn't aware she was having. She glances at the bedside clock and sees it has advanced by hours.

Woozy, she stumbles to her feet and answers the door.

Jan is there, his eyes a little wild.

'You've got to see this,' he says.

He leads her down the corridor to the stairwell, he's almost hopping with impatience. There's something electric in the air and the doors to the other flats are all open; the neighbours are milling about on the threadbare hallway carpet. Ellie sees Mrs Kiesmoski talking to Klee, her arms are folded as a defensive measure. Ellie notices the music is off. No wonder she slept as well as she did.

'Mick Dawson saw it first,' Jan says. 'He always takes the stairs going down, never the lift. Thinks it keeps him fit, though he always gets the lift going up.'

He pushes open the door to the stairwell and holds it wide so Ellie can go through.

'See how far down you can get,' he says, and he grins at her. A spoiler: *You should be so lucky*, he's saying, *you're not going to get far at all*.

Ellie frowns. She still feels a little dozy, like the sleep is still hanging from her, like she's been dragging it around and if she stays still for too long, it'll wrap itself around her again and drop her where she stands. She peers down the stairwell. It all feels like some sort of silly game, one she's in no mood to take part in. Is someone down there, ready to jump out at her?

Such *bullshit*.

But Jan's still got that grin on his face. He's daring her to prove she's not chicken and that's bullshit as well.

She glowers at him as she strides past and skips down the stairs, her hand lightly tracing the banister rail. She doesn't see what's changed until it's impossible for her to miss.

About halfway down to floor 14, the stairwell is blocked with a mass of thick roots, knotted together across the turn. They come through the wall on one side, they burst out from the floor, they disappear through holes punched in the outer wall. In the cracks around them, she can see woozy filaments of the night sky. The roots are bulky, mature; they clog the space, pressing against themselves, deforming and choking each other.

Ellie turns back and sees the evidence she missed before. Those lines snaking up the walls? They're not cracks in the plaster, they're exploratory shoots. Those pipes criss-crossing the ceiling? They're not pipes, they're more growths feeling their way.

The stairwell smells of mulch and dew, there's a thin whistle of wind through the holes in the walls. Ellie steps back, she imagines how the roots might grow further should she turn her back on them; she keeps them in view as she backs up the stairs and away.

Jan and Klee are waiting for her. Now she sees how Jan looks worn and unshaven, how Klee looks wide eyed.

'What happened?' she says. She's panting. She says it again: 'What happened?'

Jan shrugs.

'One minute they're not there, the next they are.'

'We're trying to get through to the lower floors,' Klee said. 'No one's picking up. The engaged tone sounds like birdsong.'

'What about the lift?'

'The engines spin but nothing comes.'

'Mick Dawson's got a crowbar. He and his boys are going to jimmy open the doors, see how it looks.'

Ellie turns to look down the corridor. Her neighbours hang in their doorways, looking from one to the other expectantly. Crisis has made a delicate community of them.

'We leaned out the windows to look down,' Jan says. 'I don't see any movement down there. No lights, nothing.'

'Cell phones are out,' Klee says. 'Televisions are down. Radio's just white noise.'

'What about Google?'

He looks at her, his expression pitiful. 'That too,' he says.

Ellie looks to Jan for confirmation. Klee would describe the internet as white noise no matter what was happening, but this time, Jan shakes his head a fraction.

'That too,' he says.

Ellie tries her phone anyway. She calls her mum first and then her dad. She calls Louis' mobile. She even calls Auntie B. Each time, there's a click as though someone answers, but she hears only the sound of wind in the leaves. She has to raise her voice to leave a message. She feels like she's shouting into a hole.

They go to the roof and while the fresh air is welcome, darkness robs the view of scale. Far below them, the chains of streetlights have been extinguished like birthday candles. Higher, half the city looks like it's been blacked out with marker pens. But the city's reaction to this change of state feels far too subdued. There are no shouts, no sirens, no cries of alarm. Instead, the city seems content to remain muffled in its darkness.

Ellie looks up. A fat moon hangs round and pink behind the city skyline. It's so close; she can feel it tug at her. As though it has caught her on a fishhook, and is slowly reeling her in.

Klee leans over the railing, staring down into the gloomy estate, which seems darker and deeper than Ellie has ever known it.

'It's everywhere,' he says.

Jan snorts and joins him at the rail.

'Since when could you see in the dark?' he says.

Klee looks at him. His eyes catch the moonlight in a way Ellie hasn't seen before. For the briefest moment, they glow like lanterns, then darken again.

He turns back and points.

'Look,' he says. 'There are roots everywhere. There are trees growing in the middle of the street. The vines. My god, the vines…'

Jan shakes his head and turns away, his nose wrinkling.

'Sure,' he says.

The rooftop is filling with others from the tower. Ellie wonders if the same thing is happening anywhere else. She pictures all the city's rooftops crowded with their inhabitants, staring blindly into the darkness, waiting for something, anything to happen; waiting for something to make sense. She thinks of the way birds congregate on building sites and rooftops. One loud noise, she thinks, and everyone will fly away.

Jan won't fly. Jan is turning into a squirrel, and while it's still early days, so far he doesn't look like the flying type. It takes a few days for Ellie to see what's happening to him, but now his face bristles with whiskery hair, his eyes have darkened into little black marbles and his head bobs with sharp, nervous movements. He's growing a tail too but he's pretending he isn't. He keeps it stuffed down the back of his tracksuit pants; he reverses out of doorways because he thinks people won't notice.

He's not the only one changing. Since the first night, most of the residents of the tower have left their doors open. The fifteenth floor has become one flat with many rooms, and each of Ellie's neighbours is becoming something else. People are becoming deer and mice and birds and stick insects.

Klee is becoming an owl. His eyes are fixed wide and luminous. He leaves trails of downy feathers wherever he goes. They slip from the legs of his trousers, from the sleeves of his shirt. Gold and tawny and white. He complains it itches, but when he scratches, he only sheds more.

Mrs Kiesmoski is turning into a rabbit or maybe a hare. Her ears flop down on either side of her head. She isn't ashamed of them; she ties a bow around them to draw attention to how they have grown. She plays her music louder still because she says she hears it differently now. Sometimes she sings along.

The city is barely a city any more. The estate has a beauty to it now. Where it had once been coloured in shades of concrete and steel, it is now a rich and wide expanse of browns and greens. The tower blocks are wrapped in roots and vines. They grow branches that stretch high. The tarmac at street level has been shattered into jigsaw pieces by the growth from beneath. It is now chaotic and uneven: roots and mosses and trees and shrubs. Broom and bracken, tangling and knotting through the avenues, softening the edges of what were once the rigid lines of the estate's streets.

Ellie spends a lot of time on the roof. She leans over the railing and watches the city become consumed.

She is not changing. She checks every day, standing naked before the mirror in the bathroom, inspecting every inch of herself for a sign she is becoming something new.

She wonders where her family is. Mum, Dad, Louis, Auntie B. She wonders if they have found each other. Without them, she feels unmoored, like she could just drift up into the sky and disappear. Does she miss them because she loves them? Or does she miss them because she needs them? Because her family grounded her and she is angry with herself for letting them go.

She thinks of that look on her mother's face, that pent-up fury, that stepmother scorn. She thinks of her father shaking his head. He tried, he seems to be saying, God knows he tried his best.

She wonders if they are changing too. Maybe they can turn into something new. Something that can fly or run or crawl, something that will help them find their way back to her? She appreciates how strange and selfish a wish it sounds: *change into something that will make me less lonely. Change into something that will bring you home.*

Because she wants to change. Everyone else is becoming something different, but Ellie is left as she has always been.

'I am the least loved person in my block,' she says to the city-as-was.

A blackbird rustles past. She wonders if it's a real blackbird, or if it was once someone she knew. It ignores her and arcs away, drifting lazily, then flapping fast and strong to gain the height it lost.

Ellie watches it wheel once then disappear, a tiny black speck vanishing into the avenues.

At night the city sings where once it screamed. No sirens, no shouts, no alarms. No roars of machinery or screeches of tyres. The song is one of birds and animals, the chittering of insects and the new and wilder lives of the city's residents. Its tone is uncertain, lacking fluency: it is the sound of a city learning a new tongue.

Ellie does not sleep. She lies curled up on her bed and refuses to dream because she doesn't trust her dreams to stay where they should be. She pictures them leaking out of her and infecting the world outside. She tells herself stories to keep herself awake. Once upon a time, she and Louis would play together in the park Mum used to take them to. In her story, they have the place to themselves and they play on the swings and they study the little duck pond and they pretend it's their own island which no one else can touch. All of this was true once, years ago, before Louis became a brat who preferred to play with his own friends than with her. In her story, he stays in awe of her. She tries to believe it would be better, but his attention creeps her out. He follows her around with this dumbstruck look on his face. She rolls over and thinks of something else.

She wonders if dream and reality have got mixed up somewhere, the one flipped tip-over-tail from the other. Opposites attract, they say. It's true of magnets; it's true of lovers. Mum and Dad argue like they've been together too long. The years have ground away the things that made them first fall in love and now they politely push each other apart.

Flat 1513 has become like a nest. It smells of damp fur and fresh-cut grass. Jan has stopped hiding his tail; it looks like he has a feather duster jammed down the back of his jeans. Klee can turn his head around way too far and stares at Ellie with his big amber eyes. When she reacts, he laughs, but his laugh gets all caught up with hooting coughs, which just make him laugh even more.

Jan says her name. His whiskers flicker when he talks.

'You need a haircut, girl,' he says.

She frowns. You need a shave, she almost says. A haircut! It seems like the very least of her concerns. The only people who have seen her for weeks are the upper floors of a tower block full of chimeras whose own concept of personal grooming is diminishing by the day. But when she looks in the mirror, she decides he's right after all. Her hair has grown long, so much longer than it had been when she checked herself only the day before. Then it came down to her shoulders, now it comes down to her lower back.

She traces her fingers through it, combing it gently. There is a charge within it: a pent up thrum like something electrical. If she really listens, she can almost hear it grow.

She borrows scissors from Jan and starts to hack it back. When she was smaller, she would have done anything for long flowing hair. Today she feels like being more practical. But there is little room for the practical in this newly shaped world. The scissors get stuck, they don't close over the hair no matter how few strands she stuffs between their blades; even thinned down to a single thread, it has become as strong as hardened steel.

The scissors break before the hair does; the pivot snaps and the two blades separate in her hands. She stares at them dumb with surprise, and casts them clattering into the sink. When she looks back at her reflection, she sees how she has changed after all.

The length of hair she hacked at with the scissors has bruised and thickened. It has swollen from a pale, yellow-blonde strand, to a darker, thicker, green-brown tendril. She reaches up to it and snatches her hand away again. There are thorns there, unbending silver threads as sharp as bee-stings.

She finds a comb and spends the next hour combing the thorny knots away. They soften as she combs them, but the motion only makes her hair grow further. She is in tears once the last thorn has been dispelled.

Jan holds her as she cries.

'Let it all out,' he says. 'All of it. Let it all out.'

The hair grows faster over the next few days and she twists it into braids and plaits. Whenever she tugs it too roughly, whenever it catches on something as she drags it around the flat behind her, it bruises and swells into thorny gorse that she has to spend time combing soft and straight.

It is becoming far too much for her. Her flat is filling with her own hair. It gets caught on furniture, on books, on toys, and her movements become frustrating and limited. She sits on her bed telling herself not to be frightened of it. She imagines herself being buoyed up to the ceiling, she imagines it drowning her. She drags her hair behind her and imagines that if she were to stay still for too long, it might wrap itself around her and drop her where she stands.

Ellie walks around the upper floors and her hair follows, blindly retracing her steps at one remove. The weight of it forces her shoulders back; she has never stood so straight. Her mother would be so proud.

She explores every inch of the flat she grew up in. She opens cupboards and drawers as though she might find a door to some magical world she missed. Buried in the dresser by her mother's side of the bed, she finds a wad of paperwork drawn up by a divorce lawyer, phone numbers highlighted with a pink pen. Unsigned, undelivered, her mother never was one to make a scene.

Each morning, she binds the new growth with string. She does it gently so as not to bruise it. The ends have long since turned to scrub and she no longer has the patience to comb the thorns away. Instead, unattended, they blossom and thrive. They scratch through the cheap carpet and paintwork in the hallways as she wanders through the block like a ghost.

Come nightfall, she gathers the length of her hair and coils it in her flat, so it lies beside her like a wicker basket. She goes to bed earlier and earlier each night because it takes more and more of her time to prepare.

The residents of the block have all changed by now; they're settled in their new selves, they're comfortable and content. The rooms and hallways are full of skittering and squeaking noises as they go about their business.

Ellie's own changes shows no sign of slowing down, her hair grows faster every day, longer every minute; it is intolerable. She opens her window wide, then moves her bed so it is positioned beneath it. Climbing onto the mattress, she looks down to the forest below and acknowledges one final time that it is beautiful. She looks out, as far as she can see. She takes in every detail of the changed world and stores it safe inside of her. Then she reaches for her gathered hair and begins to feed it out, into the city below.

The animals, her neighbours, they see what she is doing and they understand. They gather in her room to help her. They tend her like nursemaids. They crawl across her, gathering coils of her hair amongst them; they spin them from the open window like rappelling wires. Some are rougher than others. She sees bristling briars cast from the window as well as delicate threads.

Eventually the weight of it is too much. She turns and lies on her bed, facing upwards while the neighbours continue the work.

She wonders how the scene must look from the outside. A tangle of golden threads, curling and twisting from the fifteenth floor window like autumn grasses in a current of floodwater. It is a wonderful image, she decides, and this gives her contentment.

'Thank you,' she says. *My friends,* she would add if she wasn't afraid the word might drive them away from her.

Breadcrumbs

Her neighbours retreat; she sees them gathered in the doorway watching her and she smiles at them. She tries to lift her head to see them more clearly, but the weight of the hair and the brambles makes it impossible to move her head any further. She tells them she loves them all and it is absolutely true.

She closes her eyes and sleeps. Even the movement deep within her cannot make her stir; the movement of something flexing and stretching and growing strong.

She dreams she is Auntie B, immobile at the foot of the stairs. Facing her, nose-to-nose, she sees Louis. His cap has fallen off halfway down the stairs, leaving his hair mussed in a way that would embarrass him if he knew. His head lolls, like it had been cut off, then carelessly set back in place. His eyes are closed and he might be peaceful, but Ellie screams and cries and shouts because she has never felt so alone.

She doesn't sleep all the time. Sometimes she lies awake, staring at the dark stains spiralling across the ceiling like inexorable waves climbing a cracked and peeling shore. But there is little purpose for her to be awake. She can barely move, after all.

The neighbours tend her, all of them, Jan most of all. He scuttles up and over her, corralling the others to do as he bids. There are so many of them. They feed her, clean her, care for her. They take care of all those tiresome earthbound needs. Sometimes Jan sits on her chest, his eyes black like watermelon seeds, his whiskers flickering and alert.

They don't speak any more but, somehow, they understand each other well enough. Jan looks at her intently and the dark, mouldering shapes in the ceiling shift and resolve themselves into dancing shapes which illustrate what he wants to show her. He tells her about the forest the city has become. He scuttles down the walls of the tower to scavenge in the undergrowth below. Klee circles overhead, scouting the way, but he doesn't look at Jan in the same way he used to, and Ellie worries he will one day succumb to his new shape's predatory instinct.

'Don't let him eat you, Jan,' she says. 'I don't think I could bear that.'

Jan dismisses the idea. They've never been closer, he says.

Looking at them, even in their new forms, she see this is true. Even in their old lives, they existed in a cycle of predator and prey, forever capturing and rescuing each other in ways she never thought to understand.

Jan tells her about how her hair spills from the window like a waterfall of golden light; it drowns the avenues between the vast trees that were once tower blocks. It spreads further every day, crawling through the suburbs and into the city's central district.

He tells her how the individual strands have thickened into barbs and brambles and branches of their own, so walls of thorns pack the avenues, and climb higher and higher.

He tells her how there are still people in the city. Actual people, *hu-mans*, those who have resisted the changes that have claimed everyone else. They live with a conservatism they are fiercely proud of. They cling to the threadbare traces of the lives they once led. But their life is difficult now the city is full of predators, and the lower reaches of the brambled avenues are choked with the tangled bodies of those who have faced up to the new reality and been found wanting.

Ellie is legend to them, Jan says. Her name is whispered in the enclaves of those who remain: sometimes as a curse, sometimes a prayer. All set out to climb the tangled forest to the fifteenth floor, but when they fall to the knife-like thorns below, no one comes to rescue them. Their remains are knotted amongst the vicious barbs of her hair; their homemade armour tarnished by the rain, bones picked clean by the same carrion that finds room to nest amongst the sprawl of branch and root.

From street level, Jan says, the mass of bramble sweeps up to the open window, a great blonde arrow pointing to the room in which she sleeps. The tower is now a destination for the brave and the foolish: the men and women who view Ellie as a maiden to rescue or a monster to destroy. Let's say they congregate at the foot of the building and peer up at the room in which she sleeps. Let's say they discuss strategies amongst themselves. Whatever is said, they will fail. The hair will thicken amongst them; it will become barbed and thorny to draw their blood, the thorns will become venomous to corrupt it. It will grow through them, separating skin and bone and teasing them apart like paper dolls.

But still they come with their little swords and their little quests. She feels them down there in the city. They pluck at the nerves of her like an endless stream of little brothers, come to disturb her while she sleeps.

Sometimes, she dreams she is walking through the city as it used to be. The streets are grey and empty. Shops are boarded up and there are no cars on the road. She walks barefoot on the sun-warmed tarmac, taking turns left and right as the mood takes her. She remembers the park where her mother would take her and Louis when they were very small, but she cannot find it. A compact square of land, surrounded by smart iron fences, their rough ironwork smoothed and shining with green paint. Her own little island, her duck pond, her swings. Her mother would push her so she could believe she could fly. In her dream, she turns each corner hoping it will be there but each street is grey and long, diminishing into a distant and sterile whiteness. The streets are all the same. They are all indifferent.

She lies in her room in flat 1512, asleep and awake, waiting for something she doesn't fully understand. Not love, she thinks. Not the square-jawed kid from the network TV show. She has read enough books and seen enough films to appreciate how she is expected to believe 'love' is what every girl wishes upon herself; as though it were a prize to be won and hidden away in a glass cabinet, never to be disturbed.

Let it be something more meaningful, something that will make her engage with the world her dreams have transformed.

She wishes she could reach for her books – they at least represent a love that makes sense to her. She sees them neglected, scattered on the bedroom floor, spines crumpled, covers splayed, pages yellowing, curling and damp. Their disarray upsets her with a force that takes her by surprise. Tears well in her eyes which she struggles to wipe away.

She remembers how her mother used to tell her stories. In her quiet voice, confident with her fiction, she would spin magic for her. Ellie would interrupt her with questions and her mother would answer with barely a thought, extending the story indefinitely in all directions. And when Louis was small, she would do the same for him and Ellie would listen from her bed, her eyes closed as though the stories were for her alone. How could she have forgotten how her mother once fed her worlds?

And somewhere tucked away inside of her, she feels something move. Her *something*, which has ripened inside of her since the city succumbed to change. It is a tentative movement at first, but as she stills to give it room, it becomes more confident.

At first, she assumes it might be what she thought she has been waiting for. Some floppy-fringed hero in foil armour who has come to her aid after all; promising a kingdom, claiming a heart. She almost laughs. Who would have thought he would choose such a curious window to swing through and save her?

It only takes a blessed moment to realise it is something else. Because now she recognises the sense of it, the posture of it; its shape and movement so everyday, so familiar. It is *her*. It is Ellie. A *her* inside of her. A new and perfect self, testing at the edges of her chrysalis, impatient to be set free.

Silently, Ellie coaxes her, and feels the way she crawls from her heart and up her chest to her throat. The Ellie on the bed, the outside Ellie, arches her back in pain because the inside Ellie is simply too big, already fully grown, her eagerness threatens to choke her.

Strike off my head and my tail and cast them in the fire...

Ellie claws at her neck, but her hands are weak and while the flesh bruises, she does not draw blood. She snatches at her hair instead, worrying at a golden strand until the thorns bud and bloom along its length like a blossoming rope of razor wire. She doesn't stop to think as she draws the fattened barbs across her throat. The wound yawns open raggedly, spilling blood and sap and sawdust. The pain is thunderous, but the release is so sweet. Here at last is the transformation she deserves.

This is how she frees that which has grown within her. From the gaping hole, *she* claws out. From the gaping hole, Ellie calls out.

And once free, she is everywhere and she is complete. She is the voice to fill the world and as she draws breath, rich and heavy with such stories to tell, spring comes to the city-that-was, her cave, her monument of stone. The trees blossom, the thorny undergrowth softens and flowers. A golden, late-afternoon sunlight spills through the avenues.

In the flat on the fifteenth floor, Jan and Klee flutter around the room in concern, shrinking to tiny specks as Ellie rises, glorious and unseen. She will speak to them soon, and when they hear, they'll see. But until then, they see only what she has left behind and do not think to imagine anything greater.

Witness this: they see a battered husk, already cooling, already growing moss, already taking root. They see how its skin calcifies into plates of bark and rind. They do not see the smile upon its lips, they only see how earthbound it is, how passive, how still.

Her First Harvest

'Oh, how quickly things changed! Why didn't
happiness last forever? Forever wasn't a bit too long.'
– Katherine Mansfield, 'Her First Ball'

Nina's dress was made from synthetic silk; it was a pale silver grey which shone even in the thin phosphor lighting of Aunt Caroline's dressing room. Nina stood side-on to the mirror and twisted so she could see her back more clearly. The dress hung open from her shoulders, sweeping down in smooth symmetrical curves to meet in a discreet bow above her waist. Her exposed back struck her as looking unhealthy and pale in the thin blue light; her crop was barely more than a thick rumple of texture across her skin. It looked barely more valuable than heat rash.

She frowned. She'd hoped the shape of the dress would exaggerate the yield; she'd picked Minnie's grey one for just that purpose. Minnie said she'd worn it for her first harvest ball. That had been six years ago and Minnie's crop hadn't needed exaggerating even a little. Four months after her first seeding and her shoulders and spine had been ripe with fat clusters of button mushrooms growing in the shape of a heart centred about her spine. Everyone said they'd been so beautiful, and Aunt Caroline told Nina how heads had turned when Minnie arrived at the Governor's House.

Nina sighed. She had so hoped her own first crop would be a match for her cousin's, but her aunt shushed her when she tried to voice her concern.

'Nonsense,' she said. 'This is your first seeding, it's to be expected. Minnie was just a bit different, that's all.'

Aunt Caroline turned her back round, steering her by the shoulders. She held her at arm's length so she could get a measure of her.

'Look at you,' she said. 'You look so beautiful and you'll only become more so, I promise. And besides, Minnie won't have any crop this year. None at all.'

Nina smiled as bravely as she could muster.

Minnie wouldn't have a crop this year because she and Barnabas were trying for a baby, a very different sort of crop that meant there were both exempt from being seeded.

A voice called from downstairs and Nina's aunt smiled.

'The carriage is here,' she said. 'Are we ready?'

'Yes, Aunt Caroline,' said Nina.

'Wonderful.' Aunt Caroline's harvest gown was a pale blue and her crop was strong this season; she had been seeded with an experimental variety that was particularly decorative, fat pink toadstool caps hung from long fibrous stems. They looked like bright jewels, rippling across her back as she swept out of the room.

Nina considered her own reflection one more time. Maybe the light was just unflattering; maybe her crop wasn't so bad after all. She reached around gently to push her fingertips against the larger bulbs, growing in a line up the small of her back. They felt soft and powder-dry. They moved fractionally as she brushed them. She imagined the roots of them inside her, spidering under her skin

Aunt Caroline's voice called her from downstairs and Nina snapped her hand away guiltily.

'Coming, Aunt Caroline,' she said.

She took a final look in the mirror before she turned off the lights. She swept up her bag and her light summer shawl to wear once her crop had been harvested, then ran downstairs to meet her aunt and her cousin in the hallway.

The carriage was waiting outside the house; it looked like a balled fist of iron suspended between four enormous wheels. Its door was wide open and a walkway had been laid joining the steps of the house with the steps of the carriage.

The drivers were standing well back, buttoned up to their chins in oilskins. They each wore thick goggles and facemasks.

There was a light wind, which whipped her harvest gown up around her ankles and she caught herself pressing her hands down to keep it in check. She saw how Minnie had taken the seam of fabric in one hand to counter the slack. She tried to do the same, clutching a handful of her gown at her hip and pulling it tight.

'Don't crease it, Nina,' her aunt said.

'Sorry.'

Inside, the carriage was plush and warm. It was round like a bathysphere, upholstered from top to bottom with cushioned velvet. There were porthole windows on each side, surrounded by rubber filters which pumped and wheezed like steam bellows; but the glass was thick and so smeared and dirty on the outside that only a fraction of the late afternoon light teased through and there was little chance of seeing anything outside.

They took their seats, Nina and Minnie on the one side, Aunt Caroline on the other.

One of the drivers slammed the door shut and spun the handle to lock the seal.

Nina glanced at Minnie and smiled. Minnie didn't see her; she was staring ahead, lost in thought and blind to everything else. She was probably thinking about Barnabas, Nina thought. He wouldn't to be joining them at the ball. Since they hadn't been seeded, he said it was a waste of time. Nina had heard raised voices in the house, but she hadn't said anything, Aunt Caroline certainly wouldn't appreciate her doing so.

The carriage engines rumbled into life and the whole vehicle started to hum and vibrate. A *putt-putt-putt* sound from the exhaust chimney rang against the chassis and gathered tempo. There was a high scraping noise as the gears shifted somewhere beneath them and then the carriage lurched forward with a roar.

They reached the Governor's House in good time, and waited in the carriage as the drivers hosed the chassis down, stripping off the soot and grease that had built up over their journey. As they did so, Nina felt the temperature shift slightly, and the coolness was welcome. The journey had taken the best part of an hour and the atmosphere inside, whilst polite and silent, had threatened to superheat the air around them like a kettle and Nina was feeling quite faint.

When the door opened, she almost leapt at it, but Minnie set a hand on her knee to still her and the two cousins waited for Aunt Caroline to disembark before them.

'Are you nervous?' Minnie asked her when they were alone.

'No,' Nina said, 'of course not.'

Minnie smiled.

'There's no harm in it.'

Nina frowned. Minnie hadn't needed to be nervous for her first ball; her yield had been something special while Nina's was not. If her crop had been anything like as big as Minnie had produced, she wouldn't be nervous at all, she'd be marching down the walkway straight-backed and proud. She waited until her cousin had stepped down from the carriage before she moved to the door herself.

The Governor's House stood in the lee of the hills that rose up behind it like grey flints, hacked to sharpness by something primitive. The house was built in the same silver-grey slate that characterised most buildings in the colony, but it was bigger and grander than any other Nina had seen; three stories tall, with a wide portico, fringed with black, glittering columns. It looked to Nina like a set of jaws opened wide, inviting her to be consumed.

Their carriage was only one of many, circling the wide driveway and disgorging their passengers in pairs and groups. A light mist had softened the air, diffusing the sharpness of the carriages' edges and making their phosphor lamps flare brightly and disperse, like a procession of will-o'-the-wisps.

And then there were the people. Dozens of them, picking their way across the walkways to the front doors. Men and women, each heavy with their crops: mushrooms, brackets, bells and anemone; each extravagantly dressed in brocade, velvet, lace and muslins. Minnie had told her some people wore real silks too, imported from off-world.

'They make it with worms,' Minnie had said. 'Can you imagine such a thing?'

Whatever they wore, everyone looked so beautiful and so keen, each leaning forward with a barely contained anticipation, mirroring Nina's own.

Aunt Caroline fussed with Nina's gown. Smoothing it with her hands, standing back critically to inspect her work.

'There's my girl,' she said. She held up a hand inviting her to lead the way.

Nina inclined her head and did so, conscious she could hear Minnie and Aunt Caroline speaking in hushed conversation behind her. The walkway crackled under her shoes and ahead of her, a pair of footmen stood by the door of the house, dressed in the livery of the Governor's staff: green and gold herringbone with polished flint buttons, their hair tied back with charcoal coloured ribbons, expressions locked in neutral.

And at Nina's approach, they snapped to movement and swung the doors wide.

'Stay with me, dear, or you'll get lost,' Minnie said.

The music hadn't begun yet and Nina didn't have time to appreciate the scale of the place before her cousin had swept her through the crowds to the powder room.

The room was thick with other women, a mass of them pressing in towards the vanity counters arranged at the far end. There was a smell of rich eau du cologne mixed with the earthy, sweet smell of all the crop varieties, and the room roared with competing conversation.

Again, the variety of the guests impressed her. She watched as the other women fought to secure a spot at the mirrors, where they patted their hair and retied ribbons, inspecting themselves critically for any sign their journeys had diminished their preparatory work. They were dark and fair, old and young; their crops were wide and diverse. Many were growing simple button mushrooms like hers, but others were cultivating toadstools or other bell fungi. Some were covered with dense amorphous shapes like swirling, jagged fins that sloped around their shoulders; others were simply covered in light dustings of brightly-coloured spores, which glittered across their backs like fish scales. The crops were bred to be sturdy but Nina was impressed how, even though there were so many women squeezed in the room, everyone seemed to instinctively avoid brushing against each other's growths. 'Come,' said Minnie, 'Let me see your crop.'

It was *such* a crush, Nina felt quite overwhelmed, but she did as she was told and turned around, lifting her arms.

'May I?' Minnie said. Even though they were cousins, it was poor etiquette to touch another's crop without permission.

'Of course,' Nina said.

She felt Minnie's fingers brushing across the back of her, but she couldn't tell what she was doing.

There was an excitement around her. The women in the powder room worked around each other; there was frenetic talk and laughter. From somewhere outside, Nina could hear the sound of distorted strings.

'Minnie,' she said, 'the music—'

'Not yet,' Minnie said. 'They're only tuning up.'

She steered Nina towards the mirror and turned her so they could see her back.

'There,' Minnie said. 'How does that look?'

Nina's eyes widened. Her crop hadn't grown but there was a contrast in the colour of the bulbous shapes growing from her back that made them stand out from the paleness of her skin.

'What did you do?'

'Only powder.' Minnie smiled. 'You look beautiful, Nina, let's go find mama before the music begins.'

A broad hallway led them to the ballroom; a sizeable space in a roughly oval shape. Like most of the buildings in the colony, the walls were cut from dark grey stone that reflected the light as though it were polished glass. The walls were hung with bright pendants, embroidered with the insignia of the top tier of the United Colonies. A square dance floor was marked out by pillars in the centre of the room, above which a great glass dome showed the shifting clouds above. Beyond the dance floor, the orchestra were establishing themselves on the raised stage and around the periphery of the room, tables and chairs were gathered and the guests had already started finding places to call their own for the evening.

Nina searched the crowds for a face she might recognise, something familiar to anchor her amongst the sea of strangers. But there were so many people, men and women, and their crops were so wide-ranging! There were varieties she had never seen before: hinge fungus, brackets, black caps, gills, chains, and threads. Their colours were iridescent under the phosphor lamps, and so magnificent she felt they might overcome her simply by surrounding her.

'This way.' Minnie steered her through the crowds to a table where Aunt Caroline was waiting. She was with a pair of gentleman Nina had never seen before. The older one was stocky and plump; the mass of pink curling strips which blossomed on his back drew unfortunate attention to his receding hairline. The younger man was taller and slimmer. When he bowed to greet Nina and her cousin, the back of his jacket opened to reveal tiers of bright yellow bracket growths.

'This is Mr Yolland,' Aunt Caroline said. 'He and Mr Bracewell work for the Ministry of Agriculture.'

Nina held out her hand. She smiled.

'Mr Yolland,' she said.

The young man bowed again, he took her hand and kissed it.

'Miss Grey,' he said. 'An honour and a pleasure.'

Mr Bracewell bustled him aside and took the hand Nina still held outstretched.

'Miss Grey,' the older man said, 'please forgive my young friend. He has no poetry. An honour! A pleasure! Such inadequate expressions when faced with a beauty such as yours.'

Nina blushed; her eyes flickered back to Mr Yolland who looked amused.

'Your aunt tells us you're here from the mountains, Miss Grey,' he said.

Nina nodded.

'Near Druenin,' she said.

'Nina's father is Mr August Grey,' Aunt Caroline said. 'He owns the South Druenin mines.'

'He doesn't own them,' Nina said. 'Mr Illwood is the owner, my father manages the business.'

'Mr Illwood thinks very highly of him,' Aunt Caroline said. 'He is an elderly gentleman, and he has no kin.'

'But I wouldn't presume—,' Nina said.

'Nor should you,' Aunt Caroline said. 'That is my job and your parents'.'

Nina lowered her eyes; the reprimand stung and felt unearned. She had always been brought up to be honest, but here, closer to the capital, things worked differently. In the few months she'd spent in the town, she had concluded that society spoke a dialect she had yet to master.

'And I hear this is your first harvest,' Mr Yolland said, changing the subject.

Nina shot him a grateful smile. 'It is.'

'And how do you find it?'

'It's magical,' she said.

'In Nina's family,' Aunt Caroline said, 'only her mother has been seeded, so this is quite the novelty for her.'

Nina bit back a remark. There were others in the mountains who were seeded, but she knew how petulant that would sound if she said it out loud. Instead, she looked up at Mr Yolland. His eyes met hers and they were kind but unwavering.

'Well naturally,' he said, 'the dispensation for those who perform physical labour is an important one.'

Mr Bracewell snorted; he'd been quiet since Nina's admission that her father's status was not quite as lofty as her aunt had advertised.

'It's a waste of valuable real estate,' he said.

Mr Yolland returned a tolerant look, and it struck Nina that this must be an argument he had heard before.

'Nonsense,' he said. 'The energy of their labour would make their crops ripen far too early and the weight of their yield would impede their work. It's a question of balance, Mr Bracewell.'

Mr Bracewell shrugged and looked out across the dance floor where the crowd continued to grow.

'Well I concede that minerals are the colony's most important export,' he said turning back, his smile lodged firmly back in place. 'We did try exporting crops once, remember that? A disaster, ladies, a disaster. Those in other colonies view our harvest with distaste if you can believe such a thing.'

He laughed, a great booming sound that made Nina nervous.

'But then other colonies are not sterile,' Mr Yolland said. 'It isn't something they've ever needed to consider to be ordinary when they have acres of farmland at their disposal.'

Mr Bracewell made a disgusted sound.

'I should like it explained how that might be less grotesque,' he said. 'Growing crops in the dirt and the effluent, indeed. It's positively barbaric.'

He shook his head.

'No,' he said. 'Our ancestors understood when they came here that a new kind of farming was necessary. The ground may have been home to vegetation once, but that was a long time ago. Now there are just minerals, ores and oil. Everything that used to be alive now makes this a richer world, Miss Grey. Our ancestors had the foresight to understand that.'

He raised his glass in a solemn and private toast.

Mr Yolland looked amused, and opened his mouth to say something in reply when a bell sounded from across the room. Nina turned to see the doors at the far end open wide. The orchestra struck up the district anthem, and the guests to the harvest ball each took to their feet.

Through the door came a procession. Four men carried a broad sedan between them, upon which, lying face down, was a man covered with the largest crop of bracket fungus Nina had seen so far. Great jagged shapes rose from his back in mountains of bright yellows and reds and they did not stop at his back but seemed to cover every inch of him. It was only by looking closely that she could see a face amongst all the vibrant growth.

She glanced at Minnie for confirmation.

'The Governor,' Minnie said.

'A good man,' Bracewell added.

The sedan was set down at the front of the room and upon it, The Governor wilted a little until one of his entourage propped him upright.

Beneath the rising tide of bright fungal growth, the Governor nodded his head once and at this signal, the music picked up and the harvest dance began.

Nina had been to dances in the mountains of course. They took place in the union hut behind the mine worker's mess, and while she adored them, they were informal and their scale was so much smaller than this evening's entertainment. It was no wonder that Minnie and Aunt Caroline had considered them rather parochial when they'd arrived by carriage to collect her all those months ago. If nothing else, there was no real *purpose* to them. The harvest ball at the Governor's house felt as though it had a meaning behind it. All these people! All these crops! There was enough food in the room to feed the community for months and the sense that she was contributing gave Nina an enormous sense of pride.

Mr Yolland offered her his hand for the first dance. The music swelled around them and Nina was quite taken away by it.

'How does it compare to the mountains?' Mr Yolland said, as they circled past the dais where the Governor rested.

'It doesn't,' Nina said, watching as the colours whorled around them. 'It's a whole other, wonderful thing.'

Mr Yolland laughed and Nina was spinning again. He caught her, steering her with a blithe confidence she wondered if he was aware of any more. She followed his lead. At first, she felt she was too preoccupied remembering the steps she had learned at the academy, but together, the movement, the colours and the music combined to bleach such *process* from her mind. She felt herself existing solely in the present and it was so exhilarating that when the music finally concluded with a spirited flourish, she felt as though the energy and tempo of it had been ripped away from her. She tottered slightly, and although Yolland caught her, she felt like a fool.

Her second dance was with a serious looking young fellow whose jacket was open along the arms and shoulders, beneath which vivid blue hinges grew like epaulettes.

'Quite a good floor, isn't it?' Nina said and the man agreed.

'Best in the county,' he said, but he didn't say much else.

Nina didn't mind. The man, handsome though he was, was a vehicle to her and nothing more. He guided her through the turbulence of the dance floor, but both were under the spell of the music. Nina felt like she was caught in a fast flowing river, her speed and movement guided by unseen currents far too powerful for her to resist.

The music slowed and she glanced across the floor at the other dancers. Beside her, an elderly lady, her back shining with glittering purple barbs, was steered past by a white haired man, whose back was hunched beneath the weight of dark green, fibrous leaves. The lady's face was tight with concentration, as though every movement was an effort.

'Does everyone dance?' Nina said. 'Some people seem so very old. They must be tired.' She recalled how in the Union Hall, the older people would sit around the edges of the room, watching the revellers from behind their black-boned fans.

Her dance partner frowned.

'It's the harvest ball,' he said. 'Of course everyone must dance. We expend energy and adrenaline so our crops will be at their very best when the Cultivators gather them from us.'

He pushed her away from him a little so he could study her.

'It is a curious question,' he said.

Nina felt her cheeks reddening.

'It's my first harvest ball,' she said. 'I'm down from the mountains. When we dance back home, it is for the music, for the joy of it…'

She tailed off, quite ashamed of herself.

The man looked away again; he turned her stiffly across the dance floor.

'What a ghastly waste of time,' he said.

In the doorways around the ballroom, the Cultivators were standing, watching and waiting. They wore long, yellow mackintoshes that shone under the light from the chandeliers. Their goggles hung on straps around their necks and their scarf-filters were loose over their noses and mouths. The crops had been engineered so spores would only take root in their allotted hosts, but there were always stories where something had gone wrong and these days, all sensible precautions were taken.

On the dais at the head of the room, the Governor danced alone. His was a strange and awkward dance, his movement impeded by the sheer weight of his crop. But he twitched and flailed, hammering his foot to the ground as best as he could to keep time with the orchestra. He had hauled himself to his feet and he twitched to the music like a palsied marionette, his face turned to the ceiling, his dance ecstatic.

Like each of his guests, The Governor would be harvested that night, but only once his dance was done.

The dancing continued and Nina was taken by it. She began to lose all concept of time and almost believed she could have danced forever if the music played likewise.

But the music stopped between dances and as the revellers parted, Nina found a little space near one of the pillars to get her breath back. She glanced around at the crowds rushing about, and found herself curiously paranoid that she would not find a partner for the next dance.

At the back of the hall, she saw The Cultivators had started working, siphoning off dancers whose crops they judged to have ripened to their satisfaction, and leading them through the doors to an adjoining theatre. Nina could see others returning, their jackets buttoned down, the backs of their dresses tied up with ribbons to the nape of their necks.

She saw the Governor talking to one of his staff. A shake of the head; he wasn't done yet.

'Miss Grey, may I?' a voice spoke up to her left and relief flooded her. But when she turned, she was a little disappointed to see it was the plump figure of Mr Bracewell who had spoken. His hand was outstretched, and he was standing, half bowed, as though he was presenting himself to her for inspection, his baldness first.

Nina collected herself.

'But of course, Mr Bracewell,' she said. 'I'd be delighted.'

She took his hand and allowed him to lead her into the throng.

Despite both appearance and manner, Mr Bracewell proved himself to be more than competent on the dance floor. They turned around its periphery as though it were a carousel, and although Nina found herself adjusting her pace to compensate for the shortness of her partner's legs, she realised she was enjoying herself again.

'So how do you find your first harvest?' Mr Bracewell said.

'It really is magical.' Nina wished she could come up with a word that sounded less trite.

'Somewhat different, I would imagine, from the dances you must have attended up in the mountains.'

'Very different.' Nina smiled. 'So many colours. So many people.'

'And your family are still there? Left behind?'

Nina frowned. 'Well, yes, but it was good for me to come to the town. To be seeded, to be part of society—'

Mr Bracewell laughed.

'When I was a young man,' he said, 'thirty years ago, maybe more, I would pride myself on being the last to be Cultivated at the harvest dance. I would dance on and on into the night, and the dance floor would empty and the walls would become lined with those whose crops had been harvested, and those who were just tired and waiting for the feast to begin.'

Nina smiled sympathetically.

'I'm sure you were a marvellous dancer,' she said. 'I'm sure you could still be the last on the dance floor if you wished.'

Mr Bracewell shook his head a fraction, his smile wistful.

'No,' he said. 'That youth of mine is gone. That's what youth does. It leaves. Just as you left your home in the mountains for a better life in the town; just as the colonists left the Old World all those generations ago to set up their own, better places. The young of us set out, they seed new places, to produce crops that will be harvested, to dance until the end of the night. It is a rare sort of youth which spares a thought for those of us left behind.'

There was no bitterness in his tone, just a thin edge of sadness which, small though it was, felt at odds with the atmosphere of the ball.

Nina frowned. Her concentration gone, her rhythm went with it and she missed a step with an awful, clumsy clacking sound as her shoes struck the beautifully polished floor flat-footed. Disorientated, she pitched forwards, but Mr Bracewell caught her before she could fall. Close now, she could smell the sour sweat of him; she struggled away in revulsion but he held her tight.

'Sometimes,' he said, 'I look up to the stars and wonder how far we have progressed. Seeding our kind through the heavens like a fungal bloom. And I imagine the stars blinking out, one by one as we pass across them like a shadow.'

She felt his hand snake around her waist, his fingers pressing themselves to her back. Her eyes widened in horror as she felt him search out and then pluck a mushroom from the low reaches of her crop. With it, she felt a small convulsion run up her spine: a jolt of inexplicable pleasure, as though the lightest of feathers had drawn a delicate path down the small of her back. She struggled free and scowled at her partner.

Around her, the music and the dancing continued, perfectly blind to her own little drama.

Mr Bracewell was smiling, and Nina didn't like his smile at all.

'You really mustn't take me seriously, you know,' he said.
Nina inclined her head.

'Excuse me,' she said. 'I need some air.'

She pushed her way through the still-crowded dance floor and out of the hall.

She was not alone on the veranda; a few couples had retreated outside to engage in quiet discussion. Some who had already been harvested were there too, enjoying the comparative calm and looking across the town spread out below. They had covered their backs to hide the marks the harvest left behind, but they looked flushed and satisfied with the night.

Nina leaned on the balustrade and surveyed the view. In the dark, she had to imagine its geometry. She knew the town spread down towards the plain, where it hugged the bank of the outflow river, but her view was limited to disparate, greenish pools cast by phosphor lanterns. With the ball so full, she wondered who might be left in the town. Manual workers, of course, and those on the alternate cycle; seeded only two months ago, their own ball would be later in the year.

She looked up to the sky, straining her eyes to make out the pin-prick stars, scattered above them. She tried to understand what Mr Bracewell had been talking about, but concluded he made no sense at all and that he was a miserable little man who simply wanted to ruin her mood.

'There you are.' Minnie joined her at the balustrade and looked outwards. 'I think I prefer the view in the dark,' she said. 'Black mountains, black landscape, black river, black sky. At least the lights are beautiful.'

She turned to Nina and smiled.

'Mama thought we might have lost you,' she said.

'No,' Nina said. She sighed. 'If the whole planet is so dead and ashen and sterile, do you ever wonder why we stay?'

Minnie smiled and turned back to the view.

'Do you miss the mountains?' she said. 'The real ones, I mean. Not these bumps we have here. I enjoyed my trip to your home, you know. It's always good to see more of the world. And the mountains! Oh, the mountains. They were beautiful, in their way. Beautiful and quite frightening.'

Nina shook her head but didn't respond.

'Come here,' Minnie said; she turned Nina by the shoulders and inspected her crop. 'You should maybe take another dance and then they'll be ready for you.'

'I think I'm done with dancing for the night,' Nina said.

'Well, I'm sure Mr Yolland will be very disappointed to hear it.'

Nina turned, wide eyed. Minnie smiled broadly.

From inside, the music came to a halt and Nina heard the crowd applaud loudly with enthusiasm.

'The Governor,' Minnie said. 'He's leaving the dance floor to be harvested.'

'He lasted longer than I expected.'

'He's a good man,' Minnie said. 'And so is Mr Yolland, if you don't dawdle.'

Nina turned, wide eyed. 'Why? What did he say?'

Minnie shrugged. 'He didn't say anything, but I saw the way he watched as you ran away from Mr Bracewell.'

Nina blushed.

'I didn't run away,' she said.

'Well, don't tell him that,' Minnie said. 'Some men simply adore rescuing helpless women.'

'I'm not helpless!'

'Well of course you aren't, but don't tell him that either.'

Nina laughed, sharply and suddenly enough to draw a look from the nearby couple on the veranda.

'Does Barnabas think you're helpless?' she said.

Minnie's smile faltered a little.

'Sometimes.' She turned away from her cousin and stared out at the chains of distant lights. In an involuntary movement, she reached behind her, tracing the path of her spine as though she expected a crop to be growing there.

Nina glanced at the hall and the music reached out for her, budding a seed of impatience that made her shuffle her feet.

'I should go back,' she said.

Minnie turned to her and her smile was radiant.

'Do,' she said. She reached across and pushed a stray hair away from her cousin's face. 'And you're wrong about the planet being dead and ashen. It is beautiful. It is fertile. We make it what it is. That's why we're here.'

She smiled, but it was a sad smile which made Nina linger a moment. Minnie made a shooing motion with her hands.

'Go on,' she said. 'He's waiting.'

At the end of the hall, the staff had begun to lay out the buffet for the evening. A string of tables had been set up along the back wall, and already there were plates of foods in varieties Nina had never seen before: mushrooms in all shapes and sizes, steaks of bracket fungus, salads of hair-like growth. A procession of serving staff dressed in black and white carried plates of fungal sweetbreads and tureens of richly scented soup, spiced with the piquant varieties of powder spore.

The dance floor had thinned since Nina had last seen it, and the Cultivators had been busy, with many more people lined around the room, gathered at tables and waiting at chairs. The murmur of conversation was mounting from the harvested guests, and threatened to overwhelm the music.

Nina saw Aunt Caroline sitting at one of the tables, but Mr Yolland intercepted before she could reach her.

His timing couldn't have been more perfect. The orchestra concluded one song, and the conductor was already tapping his baton against his music stand. A shift in key signature, a gentle percussion and then the strings swelled at his command. Then came the horns and then the slow and delicate piano melody filled the room like the sun on a spring morning.

And Mr Yolland bowed his head and asked Nina for the dance.

They spun orbits around the floor; the music sent them away, then drew them back. The other dancers began to drift from the floor as the Cultivators led them away one by one. But Nina wasn't ready to go. She was too busy dancing. She would dance until the end of the night if the music would let her; she would dance until the end of the world.

If they wanted her, they would have to wait their turn.

We All Need Somewhere to Hide

The exorcism on Bexhill Road was not going as expected. Alce's arm was elbow-deep in the kid's skull, the boy was shrieking and bucking and, on the other side of the door, his mother was screaming his name and hammering her fists so hard the woodwork was splintering.

Eddie Kellogg was five years old and host to a feeder, and it hadn't taken Alce long to spot the Sculptor's mark on the nape of his neck: a ridge of skin, pinched and twisted into a yin-yang symbol by unseen fingers. To the untrained eye, he looked pretty much like any normal kid, and the demon had him playing angel when Alce and Leon had arrived. As usual, it was too much. Demons didn't understand subtlety and the kid was acting like Little Lord Fauntleroy, dressed up to the nines and playing politely with his toys in perfectly symmetrical shapes.

He'd been opened up like a biscuit barrel, and something had been stuffed inside of him before he'd been locked tight again.

The room was bare when Alce had first come in. He'd broken pretty much everything of value in the flat over the past few weeks, he'd shrieked curses and spoken in tongues, but with the flutter of those eyelashes, his mother had fallen completely under his spell. She'd shifted gears abruptly from the terrified woman who had called the number in the Yellow Pages, begging for Alce's services, to the angry momma bear on the other side of the door.

She had remained starry-eyed and oblivious, even when Alce had aimed the scrylight at the boy. Its light flattened the room's perspective and cast a shadow too enormous and grotesque for a five-year-old child, spreading its uneven bulk, fringed with horns and spikes and tendrils across the magnolia wallpaper. His mother refused to see the monstrousness of it, so Alce had instructed Leon to escort her out the way.

Bang! Bang! Bang! went the door. Parents never understood. They either didn't believe anything, or they believed everything wrong.

Alce gritted her teeth. *I need a fucking holiday,* she thought, and then she got back to work.

Darkness was waiting for them on Bexhill Road when they were done. Leon was silent as he drove the van through the late evening traffic, and Alce sat in the passenger seat watching the lights of downtown split and merge across the windows as they slid past. Too much time bathed in the crepuscular blue-grey dusk of the scrylight was always jarring. Her mother would compare it to jet lag:

'You're fast forwarding to a very particular moment of the day,' she would say. 'A frozen moment, stretched out way beyond its capabilities and folded flat. Then you turn the switch and *bam*, you're back where you started again, snapped back like you were on elastic. It's not right and your body knows it. Throws you for a loop if you're not wary. Need to keep an eye on your footing.'

Alce's mother knew all about what it was like to lose your footing, or at least Alce presumed she did; it was hard to tell in her current state. Alce hadn't visited the care facility in years, it didn't seem worth it unless she received word that circumstances changed. She paid the bills each month and received reports in the mail. *Condition unchanged. No physical response.* In the bed in her private room, her mother had barely moved for nearly six years. She didn't speak and, while her eyes were occasionally open and her pupils responded to light stimulus, Alce was under no illusion that she registered anything.

Alce had been assured her mother was healthy, she just wasn't quite at home, but Alce had seen so many bodies with an excess of souls, she was alarmed to see one with barely anything inside it at all.

'We should get you to a hospital,' Leon said, glancing at the handkerchief covering Alce's finger, the one the boy had tried his damnedest to bite off.

'It's not serious,' she said. 'Baby teeth. I'll deal with it.'

He glanced at her, sceptical.

'I'll take the jar to the Padre,' he said. 'You should turn in for the night. You look tired.'

Alce was tired. She was exhausted. 'I'm fine,' she said.

The nightclubs were dense that evening, the irrepressible energy of the mobs of revellers coalescing and slowing the city around them. Alce stared at them listlessly. They all looked so young, so careless, although she supposed a lot of them were her age, maybe even older. They whooped and howled at each other like jungle animals, slapping the bonnet of the van as they crossed the road in front of them, lapping up the glare of the headlights. Leon remained impassive. It took a lot more than drunk people – *happy* drunk people – to rile him.

Alce cradled the scrylight in her lap. A new crack had opened along one side from where it had fallen when Mrs Kellogg had finally broken the door down. It was nothing another length of gaffer tape couldn't fix.

There were newer models available, the modern versions were lighter and had more features, but she liked this one. It did one thing and it did it well, it had never let her down, and it felt solid enough she felt she could use it as a cosh if things ever got really out of hand.

Of course that was what Leon was for as well. Alce had learned at an early age how to handle herself in a fight but she preferred to avoid them, and if that was impossible, the next best option was to outsource to someone more likely to absorb the violence. Leon was a slab of a man, and she'd seen him taking on entire gangs of blood-sworn acolytes on the South Side, swatting them off him like they were a squall of autumn leaves.

Like the scrylight, she'd inherited Leon. He'd been the one who found her mother after her encounter with the Sculptor that time, and he'd carried her back to the seminary, twenty-three miles on foot without so much as a pause.

They hadn't always been so close. When the old Padre had first assigned him, Alce remembered that her mother had treated him abominably. She hadn't wanted a minder, she said. She didn't need muscle.

'We're doing fine,' Alce had heard her scream at the phone.

'We?' the old Padre's voice had crackled over the loudspeaker. 'Lyssa, your daughter isn't part of this.'

'I've trained her myself,' her mother had said. 'She's ready. She's more than ready. She's an asset.'

'She's your daughter,' the old Padre had said.

'We don't need him.'

Maybe she was right. Maybe having Leon around had given her an excuse to lose her nerve. Maybe she'd been right about Alce as well. It certainly didn't take long for the Padre to call her once her mother was incapacitated.

It was dirty, physical work, but it was second nature to Alce by now. She still marvelled at the complacency of the oblivious public she dealt with. The ludicrous way they could remain blind to the nature of the wider world until the unpleasant realities of it impinged on their own. She remembered wishing she could feel so immune. She wished she could leave the house one morning and see only the world as it pretended to be. It must be so easy to be ignorant. So happy to not know.

Leon pulled up outside Theo's block in Hewitt Gardens and Alce's stomach lurched. She looked out the window, blinking, feigning ignorance.

'Where are we?'

'Took you home.'

'This isn't my home.'

'No but your man up there's some kind of nurse, am I right? Also I figured…'

Leon reached into the backseat behind him and pulled out a plastic bag, its contents unambiguously a bottle of something, a sprig of ribbon around its neck.

'*Leon.*'

'For your anniversary,' Leon said. 'I didn't get it for you. I got it for you to give. I figured you'd forget.'

Alce took the bottle wordlessly. She shook her head.

'You're not supposed to know about any of this.' Theo was a secret. Anything outside the work was a secret.

Leon's grin would have been terrifying if she didn't know him so well.

'I know fuck-all about anything,' he said. 'But in this case, rest assured the Padre knows even less.'

Alce leaned across and kissed him lightly on the forehead.

'I don't deserve you,' she said and let herself out of the car. She tapped on the glass, a wordless goodbye, and watched as Leon pulled out, lingering until the van's tail lights had diminished into the traffic.

Theo was cooking when she let herself into the flat. She could smell his signature casserole from two flights down. He had the radio on loud and was singing along to Mark Bolan. She set the keys and the scrylight down on the bookshelf, then hesitated in the kitchen doorway, reluctant to interrupt him.

Theo wasn't a nurse; he edited biology journals at the university. He had one of those faces that looked too youthful, but he was only younger than Alce by a couple of years. He was almost-slim, he was almost-fit, he was white-guy dancing in the kitchen in stockinged feet. He had a wooden spoon in one hand, a pair of tongs in the other. It was awkward, but Alce smiled anyway. It was what normal people did after all.

He saw her mid-lyric and started with surprise, then he clutched his hand to his chest as though he'd almost had a heart attack.

'Holy shit,' he said, stumbling against the counter.

'Hey.' Alce brandished the bottle half-heartedly. 'Anniversary, right?'

'Right.' He dropped his tools and stepped forward, taking the bottle off her with one hand and setting it on the counter without looking at it. 'I didn't hear you come in.'

'I tip-toed.'

He rested his hands on her shoulders, and leaned in to kiss her. She could taste the garlic on him, like it had breached his pores as he'd sliced it, and now inhabited him. He slid his hands down her arms, and it was only then that he saw how she had injured herself.

'Jesus,' he said, pushing back and holding her hand up. 'What the hell happened to you?'

'Answer's in the question.' Alce managed a smile. She let him hold her hand, examine it.

He frowned. He only had the vaguest idea of what she did for a living, and even that was under sufferance on Alce's part.

'We need to get you to a hospital.'

'I just need a dressing,' Alce said. 'I'll be fine.'

'Jesus. You've lost the top of your finger.'

'I know,' Alce said. 'I got bit.' She closed her eyes. She shouldn't have told him that.

'Someone *bit* you?'

'It's complicated. I just need a dressing. It didn't hit the bone. Really, I'll be fine. I've had worse.'

His look reminded her that she probably shouldn't have told him that either. She tried changing the subject.

'Smells good,' she said.

'It'll keep.'

Theo led her to the bathroom and sat her on the toilet seat. He fussed over her hand, gently unwinding the handkerchief and washing the wound it revealed: an elliptical cross-section, beading with spots of blood. He dressed it with care and she watched him work, moved by his delicacy, by the stark contrast between how he treated the cuts and bruises of her, and the brusque way her mother used to patch her up.

'You know,' he said, 'you're not really supposed to leave bits of yourself behind when you go to work.'

'I'm careful,' Alce said. 'Could have been more than just the fingertip. You know how it is.'

Again, his expression underlined how he didn't.

'Either way,' he said. 'Maybe you want to think about doing something else? Something a bit safer.'

She laughed and it sounded hollow.

'I don't know how to do anything else,' she said. 'My mother took me out of school so I could learn from her. No one else would take me.'

She stopped. She wasn't going to talk about this with him. She'd said far too much already. But his smile was good humoured, he'd learned well enough over the past few years not to pry.

'I'll take you,' he said.

She gave him a look for that. Not *the* look, not the one she'd cultivated to freeze acolytes where they stood, but something softer. Reproachful. It was something else she'd had to learn: a shade of darkness to colour her amusement.

'How's the casserole?' she said instead.

'Like I said, it'll keep.'

They kissed again, and for a brief moment, she lost herself in him, then she opened her eyes and caught sight of the pair of them in the mirror. It was an absurd tableau. She, sitting on the toilet seat, her bandaged hand still raised like she was asking attention in class.

Despite herself, she laughed. He pulled back, his smile uncertain.

'What?' he said.

Her phone broke the mood. Trilling in her jeans pocket until she fished it out and gave it full voice.

'Bollocks,' she said. 'I should take this.'

'I'll get the veg on.' Theo smiled at her. 'You are staying, right?'

'Of course I'm staying.' She gently pushed him out of the bathroom and closed the door to, then tapped the answer key and raised the phone to her ear. 'Padre,' she said.

'What happened?' The Padre's voice was filtered through both a lifetime of smoking and the old analogue phone he kept on his desk. He sounded the part, but he didn't have the steel of his predecessor.

'Didn't Leon get back?'

'He did. Along with six-and-half kilos of feeder ash, but you weren't there. What happened?'

Alce sighed.

'I was tired, Leon dropped me home.'

A pause. A click. A harrumph. Percussive placeholder sounds as he tried to figure out the best way to reprimand her. She waited patiently.

'Well it's irregular. You know you need to come back to debrief.'

Weak.

'As I said, I was tired. I'll be in tomorrow morning.'

'Well is there anything you can tell me about the job?' The Padre was going through his list.

'For the most part, standard feeder. I'd estimate it had been there for nearly two weeks judging by its size.'

'Any idea how he contracted it?'

Alce hesitated.

'A Sculptor,' she said. 'He was marked. Back of the neck. At a guess, I'd say it wanted us to know it was there.'

She heard the Padre inhale sharply.

'Oh shit,' he said.

She'd never heard him swear before and was surprised by the way it endeared him to her a little.

'You should interview the boy when he's had a little time to recover,' Alce said. 'Figure out where he's been, where he might have met it. You might have to get the mother to agree to hypnosis as he likely won't remember. I doubt she'd want to see me again.'

'Alce, this is *very* serious.' The Padre sounded flustered. He'd had a relatively easy time of it since taking the role. A few standard possessions here and there, the occasional outbreak of acolyte activity, but nothing on this scale – and he knew fine well that a Sculptor had led to his predecessor's downfall.

'I know,' Alce said.

She heard his breathing at the other end of the phone.

'Is it the same one?' he said again. 'The one that… your mother…?'

'I don't know.'

'Shit,' he said again.

'Get in touch with the diocese, let them know what we're dealing with. They'll probably send Benway over. He's dealt with Sculptors before, so he can take the lead.'

He didn't say anything. She heard only static.

'I'll be in first thing tomorrow,' Alce said. 'Get some sleep.'

It amused her that she should sound like the employer and he the employee. She didn't wait for him to answer before she hung up.

They ate in the lounge. Theo had set up the table under the window where the television was usually positioned. He set it pretty with wine glasses and napkins and even pulled out the chair so Alce could sit down. The food was good, simple but tasty. He'd made the dish often enough that even he couldn't screw it up by now. It was nice, it was *pleasant*, but there was the familiar shadow of something unsaid that fell between them; something which prevented the meal from being quite as warm and comforting as Alce had hoped, something which had not been quite so prominent when she had first arrived.

She'd sensed it before over the past few months. It came and went like a tide. It wasn't a cooling between them so much as a certain prickliness which Theo seemed to be doing his best to hide. Sometimes he was just quiet and brittle. Sometimes he would back away from her, flinching when she touched him as though he was afraid of her. It was only his own discomfort with his behaviour that had postponed her asking him about it. Unchecked, she knew it might grow into something unsolvable, but she also knew from experience it was a manner of confrontation for which she was ill-equipped.

That evening, she assumed it was just her. She knew the situation was as serious as the Padre had said, and when the time came to devote herself to it, she would do so completely, at Theo's expense. He *would* understand, she knew that, but it bothered her that he should need to, just as it bothered her that she was putting it off at all. She could pretend she was doing it for him, but that wasn't true. She was doing it for her. She just wanted one evening off, one evening away from the rising tide, before it broke and took her over completely.

'What's a Sculptor?' Theo said unprompted after they had cleared the table.

'Were you eavesdropping?'

'Thin walls.'

'You don't want to know.' *I don't want to tell you.*

His shrug looked a little too affected.

'Just sounded serious, that's all.'

He ran the taps and held his hand under the flow, waiting for hot water to come through.

'We can do that in the morning,' Alce said. She reached out a hand to him.

'I'll get them out the way now.'

He worked silently. He didn't look at her and Alce watched him but didn't offer to help. She checked her phone, then set it on the bookcase next to her her keys.

'A Sculptor is someone who can reshape flesh,' she said eventually. 'They touch living cells and restructure them, reproduce them, and then make something else. They're dangerous, unpredictable. They're whimsical, capricious. They can open people up to put demons inside. They can reach into people's heads and let their memories run out.'

Still he didn't look at her. He concentrated on his work. She tried to remember what she had told him about her mother. She tried to see if he might connect the one thing with the other.

'Are they demons themselves?' Theo said.

Demons. There had been a time when he could only pronounce the word like a sceptic.

'Not really, no,' she said. 'Demons are as frightened of them as we are but sometimes they're used by the higher orders. They don't really have any affiliation. They have their own agendas.'

She sighed.

'They're rare, which is a mercy. But they're difficult. The last one we had in town caused all kinds of chaos. We're barely recovering.'

She reached up and touched his shoulder, feeling him tense. He shot her a quick look over his shoulder, and she saw his cheeks were pink, before he turned away again.

He drained the sink and dried his hands.

'Theo,' she said.

'I know where she is,' he said.

'Who?'

'Your Sculptor. I know where she is.'

Alce dropped her hand and stepped back. Even in the small kitchen, warm from the steam of the washing bowl, a cold current pricked at her. Theo didn't turn around. He stood with his hands on the side of the sink.

'I didn't know what she was,' he said, then his head ducked a little, catching himself. 'Well I suppose I could have guessed. I just didn't know how to tell you.'

Now he looked at her. His face red, his eyes raw.

'Al,' he said, but she had already turned away, fast pacing down the hall to his bedroom where her overnight bag was stored. She could hear him following her.

'I've been wanting to tell you,' he said. 'But I didn't know how. They made it difficult. They want you to— *holy shit* what is that thing?'

Alce's mother called it a howitzer; she didn't know its proper name. It certainly looked tank-like: it was strange and boxy with a fat barrel. The hand grip looked like an afterthought, but it was worn smooth and comfortable and Alce aimed it directly at Theo's chest.

'It burns through the human epidermis and dissolves the foreign cells living beneath.' She probably didn't need to have said that.

'Jesus, Al—'

'It's a last resort.'

Their directions inverted. Theo backed down the corridor towards the kitchen and Alce stalked after him. She steered him into the lounge and snatched the scrylight from the bookshelf where she had left it.

'Start at the beginning,' she said. 'Don't lie to me. Don't leave anything out.'

Theo set his hand on the back of the chair Alce had been sitting on during dinner. 'Can I sit?'

Alce shook her head.

'Stand,' she said. 'It'll focus you.'

Theo nodded, then shook his head. Then nodded again.

'I don't know her name,' he said. 'She said she was called Diana but I don't believe her anymore. Do you remember when I went for that job interview?'

'What job interview?'

Theo stared at her.

'Four months or so back? It was a publishing job. I was terrified. I could do it, but it wasn't my area, Greek myths or something. Ovid?'

Alce shook her head. 'Remind me.'

'The job isn't important. There was no job. That's what I was trying to say. Jesus, Alce. You don't remember? I was in pieces when I finally got home. I slept on the sofa for a week and you didn't notice?'

She didn't reply. He sighed.

'Look,' he said. 'I met this woman at Barney's leaving do. Remember that? You said you couldn't make it, so I went on my own. Anyway, there she was. Tall. Brunette. We weren't introduced or anything, I just thought she was one of Barney's friends. Anyway I got drunk that night, you weren't about and we ended up talking. I don't remember what about, honestly I don't. Just work stuff mostly. But... don't look at me like that, nothing happened. Really it didn't.

'Then a few days later, I heard I got an interview, so I spend the week swotting up for it. You must remember that? No?

'But it wasn't an interview. It was a set up. I don't know what I told this woman, but I must have said what I did. Maybe talked about the job I'd applied for. Maybe I talked about you.'

He raised his eyes to look at her. The look she returned was steely enough to make him turn away again.

'It was in a building out in the old town, one of those new offices under the railway arches. Half a building site really, I don't know if they'll still be there. They offered me a coffee at reception and I took it and... the next thing I know...'

He blinked.

'It must have been drugged or something. I don't remember passing out but I must have. Because when I woke up, I was tied up and... I was... naked—'

He choked on the word. Embarrassed by it, and embarrassed to be so.

'They'd moved me to the back somewhere. It was like a warehouse and I was tied to this pillar in the middle of the room. Standing up, but really tied, you know? I couldn't move. And there's this woman sitting on a chair in front of me. This little smile on her face. And do you know what she wanted to talk about? You. She asked me all about you. She knew more about you than I ever have. She told me about your mother. She said what she did to her. And she said—'

'What did she do to you?'

Theo swallowed hard, stalling for time before answering her.

'She changed me.' His voice rose in pitch as though he still struggled to believe what he said. 'When she... touched me, I changed. It was like she was moulding me out of clay. There was nothing I could do. She just... She took hours. Hours.'

'What did she change?'

'Everything.'

'You don't look different.'

'I am.' He looked frustrated. 'I'm getting ahead of myself. There were men there too. I didn't see them at first. Tall, bald, wore suits. Very sharp.'

'Acolytes.'

'Three of them. And before she started, one of them came and took some of my blood. They didn't say much, and they disappeared early on, only coming back in at the end, but the woman told me they were on the black market. They used the DNA to make... to make a skin suit for me.'

He looked at her, pleading, as though desperate that his own jargon might overlap with her own.

'A *skin suit*?' She didn't hide the contempt in her voice. For a moment, it felt as though the room was lengthening, pushing Theo further away from her. When he laughed, it was a stark, echoey sound. It was out of place, a long way away.

'It's ridiculous isn't it?' he said. 'If anyone had told me a few months back what I'd be saying now, I wouldn't know what to say to them. But now? My god, Al. Before this, I considered myself a scientist. I knew what you did. I knew what you dealt with. But it seemed so far away. I thought I had a good understanding of the world. Now I'm a child again. There are just so many things...'

He looked away. His hand reached up to touch his face, but he hesitated as though he was unwilling to make the contact now he understood what it meant. He blinked and his face turned pink, and for a moment she thought he was going to cry in front of her.

'This,' he said eventually. 'This isn't me. It's something synthetic, I don't really understand it. The *me* they made is underneath it. It's monstrous and I hate it. I wanted to run away but I didn't know where I'd go. They're making me pay for the suit. A few thousand a month for as long as it takes or they'll strip it off me and leave me as they made me.' He looked up. 'But I don't know if they really care about the money. I think they just want me to be scared of you. They said they'd leave me for you to kill. Because you will, won't you? You didn't even notice when I was crying all night and puking in the bathroom because up here you were just thinking about what monsters you were going to kill next. It's what you do.'

Alce steadied the howitzer.

'Show me,' she said again. She'd always thought she would hate using that voice on Theo. But it occurred to her then that this scene had always been inevitable. He would always have betrayed her. Not consciously. He would most likely have only got in the way through his own naivety; he might have been taken hostage, or someone would have killed him to spite her. Anything would have been a betrayal. It was always the same. In her turbulent world, any island of normality, no matter how small, stood little chance of remaining a sanctuary. She had let Theo in closer than most. She had let her guard down for him. She'd opened herself to him more than she had done to anyone since her mother.

And look what happened to her.

'Al,' he said.

'Alce,' he said.

He'd had the voice. Now he got the look. He blanched; he really didn't know what he was in for. He looked to the floor.

'Okay,' he said. 'But I never wanted to you see this. I thought I could fix it, and...' Maybe he realised how idiotic that sounded. 'I'm sorry,' he said again. 'But it's still me. She just made me look different. But it's still me.'

Alce didn't answer and Theo nodded once, then started unbuttoning his shirt.

'If I show you,' he said, 'will you promise not to kill me?'

It was too preposterous a question to reply to and Theo seemed to understand. Shaking his head helplessly, he continued undressing in the face of Alce's silence.

Shirt, vest, watch. He folded them roughly and hung them over the chair beside him. She watched as he unbuckled his belt and slid his jeans down. She tried to image how such a striptease might have appeared without the shadow of foreknowledge. It all seemed so prosaic. So unerotic. There was no sensuality here, just function, tension, threat.

Theo dropped his boxers and kicked them away. He stood naked and awkward, his cheeks now a different shade of pink. He was a pale, skinny figure. A little paunch on his stomach and some token definition in his musculature that he didn't tend. His penis hung limp and shrivelled as though the temperature had dropped.

Alce gestured with the howitzer.

'Go on,' she said.

Theo sighed. He reached up both hands behind the nape of his neck and ran his finger up the top of his spine. Then he shrugged awkwardly on his left side and using his right arm, gently, uncannily, teased the skin from his left – beginning with the fingertips, moving up to the palm of his hand – and then gently tugging the skin on the forearm down. It rucked and bunched at his touch.

Almost immediately, the artifice of the human arm was obvious to her in a way it hadn't been before. The now-empty fingers were thin like latex, nearly transparent.

Theo twisted his shoulder, extricating the bulk of his left arm by hauling it up and back, leaving the pale skin sleeve hanging like an empty silk stocking.

The arm was huge, impossibly so. It latched onto the side of his slim frame looking as though it should unbalance it. It was as thick as his thigh, maybe thicker, knotted with muscle and sinew. The skin was a rich, unmistakable crimson colour, brushed with coal black hair.

He stopped and looked at her, his unequal arms hanging at his sides, his expression searching hers for a sign of clemency.

She didn't say anything, she offered neither encouragement nor reproof, but her silence was damning enough to make him sigh. He gathered himself and continued.

He used his new arm to aid himself as he unclothed its matching pair, the skin easing off much easier this time like a snake shedding. He was more balanced now, but still preposterous. His arms together seemed bigger than the rest of him, his shoulders like medicine balls. He ducked his head forward and reached behind with both enormous hands then gently unpeeled the skin and scalp from the back of his head.

For a brief moment, she saw his familiar features distort and then collapse, then the head was free, and he rolled the remains of his old familiar face down like a mask. The face stretched grotesquely as he teased it, gathering up his chin and his shoulders and pushing them down over his chest, becoming mercifully unrecognisable once it had distended and folded down to his waist, revealing the new head and the trunk of him.

Now he looked more evenly proportioned. His chest was a piece of brutalist architecture, pectoral muscles like slabs of concrete, shoulders like flyovers, the red skin rough like gravel, sheened with dewy sweat where it had been covered.

When he lifted his head, Alce was surprised by how much of him was still there. His eyes hadn't changed, and while the shape of his face was distorted by the snout and the tusks and all those horns, there was still enough of Theo inside of it for her to recognise him. The mortified embarrassment, the weary acceptance of it all; the expression *alone* was his.

He reached down and freed the rest of himself from the skin-suit as though they were a pair of increasingly ill-fitting tights. Swollen goat legs, thick with black fur, stepped out of his slim human ones. Gnarled hooves settled on the plush carpet where his feet had stood. He stretched to his full height, near two foot taller than his previous five-foot-nine, ducking only when his horns scored lines in the plaster moulding on the ceiling.

He took the skin-suit delicately in his clawed hands and folded it with a gentle reverence. When he turned to set it safely on the shelf, she saw how he also had a rope of tail, ending in matted brush. It arced out of him and trailed like a pitifully ironic question mark.

He turned back, his hands moving instinctively to cover his phallus, which, to his clear embarrassment, had grown thick and erect with its reveal.

Alce aimed the scrylight at him and threw the switch. He winced under the glare but didn't move. The lights flickered precipitously but the shadow he cast was still small, still very human, cowering on the wall behind the enormity of the creature he'd become.

Alce shut off the light and set it and the howitzer aside. She stood up and realised for the first time that evening how tired she was.

'This is ridiculous,' she said. 'Demons don't even look like that. They're tumours. Digestive systems with teeth. They're all spikes and tentacles. Nothing else.'

She approached him, walking around him while he stood stock still.

'She said was doing a course in medieval art,' Theo said. 'She thought it would be funny.'

Funny. Yes, a Sculptor would think that. Alce frowned. Something occurred to her.

'How long have you been like this?'

'Four months. Just over.'

'We've fucked since then,' Alce said. 'You were like *that*—'

'I was wearing the skin-suit!' Theo said. 'It's… expensive, like I said.'

'Jesus, Theo.'

'Al—' He turned around to face her, too quick; his horns caught on the ceiling again and jerked his head back, making him growl in surprise. The moment was so slapstick, Alce laughed before she could catch herself, and once it was out, the sheer absurdity of the situation coupled with her own exhaustion set her off. She laughed longer and harder than she had for years. Theo had always known how to make her smile after a long day, he'd always been able to raise a laugh with something wilfully ridiculous, but *this*? This was something else.

Short of breath, she reached out to him to support herself. His skin was unfamiliar and calloused, but warm and oddly reassuring in its weight and mass. He shuddered at her touch and for a moment she thought her laughter had set him off as well. It took a moment for her to appreciate it was something else instead.

The monster, crying.

If anything, he had turned even redder. His eyes were puffy, bloodshot and raw, and tears cut new paths down the reconfigured contours of his face. Snot and mucus ran from his flattened nose as he cried. His mouth, misshapen by the mass of teeth and tusks he had acquired, was ill-designed, and drool spilled down his chin. He wiped his face with the back of his arm, the fur matting.

'I'm sorry,' he said, over and over again. 'I'm so sorry.'

He crouched low, head down like a child who knew they'd done wrong, his body wracking with his tears to the extent that the floor shook beneath him.

Instinctively, Alce reached out to him and held him. He was too big, too ridiculous. But she held him anyway, turning her cheek to rest on his chest. He smelled of leather and iron, but the sweat of him was still familiar, still him.

'Why would she do this?' he said, his voice broken to a leonine gruffness that almost suited his new appearance.

'To hurt me,' Alce said, aware of both the truth of the answer and the selfishness of it. 'Because my job is to kill people like her.'

He choked on that.

'It's okay,' she said, not knowing as she said it how it could be. 'We'll fix this,' she said, not knowing if it was possible.

Reassurance didn't come naturally to her. She knew it

sounded forced, but something connected. She felt him shift his arms so they surrounded her, holding her gently and she froze, feeling only the heavy threat of him. When he sensed her discomfort and released her again – holding his hands to his sides slack and impotent – she felt inexplicably awful.

She shook her head.

'Let's get you to bed,' she said.

Theo slept on their double bed which now seemed far too small for him alone. He had curled up into a foetal ball, bringing his goat-legs up to his demon chest. His horns had punctured one of the pillows, but he slept anyway, whimpering slightly as he did so as though he was still crying, even if he wasn't awake enough to realise it.

Alce had waited with him until he had fallen asleep, then watched him a little while longer.

Theo was her normal. At least he had been before. He was dull, bland, useless. He was funny, sweet, silly. He was far too sensitive for her world, he was her anchor point to the lightness of the real, while she spent so much of her time in the dark.

Her mother never had any time for a partner. She'd never had any time for anything other than the work. Alce certainly never knew her father and the only time her mother had spoken of him was to firmly dispel the fantasy that Alce had been brewing, the idea he might have been someone special or magical.

'He was a mistake,' her mother said. 'Nothing more. He was weak. I don't drink anymore.'

And that had been that.

Alce had grown up in her mother's rooms in the annex

behind the seminary where the word 'father' referred to the Padre, to visiting priests, to churchmen and no one else.

On one of her first trips to the field, she helped her mother exorcise a demon from an elderly man and watched in horror as the man wailed as he reconnected with the cardiovascular pain the demon's presence had muted.

'He's better now,' her mother told her as she steered her out of the room. 'He's human again. You don't know what it's like to have someone else living inside of you. I do.'

The look she had given Alce had been sharp and final.

She had never known about Theo. She hadn't known about any of the people Alce had been with.

'Someone once told me,' she told Alce one evening, 'that everyone needs somewhere to hide, but that's dangerous nonsense. Giving in to the instinct to hide is what makes you vulnerable. You don't need sanctuary, you need strength. Remember that.'

Alce had never believed it. Seeing her mother in the care facility, she wondered if she still believed it either. People just needed the *right* place to hide, that was all.

Theo whimpered in his sleep again.

She leaned over him, and with a light touch, traced the contour of him from his shoulder to his hip, to his thigh. He didn't wake, but he stilled a little, as though her touch had chased away his nightmare for a spell, and let him sleep in peace.

It was late but although she was exhausted, she didn't know if she would sleep. She took a long shower instead, wrapping a towel around her when she was done.

In the kitchen, the dishes were still half-done; in the

lounge, Theo's clothes were still laid out over the furniture.

She picked up the skin-suit from where he had left it and examined it with what she hoped was a professional disinterest. Without him, it looked anonymous and grey. She turned it around to try and find the trick of it, but it appeared to be dormant in her hands. She held it up by the shoulders, and it unrolled before her like a plump stick man, its head lolling forward on its chest.

She wished she could see his face in it somewhere. Something of him she could recognise and claim, but the face was a grey blank, an empty hood betraying nothing.

There was an opening at its back. A long line which ran from the nape of the neck to the coccyx.

Curious, she fed her hand inside it, feeling the path of one of the arm holes and running it up her own forearm, so her fingertips found its fingertips. The suit felt slightly elastic, she pulled it taut and snug, it found her shape and used it, the texture of it resettling and taking on the appearance of flesh. Now it was no longer a glove, but a hand. Her hand, his hand. His scuffed knuckles, his dirty fingernails, his life line stretching and splitting across his palm. She turned it back and forth. His light fuzz of red-brown hair thickening across the forearm, the constellation of freckles at the root of the thumb. She put it to her cheek and felt his touch; she put it to her lips, and it was his taste.

She heard him move in the other room, and she stepped into the corridor to see him framed by the bedroom door. He was now on his back splayed across the covers, one giant arm trailing on the floor. She saw the give of the bedsprings under the size of him and heard the catch in his throat as he snored.

She tried to reconcile the touch of the old him with the

shape of the new one, but the disconnect was too great, the rift too wide. She went back in the lounge and closed the door gently behind her.

She let the towel loosen and fall to the floor, and guided his hand from the nape of her neck, over her the curve of her breast and down the flat of her stomach. She traced his fingers over the edges of her scars as he sometimes did. He was so much more gentle, so she tried again until it felt more right: the barest touch of his fingertip. It was like tuning a radio. She guided his hand down between her legs. If she closed her eyes, he may as well be there.

Later, she teased open the gap in the back of the skin and stepped inside. She pulled his feet on over hers, his chest, his arms, his face, his head. She reached back over her shoulders and touched the seam on the back, feeling it close up around her, tightening, then relaxing as it settled. It felt comfortable, cool. She looked down at herself, and saw only him. She cupped his penis and balls gently in her hand, but they felt light, illusory. Too much to expect, she supposed, that the suit would make meat of them as well.

The bathroom mirror was still clouded from the shower, so she swept it clear with a towel to see him standing there facing her. His face, his body, his hair mussed from sleep. His lopsided grin smiled back at her and it was such an easy expression, she found herself disappointed. Something she had loved in him was something he had never put any thought into. It was just a part of him, not something he did for her alone, not something either of them had earned.

In the bedroom, she lay on the edge of the bed. She faced Theo and watched him sleep through his own eyes. She lay there for long enough, she wondered if she was daring him to wake and see her. But he didn't, he slept sound and oblivious; his monstrous features softened and strangely childlike.

'This is a job that is never done,' her mother had told her once. 'It's an enemy we can't defeat, we can only keep at bay.'

She remembered seeing a documentary when she was young. Scientists used a microscope to prove just how many *things* lived on the human body unseen. The eyebrows alone were crawling with tiny bugs and parasites and Alce had spent the next two weeks scrubbing her face so hard her pores glowed, giving her an expression of bruised surprise.

For the past ten years, she felt as though she had been scrubbing the city raw in the same way. It only felt more futile as the years had gone by. There was always something there, always something coming.

Why would she do this? Theo had asked her. *Because I keep trying. Because I don't know how to stop.*

It was nearly dawn when she dressed. Theo was still asleep, still snoring where she had left him in the bedroom. She put on the clothes he had worn the day before: boxer shorts, jeans, t-shirt, boots. She retrieved his coat from the cupboard and found it contained his wallet and his phone. She took his watch from the bedside table and looped it onto her wrist. His mother had given it to him the year his father had died, and although the strap was fraying, he wore it every day.

She kissed him once, gently on the forehead.

At the front door, she hesitated, then took out her own phone and dialled Leon's number. It rang three times before he answered it, his voice hoarse as though he had only just woken up.

She didn't answer him when he asked why she was calling. She listened to him say her name, the syllables escalating in the face of her silence, then she dropped the phone on the doormat and his bass note of worry became tinny and shrill in panic.

She glanced one more time at the shape sleeping in Theo's bedroom, then she let herself out, and let the door shut fast behind her.

Dogsbody

Gil McKenzie didn't get the job in the marketing agency on account of the fact he turned into a werewolf that one time.

The rejection didn't come as a surprise; he'd been through the process often enough in the past five years. It had become almost as routine as the labouring work he took to cover the bills that had continued to stack up no matter who employed him.

The interview had taken place well over a week ago, and the young woman in the grey tweed suit had not taken long to make up her mind. She'd introduced herself as Vicki, and of the three panellists, she'd been both the youngest and the least susceptible to his desperate charm. Unlike her colleagues, she hadn't laughed at any of his self-deprecating jokes about the gaps in his employment history and when she'd turned over the diversity form to examine it in greater depth, he registered how her eyes scanned down it, mechanically switching left and right until she hit the small checkbox on the bottom left of the page. Gil knew the wording by heart. *On November 17th 2010, were you affected by Lunar Proximity Syndrome?* A little superscript asterisk pointed to a lengthy paragraph of small print at the foot of the page: a promise that an affirmative answer would not invalidate the chances of employment; a warning that a dishonest one would lead to disqualification.

He'd completed the form while waiting in the reception area and his pen had hovered over the checkbox. The weekend tabloids were full of angry stories about once-upright employees having lied about not being LPS, and while the articles focused on how they'd been caught out and punished for their transgressions, to Gil, they demonstrated it *was* possible to game the system, at least for a spell. But Jackson and Broome was too big a company to be careless. They would have access to the government register and as such, the question seemed cruel. It felt like a dare.

With a flick of his pen, he told the truth, and he remembered how Vicki's eyes had sharpened, and how she'd looked at him anew, staring into him as though she could perceive the monster he'd briefly been, still hiding, uncomfortable under his human skin. Then she'd promised they'd be in touch in such an abrupt tone, it had taken the other two panellists by surprise.

One week later, and he was standing in the narrow hallway at the entrance to the block of flats where he lived, holding the letter he'd been surprised to find waiting for him in his mailbox.

He held it closed. One week was enough time to make him wonder if he'd misjudged them. Maybe they had a quota they needed to fill? Maybe Vicki's expression hadn't been one of horror but one of fascination? Maybe they wanted him *because* he'd changed?

He tore open the envelope and knew what it said before he read it.

We regret to inform you, etc. etc.

The date on the top of the letter was the same as the day he'd attended the interview, and it was only when he examined the envelope more closely that he realised it was addressed to Flat 12 rather than Flat 12a. They hadn't wasted any time, but Rob next door had.

It didn't matter now. The envelope was open, the letter read, its promise was already spent. Gil tore both into pieces and crumpled the fragments in his fists. He held them over the paper basket on the floor beneath the mailboxes and let them fall, spinning like broken sycamore seeds.

He stopped in Sharmin's on Ledgerman Road for a pack of Marlboro Reds, and as Sharmin himself hunted through the back room in search of fresh packs of lighters, Gil caught sight of himself in the reflective glass of the cabinet behind the counter, where the bottles of whisky and rum were kept locked in the mornings like a holding cell.

It alarmed him how quickly he'd become comfortable with his site clothes: his grey tracksuit pants, the khaki zip-up hoodie now forever tangled with the hi-vis vest. It was a brisk November morning and he was dressed warmly with a beanie and an extra layer he'd end up peeling off as the day wore on. His face was lean and ruddy, and the beard he'd grown in a conscious attempt to look less like an office drone suited him now he'd grown into it, even if it was greyer than he'd have preferred. The neatness he'd trimmed into it for the interview was growing out and he didn't look like the experienced and capable marketing executive his curriculum vitae still described him as.

He shuffled idly through the tabloids stacked on the counter. Most had something about the anniversary, but it was the same not-quite-news the media had been peddling since the event five years earlier. Old stories repeated with limited hindsight, the same hypothetical questions asking what was being done to keep everyone safe, and a few inevitable column inches about Chrissy Linderman's upcoming appeal. Some lip service was paid to some unlikely new theories to explain what had happened (A genetic disorder! Blood disease! Aliens!), but none had anything new to say. He leafed through the pages and recognised some of the photographs inside. Familiar stills of sleeping monsters, incongruous in offices, underground platforms, town squares.

Sharmin returned red-faced and panting, and slammed two shrink-wrapped slabs of plastic lighters down on the counter. He was close to retirement, and looked like a man who found the gradient steepening now the summit was in sight.

'We got stars or spots,' he said when he got his breath back.

'What's the difference?' Gil said.

'No difference,' Sharmin said, 'except one's got stars on them, the other lot have spots.'

Gil tapped the top package.

'I'll have a couple of those.'

'Stars it is, then,' Sharmin said. 'I did have some with stripes on them a while back. But they were a bad batch. Tended to flare up and I'd have people in complaining how they took their eyebrows off.'

'Stars is good.'

Sharmin tore open the packaging and rang up the till.

'Stars it is,' he said again.

'What happened to the window?' Gil gestured at the board taped up over a broken pane on the door.

Sharmin shrugged and pushed a few coins in change across the stack of newspapers.

'The usual drunken animals,' he said. 'On this street, a good night is one I don't get woken by the sound of broken glass.'

Grisham set Gil to work for the morning, painting the plywood hoardings that masked the site from Mendell Road.

'Doesn't have to look good,' Grisham said. 'Just has to look clean. And mind how you drip on the pavement, the council will have us otherwise.'

Grisham was one of the older supervisors. He had a grey walrus moustache and his hi-vis anorak was zipped up to his chin.

He left Gil with a can of industrial grey-blue, the building company's brand colour, and Gil spent the best part of the morning painting his way from the corner of Bury Street to the remains of the bookies at the top of Mendell Road, which looked like it had been cleaved in half by an enormous blade.

At Muirhouse & Partners, where he'd worked for six years, he'd often sat at his desk in the bright, open plan office and pored over brand proposals submitted by agencies. They'd fascinated him with their intricate pedantry. The minutiae of logo placements, the bizarre laws of typefaces, the curated subset of Pantone colours. Now here he was with a bucket of brand to apply in person. No longer a swatch on a page, but a tin of pure corporate pigment that spattered like buckshot across his tracksuit trousers. It was clean theory made grimly practical. He felt like a disgraced officer sent to die on the front line.

Like most of the jobs he was given on the site, it was dull, repetitive work, but anything which put some distance between him and the apprentices was a job worth taking. They were young and rowdy, getting trained up for the beginning of their careers. They knew his story, or some variant of it. To them, he was old, and cast out of his career, forced to start further down the ladder from where they found themselves. In other words, he was fair game for their taunts, and there was nothing he could do about it.

The last site the agency had him working was a series of low-rise office blocks out past the ring road, now he was on a crew building the new multi-storey behind the Kroner Centre. It was a big job – fifteen months or so – and Grisham had assured the labourers there'd be work for them for the best of it. This was good news, but its location in town increased the likelihood Gil might run into people he knew or worse, people he once worked with. He was sure he'd seen Stephanie once. There had been something about the way she walked through a crowd that seemed so familiar to him. He felt like he was seeing her as strangers saw her and the thought made him feel uncomfortably like a voyeur. He'd stepped well out of sight until he was sure she was gone.

But it wasn't so bad on the site now he was used to it. He knew his place as an unskilled labourer and everyone else knew it too. He was expected to do as he was told and do it as efficiently as he could, but no one really expected him to excel and that was liberating. He was mostly there to carry materials and equipment, to screw in fixtures, to clear rubble, to sweep up the detritus at the end of the day. Occasionally, he almost convinced himself that he'd grown comfortable with the work over two years. Even when it rained, he told himself, he liked the fact they just ploughed on regardless.

When Gil was a kid, his father would pick him up on alternate weekends. A painter and decorator with his own modest company, his father owned a stubby little van that was thick with plaster dust, its smell sharp and dry with paint and turpentine. His overalls would be stuffed in the footwell of the passenger seat and the ladder would be angled over the seat, forcing Gil to crouch to fit in. He'd resented it at the time: the van, the smell, that desperate, over-eager smile, all come to drag him away from his comfortable home in the well-manicured suburbs.

When he was a little older and the school holidays were feeling shorter than they used to, his father would sometimes take him with him to sites he was working on, and to Gil's embarrassment, he'd call him his *mate*, and pretend he was one of the lads he employed. Even then, Gil felt like a fraud. He would try to maintain the complex illusion he knew what he was doing, but the swagger, the surly insolence, and the estuary vowels were all a front. He got the impression his father was proud of him – he'd laugh and ruffle his hair as they walked back to his van – but Gil never felt he deserved it, and when he saw his mother's face when he got back home, he remembered how he didn't want to deserve it either.

On Mendell Road, Gil worked briskly and without complaint, shifting his set of steps along with him as he progressed, leaving a trail of cones, demarcating his work. Later, as he was stringing up yellow and black tape to secure the area, he watched as a man in a neatly-tailored suit veered towards the glistening hoardings, distracted by his phone.

Instinctively, Gil called out to him.

'Watch what you're doing,' he said. 'Wet paint.'

The man glanced back, his course corrected absently as though he didn't quite take the warning seriously. He didn't seem to see Gil at all, seeing only another scruffy workman in a hardhat and boots, but Gil was appalled to recognise him, having drawn his attention. It was Mark Jefferson, who used to work in the finance department at Muirhouse. They'd been in the same meetings, the same presentations, the same awkward conference parties and bland hotels, but if Jefferson recognised Gil, he made no indication. Gil stared after him as he folded into the crowds and disappeared.

'If you ask me,' said Graham, of whom no one had asked anything at all, 'they should ship them all off to an island somewhere. Only real way to be sure.'

He glanced up over the top of his copy of *The Sun* and nodded towards Gil.

'No offence,' he added.

'None taken,' Gil said. 'Just make sure you get me something with a sea view. Or a penthouse. I'll have one of those.'

There was a murmur of amusement in the hut, but Graham frowned. He was the oldest of the labourers, salt and pepper hair trimmed to an even fuzz over his scalp and chins. He didn't really have a face suited to smiling, so the frown was hard to judge.

'I'm not joking,' he said.

'To be clear,' Miro said, 'would this be the same island where you want to put all the gays? Or would that be nearby?' He grinned, his façade of innocence falling with a clang. 'And where would you put all the gay werewolves? Would they get dual passports?'

Graham scowled unambiguously and clambered to his feet, slapping the paper down on his chair.

'Fuck you, you gobby gypsy cunt,' he said. He jammed a cigarette in the corner of his mouth and barged out the door, sparking the lighter he held in his fist.

Miro sat back in his chair, beaming. He was a stocky figure, a wide-eyed face beneath spiky black hair. His grey sweatshirt was printed with the album sleeve of The Sex Pistol's *God Save The Queen*. He only wore it because he knew it pissed Graham off.

'You know, on second thoughts,' Miro said, 'if gypsies get their own island too, I might see if I can sign up. Although my mother would never speak to me again. When it comes to gypsies, she's worse than he is.'

On the other side of the room, Otto bobbed his head in agreement. He was slimmer than Miro. His patchy hair shaved tight so it looked like the shadows of continents mapped on a tall, distorted globe.

'Well they are all thieves,' he said, studying the tea swirling in his plastic cup.

'Otto.'

'I'm not joking either,' he said. 'Where I come from, they're all thieves. You see them coming into town, you lock your door. Don't give me a look like that. You don't have them here. But everyone has someone to lock the doors to. What do you have here? Scousers? The Irish, am I right?'

'Romanians,' Gil said.

'Fuck right off,' said Otto. He aimed a kick at Gil's shin, but Gil shifted out of the way.

Still grinning, Miro picked up the paper Graham had left behind and refolded it to the front page. There was another blurry picture of a monster. It still surprised Gil how few decent photographs there seemed to be of the event; most were low resolution mobile phone shots, or unspecific security footage. The most famous one was the businessman in the empty tube car, slumped on his seat, his now-enormous head awkwardly jammed against the partition beside him. His stockbroker suit was in tatters, unable to contain the new bulk of him. He was all teeth and snout and tail; there were outcrops of bristly fur punching through the remains of his silk shirt and bear-claws breaching the perfect uppers of his patent leather shoes.

The *Sun* had gone with something else for their front page. Uncharacteristically avoiding the celebrity angle and opting for the political instead, they'd chosen the picture of the former Labour MP Kevin Wilkes splayed out and transformed on the floor of the House of Commons. The picture was too grainy to make out many details, snapped by some fleeing backbencher with his smartphone.

The headline was typically flippant: 'Animal House', it read. The subtitle was more portentous. In stark bold letters it promised: 'It will happen again'.

'Inevitable, it says here,' Miro said.

Gil snorted.

'Bullshit,' he said.

'Well, I guess we'll find out tomorrow.' Miro turned the page and a photograph of Chrissy Linderman stared back. Blonde curls, big chinned, a look of dangerous defiance in her eyes. Gil turned away. For a moment, he felt as though she was looking straight at him from the page.

'Bullshit,' he said again. 'And tomorrow doesn't mean anything. Why would it happen at the same time? Like it keeps a diary. Makes no fucking sense.'

Otto nodded.

'But this time the moon is full,' he said.

'The moon's got nothing do with it either,' Gil said. 'You know why they call it Lunar Proximity Syndrome? Because they don't know what else to blame. No other reason. It's as if when science doesn't fit, people turn to the movies for an explanation instead. It's bullshit.'

There was a pause, the clock ticked closer towards quarter-past.

'So are you working tomorrow?' Miro said, his face all-innocent again.

Gil scowled at him.

'Grisham thinks it best I stay at home,' he said.

'What you going to do? Lock yourself in a cage somewhere?'

'Nah, mate,' Gil said. 'I'm gonna sit in my Y-fronts and jack off to *Loose Women*.'

Miro looked at him, perfectly deadpan.

'Never let it be said that you English have no class.'

Gil raised his tea. 'Amen,' he said.

'Ho, wolfman!' The voice was a high-pitched whine but it was the accompanying whistle that made Gil look up. He straightened, and leaned on the yard brush.

Three of the apprentices were standing near the hut. The one in the middle was thin and pasty white, his clothes hanging off him to the extent they almost pooled on the floor at his feet. He wore a trucker's cap backwards on his head but it mostly served to emphasise how narrow his features were. But he was smirking through his glistening acne at Gil, an electric sparkle in the pits of his eyes.

'Alright,' Gil said.

'You feeling yourself, wolfman?' Ollie's hand cupped his groin, his laugh a reedy, grating sound. His friends laughed with him. Troy on one side, Benny on the other, they sounded like a tone-deaf a cappella trio.

'Doing good, Ollie,' Gil said. 'Doing good.'

'Valuable work you're up to there, man,' Troy said. Nearly twice the size of Ollie, Troy looked as though he had been hastily built with a surplus of something denser and thicker than the concrete foundations they stood on.

'Well he's got that expensive education, hasn't he?' Ollie said. 'Degrees and shit. So Grisham only sets him to work on the best there is. He's *earnt* it, man.'

'University of cleaning shit up?'

Dogsbody

'Must have been crap at it,' Benny said, dropping his sandwich wrapper at his feet. 'He keeps missing bits.' Benny was lanky and gym-lean, his features tense and wired. He was the sort of kid who wore his athleticism as though it might be a weapon.

Troy grinned and threw the plastic Coke bottle he'd been drinking from so it spun across the site.

'Go on, boy,' he said, 'fetch.'

Laughing and whooping, they set off back across the site and Benny threw his head back and howled, which only set Troy off again. They hadn't got far when Ollie broke away, and swaggered back to Gil.

'Hey, wolfman,' Ollie said. 'Check it.'

He glanced around him to confirm they weren't being observed, then fished in the back of his work trousers and pulled out a short-bladed hunting knife, blade bright and serrated.

'Tomorrow,' he said. 'When the moon comes out and all you freaks turn into whateverthefuck, me and my boys are heading out and we're going to cut ourselves a wolfskin.'

He turned the blade so it grinned toothily in the light.

'*Swick! Swick!* How's that sound to you?'

'Guess you'd better hope they don't wake up this time,' Gil said. 'You might need bigger balls starting a fight with something that could fight back.'

Ollie blinked, dead eyes, humour gone. The knife dipped in his hand, point-down towards Gil's crotch.

'Oh,' he said. 'I'll take their balls and all.'

'Well if that's your thing, I guess.'

'What did you say to me?'

'I said fuck off, Ollie,' Gil said. 'Haven't you got a wall to build?'

Ollie froze, his stare dull and empty, the knife unwavering in his hand. Gil wondered how quickly he could move the broom. He could probably knock the boy's legs out from under him if he was fast enough. He wondered where the knife would land—

Grisham's voice called Ollie's name from across the yard and, as though he'd been in a trance, Ollie pocketed the knife and backed away, his lip curling.

'Coming for you first, wolfman,' he said.

Gil didn't say anything. He kept a hold of the broom a long while after the boy had gone.

Gil was about to leave for the day when Grisham called him over.

'Decent work today on the hoardings,' he said, although to Gil it sounded like he wasn't comfortable with the compliment. It wasn't work that could easily be done wrong, it didn't need any validation and they both knew it.

'Any word back from that job you went for?'

Gil winced, glancing away, and Grisham sucked his teeth and shook his head.

'Shame,' he said. 'Well you're off for a few days, but when you're back, I was thinking I might hand you over to Hamley if you're keen? He's working on the Yarrow Road offices at the moment. Said he was looking for some new lads.'

Gil frowned. Hamley was a contractor: a painter and decorator with his own boys. Gil had seen them around on the last site he'd worked, but he hadn't really spoken to them, just a brief nod as he passed them, lined up in their whites, finishing their morning coffees.

'You're too old for an apprenticeship,' Grisham said, 'but Hamley said he'd be up for trying to get you some on-the-job training, if you're interested?'

'He did?' Gil frowned. Bulky, thuggish, forearms spiderwebbed with home-made tattoos, Hamley didn't quite fit Gil's idea of a philanthropist.

Grisham shrugged.

'He knew your old man,' he said. 'They used to work together. Went back years, they did. When Hamley realised who you were and, you know, *what* you were... Well, he was right put out. Said he wants to do good by your dad, you know? Said your dad was always good to him and he wouldn't be where he was without him. So he wants to pay that back in some way.'

Grisham spread his hands. 'And seeing as you're not getting anything else in those interviews you go and do, I figured...'

'If this has anything to do with that thing with Ollie—'

'Nothing to do with Ollie. The lad's a punk but he'll straighten out in time, they usually do.' Grisham scratched the back of his head. 'This is me playing nice. Pays in this trade to realise when people are doing you a favour and not be a complete tit about it.'

Gil lowered his head. He knew this sort of talk didn't come easy to Grisham. He'd known him for two years now and it was most he'd ever heard him say.

'Cheers,' Gil said.

'And as I was saying,' Grisham said, 'you did an alright job with the hoardings, so it kind of makes sense. I mean your dad was a craftsman. One of the best I knew. Really good he was. Maybe he passed some of it on to you? Would be a crying shame if his skills died with him, wouldn't it?'

Gil's smile stiffened.

'I suppose you're right,' he said.

Grisham nodded and turned away.

'So next Monday,' he said. 'Go to Yarrow Road and look up Hamley. I'll have a word with the agency, they'll shuffle the paperwork. Hamley'll show you what's what. Be on time mind, he doesn't like any fucking about, that one.'

He glanced up at Gil again.

'You look like your dad, you know,' he said. 'You might take after him yet.'

About halfway down Brook Street, Gil realised he wanted to get drunk.

Autopilot had set him on a course back to his flat out past the bus station, but now, surrounded by the tide of early evening pedestrian traffic, he stopped in the middle of the pavement to give the thought more room. He dug out his pack of Reds and lit one.

It was Thursday and almost everyone without LPS would be working the next morning. If this was his last day as a human, as the papers were keen to imply, he wondered how he should spend it.

He dug out his phone and paged through his contacts. He'd seen his mother a few weekends back, one of those awkward Sunday dinners where he'd sat at the end of the table feeling like he was intruding while his half-brothers – ten and fourteen, and smug with it – had screamed and thrown vegetables at each other.

Her mobile phone was off so he tried the house number and got the answer machine. It was Geoff's voice and the recording made him sound even more nasal. None of the family were in right now, his message said, and the way he said 'family' sounded pointed and exclusive. Gil hung up without leaving a message.

Geoff was in plastics, but not in the way Gil's father was in paint. Geoff's job came with a new BMW every six months and a company card to cover the fuel. Gil had been nine when his mother had remarried and he and Geoff had ground away at each other until they no longer got in each other's way.

'What's he like?' his real dad had asked when he picked him up one weekend.

Gil had shrugged. 'He's alright,' he said.

It was supposed to be non-committal, but he noticed how his dad couldn't look at him, concentrating too fiercely on the road, as though it might suddenly convulse and throw them off at any moment.

'I mean, he's a dick, obviously,' Gil had added, but it was too little, too late to salvage anything more than a brief smile.

'Sure he is,' his dad said.

Geoff wasn't really a dick. He was a good man, Gil had eventually concluded. He had no idea how to talk to the son he had acquired, but he treated Gil's mother with a respect she wasn't used to. She was happy with her new family, she was doing it *right* this time, and Gil had no wish to get in the way.

He put his phone away. New plan: he could just go to The Volunteer and get hammered. He tossed the cigarette to the drain and cut down the alley beside the newsagents, crossing through the car park and slipping back out onto the main drag.

'Gil.' The voice came from one of the side streets and sounded familiar enough to make Gil stop to hunt down its source.

A figure was jogging towards him, a slim man in a long tweed coat and a flat-cap. It was only when he said Gil's name again that he realised who it was.

'Toben?' he said. 'Jesus, I almost didn't recognise you. Where's the rest of you?'

Toben grinned and stuck out an elegantly gloved hand. Gil shook it awkwardly.

'Tash's got me on a diet,' Toben said, thumping his stomach. 'Plus I'm hitting the gym these days. Since that thing happened, everyone's working on their cardio, just in case you all go crazy again. Give us a head start.'

Gil blinked, which made Toben bark with laughter.

'I'm screwing with you,' he said. 'Jesus, were you always so sensitive? How are you doing? You're a hard man to get hold of, I tried calling, emailing but…?'

Gil looked at the floor.

'Oh,' he said, 'you know. I got a new phone.' After he got out of quarantine he'd cut himself off from most of his colleagues at Muirhouse. He didn't know which of them had given his name to the authorities; it could have been anyone, maybe even someone who'd witnessed him stumbling home in ragged clothes. He still remembered the knock at the door, the black van, the dull sinking feeling he'd been betrayed.

Toben looked oblivious.

'Off the grid, huh?' he said. 'Yeah, I get that. Well, I caught you. I win. Prize is that I get to buy you a pint. Does that sound good to you?'

He glanced down at Gil's clothes, his expression critical enough to make Gil feel his cheeks turn pink like he'd been caught red-handed in fancy dress.

'Well,' he said. 'I was heading to The Volunteer—'

'The Volunteer?' Toben pantomimed his disgust with a spluttering noise. 'The *were-bar*? Fuck that. We're going to The Bank. They got cocktails and I'm getting you a cocktail.'

'Toben.'

Toben put a hand on Gil's shoulder.

'Gil,' he said. 'If you stay scared of horses, you'll never get back in the saddle.'

'What?'

'Something my mum used to say,' Toben said. 'Actually, no, I'm fucking with you again. I just made it up. Sort of thing she would say though.'

'Right,' said Gil.

'I've missed you, man,' said Toben. 'You have the best "what the fuck are you on about" expressions and my life has been poorer without them.'

'You never used to be sort to turn down a cocktail,' Toben said, slopping a pint of IPA across the table.

'I'm planning a long one, this evening,' Gil said. 'I figure it's best to drink sensible when you're sober if you're going to drink stupid when you're drunk.'

'You and my mum would get on,' Toben said. He raised his mojito and they clinked glasses.

Gil's glass had been chilled so the beer was too cold; he could barely taste it, but something satisfying connected. Self-conscious, he wiped the foam from his moustache with the back of his hand and glanced across the floor.

Even for a Thursday evening, The Old Bank was dense with lawyers, brokers, marketing executives, whatever the hell they were. The air was thick with day-old deodorant masked with too much aftershave, but there was piss and spilt beer in the mix too, a reminder that while the pretensions of the clientele may have been lofty, The Bank's purpose was the same as any other pub in the town. Gil hadn't been there since he'd worked at Muirhouse and he was keenly aware he looked out of place. He caught some of the younger men staring at him with unmasked hostility, but when he met their looks with an unwavering dead-eyed gaze of his own, they turned away again and this made him feel oddly pleased with himself.

'I saw Jefferson, this morning,' Gil said. 'I called after him, but he didn't recognise me.'

Toben cocked his head.

'Well he's head of finance these days,' he said. 'He doesn't recognise anyone unless they've got the Queen's head on them.'

Gil whistled.

'They made him head of something?' he said.

'Big shake up since you left,' Toben said. 'You wouldn't recognise the place. Let's see. Ahmed, remember him? Ahmed Farah? He's doing okay. The man's a machine and they'd be a fool to keep ignoring him, but you know the shit I've had to put up with from the old men up top? Same deal. Oh, but Kima just got promoted. She's an account manager now, so that's a thing at least.'

He stirred his cocktail. The mint leaves swirled.

'And Stephanie?' Gil said.

'Stephanie's still there,' Toben said. 'Made an impression with her handling of the Dewley account. Got her some high-profile fans. She's going places.'

Gil wasn't going to say anything. Then he said, 'How is she?'

Toben smiled awkwardly.

'She's good,' he said.

They drank in silence for a moment. The Old Bank was a grand looking establishment, its brightly painted, vaulted ceiling was supported by ostentatious pillars and the room was separated into private alcoves by wrought iron dividers. The bar was a circular counter in the middle, and above it, flat screen televisions showed the highlights from some lower-league game, to which no one was paying attention.

'So what about you?' Toben said.

'I'm no longer in marketing,' Gil said.

'I figured. Are you looking anywhere?'

Gil nodded. 'Had an interview last week.'

'And?'

'The job part was great,' Gil said. 'The *"are you now or have you ever been"* bit, not so much.'

Toben stared at him, wide-eyed.

'Seriously?' he said. 'They turned you down because of that?'

'Not the first time, either. Had dozens of interviews over the years. They all end the same way.'

'Can they do that?'

'Maybe I'd exceed their insurance premium. Change again, go crazy, you know.'

'Shit, I had no idea.'

Gil shrugged.

'Why did you think I got fired from Muirhouse?' he said.

'Aw, I don't know,' Toben said. 'They said the government had you all locked up somewhere. Like you'd got together and robbed a bank or something.'

'They called it a "quarantine facility", but it may as well have been a jail. They had to set these things up in a hurry, you know? It was one of those detention centres they set up for immigrants. A pop-up prison. Up in Kingston.'

Gil spread his hands.

'I mean this was when they thought we might change again straight away, so I guess there were good reasons behind it.

Next time, we might not all stay asleep, that was the fear. So it was in the *public interest* that we were put somewhere safe. So they lock us all up, scan us for serotonin, excess testosterone, the warrior gene, all that crap. No correlation. Makes no sense, drives them up the wall. Six months or so go by and nothing happens and we're a waste of tax payer's money instead. Tabloids found something else to moan about and we were just a bunch of confused people living in dorms, getting fat.'

'You don't look fat.'

'Thanks, man. I appreciate that.'

Again, they measured the silence with drink and Gil was conscious he was drinking too fast.

'You working tomorrow?' Toben said.

Gil shook his head. He made curly finger quotes with his hands. 'Holiday,' he said. 'I got an official letter advising me to lock my doors and stay inside, preferably alone.'

'Think it'll happen again?'

Gil shook his head. 'It's all a PR exercise. Some merry dance to placate the idiots who wanted to know why they didn't do more last time round.'

Toben turned his glass around idly.

'But that's the thing,' he said. 'The anniversary isn't really about you. No offence, but you don't realise how frightening it was back then.'

'I had other things on my mind,' Gil said. That wasn't strictly true. From his perspective, the event had passed as a heavy, dreamless void. He may as well have been struck on the back of a head with a shovel.

'In the office, you fell close to where I was sitting,' Toben said. 'I had a front row seat. First I thought you were having a seizure, then there were other people shouting for a first-aider to come over. But they were calling from other parts of the office. Because it was happening there too. Crazy.'

He smiled as though the memory was now too preposterous to take seriously.

'And it was like everyone realised how strange it was at the same time. It was like we all collectively saw the bigger picture, and it was frightening.'

Gil stared into his pint. 'And then we changed,' he said. He'd heard this story before.

'Damnedest thing,' Toben said.

Gil swallowed the remains of his pint and stood up.

'And three hours later, we all turned back,' he said. 'Another one?' He gestured with his empty glass.

Toben reached for his wallet. 'Let me,' he said.

'Fuck off,' Gil said. 'I got paid today.'

He took the few steps down to the main floor of the bar and steered his way through the crowd. He felt drunker than he had any right to be. He was conscious he hadn't eaten anything since the pack of sandwiches he'd polished off at noon.

There was a bit of a crush at the bar, but one of the benefits of being the scruffy one in the crowd of suits – one with steel toecaps at that – was that he didn't care if he was mussed or spilled or trodden on. He picked his way forward with a bullish confidence, turning like a dancer to avoid the drinks being carried the other way.

He didn't have to wait long to get served.

'Pint of IPA,' he said. 'And one of the cocktails. Small one. With leaves in it?'

'Mojito?'

'Yeah, let's have one of them.'

The barmaid smiled, a delicate little expression, and poured the beer first. He started on it, and while she set about mixing the cocktail he looked about him. Everyone seemed so young and in a strange way, they reminded him of the apprentices on the site. Fired up, boisterous and painfully keen. They were all learning their trade, securing their place in the world with their first, increasingly confident steps. They each assumed themselves locked on a path to a particular future and couldn't imagine how circumstance could drive them off course. Gil sighed. They didn't know it yet, but they were all in training to become as old and cynical as he was.

Someone jostled him from behind and he turned to see a young man in an expensive looking suit. Nearly interchangeable from his peers, this one was pale and lanky with a floppy blonde fringe, and was making an effort to wedge his way forward to the bar. The youth's eyes were already slightly unfocused, and for some reason this only darkened Gil's humour further. He looked a little like Ollie, the same high cheekbones and pitted eyes, the same curl of the lip.

Glowering, Gil could feel something stubborn and combative brewing deep within him and he welcomed it, tensing up to make himself a solid, immovable obstacle. He could almost hear the whine of annoyance from behind him.

The barmaid set the cocktail on the bar. The round cost more than twice what he'd expected, so when he turned back with his drinks, his mood had blackened further.

The young suit tried to strong-arm him out the way.

'When you're done,' he said, 'there's a blockage in the gents that needs fixing.' His voice was as reedy and imperious as his appearance, but there was a trace of an accent there too, betraying a background Gil hadn't expected.

Gil stared him down and when he spoke, his voice came out with enough resonance to quieten the room.

'I'm too sober to start a fight kid, so back off.'

'Fight?' The kid spluttered. 'I was just making a joke. Why would you do that?'

'Because you're a cunt,' Gil said, 'and a broken nose might give you some character.'

He didn't wait for a response beyond a startled look he couldn't ever imagine seeing on Ollie. Instead he barged past and the kid lurched out of his path with a gratifying whimper, stumbling into someone else and causing a minor chain reaction of chaotic alarm like a herd of wildebeest sensing the presence of a lion. There were still raised voices by the time Gil was back at the table.

'What kept you?' Toben said. He craned his head around the metal fence to see what the commotion was.

Gil grunted, setting the drinks on the table.

'You might want to down that,' he said. 'I'm not sure we're still welcome.'

Toben stared at him, then spluttered with laughter.

'Still got that touch,' he said.

The Volunteer was a different sort of pub with a very different sort of clientele. Gil had tried to convince Toben to come with him but Toben had demurred. They'd parted ways at the top of Ship Street and there'd been an awkward handshake followed by an even more awkward straight-man-hug that only served to embarrass them both. Toben set off down the street and Gil saw him brush his coat down as he went.

As Gil had expected on the evening before the anniversary, the pub was heaving, thickly overheated and ripe with the smell of beer and bodies. Gil pushed his way into the warmth of the mob, plotting a course to the bar. The crowd swelled and eddied around him, his presence accepted then ignored.

They weren't all werewolves here, but a lot of them would be. The others were friends or hangers on, or those who simply wished they'd turned themselves. Some had witnessed people change and that tiny fragment of magic was intoxicating enough. Now they followed the werecrowd, greedy to see more. Finally, there were those who just wanted to fuck a werewolf, either in human form or otherwise, they weren't really fussy. This group were easy to spot: they were the ones in the three-wolf-moon T-shirts, the 'BITE ME!' pin badges, the felt and taffeta tails hanging out the back of their shorts and skirts. Gil had seen it all before. The Volunteer took all sorts.

As he waited his turn at the bar, Gil let himself be distracted by the TV in the corner. The news was on with more talk about the anniversary, more footage of monstrous bodies lying unconscious in public places, more vox-pops from the day which already had the appearance of something vintage and irrelevant. Then there were the crazies: the elderly woman who'd tried to convince the police her husband had been killed by a werewolf; one who had apparently stabbed him eight times in the neck with a letter opener; and the guy in Covent Garden whose rant had gone viral on Facebook.

'The rapture has already happened!' he said, eyes wide, arms flapping, 'No one deserved to be taken to grace! We've all been left behind and the demons are already here!'

By his calendar, the world should have ended by now. Gil wondered if he was disappointed it hadn't.

'Gil.' The barman was waiting in front of him. Big guy,

bald and bearded, Sepultura T-shirt stretched tight across his belly.

'Alright, Warren,' Gil said. 'I'll have a pint of that one there, and maybe a shot of Grouse to keep it warm.'

Warren barely reacted.

'Starting sensible, Gil?'

'Done that. Aiming for insensible now.'

Warren's grin was broad enough to split his beard in two.

There was a loud jeer, and Gil turned back in time to see Chrissy Linderman's doughy mugshot on the television. The program cut to the footage she'd taken five years earlier with her headband-mounted video camera. A fiercely opinionated gun-rights activist, Linderman had been shopping with her sister in a mall outside Atlanta, when the event had occurred. She'd filmed herself taking out six werewolves as they slept. Double-tapping each in the skull with the AR-15 assault rifle she kept in her Chrysler Aspen. One of her victims had been Justin Gethen, who had been celebrating his sixth birthday with a trip to the toyshop in the mall with his family. Her supporters remained unrepentant.

They interviewed the protestors crowded outside the courthouse.

'I seen all them videos from Africa or someplace where all the monsters are being killed,' said one, 'but no one does a damn thing about them. It's only 'cause she's white, isn't it? It isn't fair.'

'If they'd woken up,' said another, 'Chrissy would be considered a hero. She is a hero.'

In the pub, the jeers turned to shouts of outrage, raised fists blocked the view and Gil turned away.

'Nothing else on, Warren?'

'Nothing else.'

He planted the drinks on the bar and Gil checked his wallet.

'Can I get a tab?'

'Not if you're going to be insensible.'

'I won't be that insensible.'

Warren shook his head and took Gil's bankcard.

The Volunteer was a large place, but every inch of it seemed occupied. Gil recognised a few people, most from his previous visits, but there were some he hadn't seen since quarantine. He nodded in curt acknowledgement, a little alarmed how they all looked so similar these days, but he wasn't in the mood to talk to them. In a strange and almost childish way, they felt like the 'bad crowd' his mother used to worry about him falling in with at school.

He found a table occupied only by dead glasses. It was small and sticky-surfaced, wedged under the staircase, but it gave him a good enough view of the outlay of the pub. He sat himself down and downed his Scotch, swallowing a finger or two of beer to soften its burn.

The game at the nearest pool table was being interrupted by raised voices, so Gil dwelled pointedly on his phone and considered dialling his mother's number again. He didn't really have anything new to say to her. He could tell her about the job rejection but it would only start a lecture and he wasn't in the mood for that. He scrolled through the numbers idly and was almost surprised to find Stephanie's was still there.

Stephanie would have hated it here. Too noisy, too unrefined.

That wasn't fair. It frustrated him that he could only view

his past relationships in the context of how they had failed. There *had* been better times between them, they'd had fun together over the four years they'd been a couple, and it had never really mattered where they'd been. They'd met in a pub worse than this one, and that mad early rush of romance had a searing brightness, if no real depth or connection. Maybe they were still too young back then? By the time the event came round, they no longer smiled at each other in quite the same way, so maybe it was just the excuse they needed.

He remembered her look of distaste when she came to visit him in quarantine. He'd been there for nearly two months by the time they'd opened the facility to visitors, and Gil's presence there seemed to embarrass her. It didn't help that the conditions were so strictly controlled in those early months, and the glass between them exacerbated the prison feel.

Stephanie had sat opposite him. She'd brought a bottle of antiseptic gel and constantly dabbed it on her hands, rubbing and kneading them. She'd barely looked at Gil; her eyes darted around the glass instead, looking for neglected breaches where some infection might find a way through.

He remembered she mostly talked to him about work and he remembered how that had annoyed him. He didn't remember what he'd said to her, but he didn't think he deserved the email she'd sent him four days later:

We regret to inform you, etc, etc.

'This seat taken?'

There was something familiar about the voice that made him look up. He almost didn't recognise her to begin with; the rock-chick look was so far removed from the neat tweed trouser suit she'd worn during the interview a week ago.

'Vicki,' he said, 'is that right?'

'That's right,' she said. She gestured at the stool tucked half-way beneath the table. 'This seat—?'

'—is free, sure. All yours.'

She surprised him by pulling it out a few inches and sitting down to join him at the table, setting her fizzing high-ball next to his flattening pint. Gil glanced around the room as though he could figure out where she'd come from.

'You here with friends?' It was a bit of a struggle to keep his tone civil.

'I'm meeting someone.' She smiled, not like the small, curt smiles she'd used so sparingly during the interview; those had been professional, on/off expressions she'd deployed like punctuation. This was something warmer, conveying sentences rather than silences and for a moment, Gil felt it was an opening, a way in.

'I have to admit,' he said, 'I'm kind of surprised to see you in a place like this.'

'Last time we met,' she said, 'I was interviewing you, not the other way around. So you don't have to be surprised by anything really. We may as well have just met.'

Gil extended a hand.

'Gil McKenzie,' he said.

Her smile widened as she took his hand and shook it. 'Of course, I have read your CV,' she said. She picked up her glass and chased the straw around the rim.

'Yes,' he said. 'About that.'

Her smile shrank a little. 'Yeah,' she said. 'Sorry.' She studied him for a moment, then set her drink back down on the table. 'Listen, I shouldn't be telling you any of this. It's very unprofessional. But we didn't turn you down for the job because you were LPS. That's what you're thinking, isn't it?'

'Why then?'

She shrugged. 'You haven't worked in the industry for over five years. Your projects and references were out of date. In comparison with the other candidates, you just seemed... a bit out of touch.'

'Not my fault.'

'I'm not saying it's easy,' she said. 'But there are ways you could've kept on top of things. Programmes, college and so on.'

'Bullshit.'

'Okay,' she said. 'I'll drop it. But just so it's out there.'

They fell to silence for a moment and the argument at the pool table, violence brewing, filled the gap.

Vicki said, 'Do you smoke?'

'Sure.'

Her eyes flicked across to the pool table. 'I could use some air,' she said.

'Let's get some more drinks in first.'

There was that smile again.

'Deal,' she said.

The smoking area around the back of the building: an abstract negative space between the pub and the student flats behind.

'Stars,' Vicki said, lighting up. 'Pink stars. Very classy.' She handed the lighter back to Gil.

The benches outside were already full of people, so they found a small corner in range of one of the patio heaters, where a wooden shelf had been bolted to the wall.

'When are you expecting your friend?' Gil said.

Vicki shrugged.

'Whenever,' she said. 'Listen, I realise this must look terrible, but meeting you here is a complete coincidence. I mean, obviously I figured you might be here, what with being LPS and the anniversary and everything, and yeah, it could have been awkward, but... just coincidence, that's all.'

'So you don't use your knowledge of people's CVs to flirt with them at pubs?'

'God, no!' she said. 'Wouldn't that be awful? No, I'm normal. Totally non-stalker.'

'And you hang out in were-bars because...?'

'I don't as a rule.'

Gil was surprised to realise he was enjoying himself. They talked on, and easily; the crowds sifted and the empty glasses stacked up between them. The drink loosened him, and he found himself talking more freely about his current job, about Grisham's suggestion he work with Hamley, about his time at Muirhouse. They talked about the event too. It was in the air that night, and there was little sense avoiding it. They talked about Chrissy Linderman's appeal and how they both hoped she wouldn't get off. Gil told Vicki about the YouTube clip he'd seen where someone had taken the footage from the mall and added HUD graphics and sound effects, so it looked like a first-person shooter. They were both appropriately appalled, both secretly amused.

'If you don't mind me asking,' Vicki said after a while, 'is your dad LPS? I read somewhere that there's sometimes a genetic link on the father's side.'

'I heard that had been disproved,' Gil said. 'But yeah, he was.'

She caught the tone in his answer. 'Was?' she said.

'He was driving across town when he lost consciousness. The van veered through a wall and ended up in the canal.

He drowned, but they found his clothes had been all torn up, so they figure he changed first.'

'Oh, shit, I'm so sorry,' Vicki said.

'I'm not,' Gil said.

He pictured the van sinking in a way it could never have done. He imagined the letters peeling off the side one by one. The face inside too busy becoming something new to appreciate it was dying.

'Fuck, I don't know,' Gil said. 'That's not true. I am sorry. But... I didn't really know him that well. I used to work with him over the holidays sometimes. Weekends, you know. He was just some guy who came round once in a while. But there's a reason mum left him... There's a reason... she finds it hard to look at me. Now I've grown to look more like him.'

Uncomfortable, he backtracked. 'But it happened to a lot of people. That plane, for instance.'

'Terrible,' Vicki agreed.

Many had died during the event, the change taking them at inopportune times when they were balanced at the top of staircases, on the edges of train platforms, while crossing the road, driving cars and buses. In China, a pilot had changed mid-flight, slumping over the yoke and driving the plane down into the sea. It was a late night red-eye flight and barely half full, but there had been no survivors.

Vicki set her drink down on the still.

'So I'm going to tell you a story,' she said. 'And you're not going to interrupt. Deal?'

'Deal,' Gil said.

'Good. So I was in Australia. I had a work-holiday visa there, got it just in time; the deadline was thirty and I got there just before my thirtieth birthday.'

'I thought you were younger,' Gil said.

'Smooth, but you said you weren't going to interrupt.'

'Sorry.'

'So I was in Melbourne. And I was working, mostly doing shit jobs. It's what people do when they're on work-holiday visas. No one goes there for a proper job. I'd done fruit picking, I'd done bar work and at this time I was working as a waitress in a pizza restaurant out on Brunswick Street. And it was all right, you know? The crowd were good fun and I was sharing a house with someone else who was working there and when we had time off, we'd go out together. Go to the beach. It was okay.

'I was seeing someone. Sort of. He was called Lance and he was an idiot, basically. Rugby player build, crew cut, stubble. Wanted to be an actor but refused to play gay, even though he'd tell me he "dressed gay" to pull women. True story. Used to walk around in a singlet all the time to show off the work he'd done on his muscles.'

She laughed.

'The point is, Lance was a dick. A dick with a stupidly high opinion of himself. And so when I say I was seeing him, I mean we would sometimes fuck and that's about it. He wasn't exactly sensitive, but – I don't know – sometimes you just settle for someone who knows what they're doing down there, you know? He was the sort of prick who figured out how to give a woman an orgasm, because it made *him* feel good. It was an ego thing.'

She touched Gil's arm.

'Am I making you uncomfortable?'

'Not at all, just trying to figure out where this is going.'

'I'm getting there. So one night I was back in the flat. I was alone and it was late, like three in the morning, and I'd had a hell of shift. Jesus.

'And then Lance comes along, banging on the door. He's so drunk he can barely stand. God knows how he got himself up the stairs. And I let him in, which I know was stupid, but there you go.

'And he's being all amorous, drunk-amorous. *I Love You, I Can't Live Without You*. Someone else has clearly told him to fuck off that night so his G-spot-PS has directed him to the nearest soft-touch.'

She pointed to herself with both thumbs.

'So I know it's all bullshit, and I'm just not in the mood. And I tell him he should just go home, sleep it off. But he won't budge. Tonight, he's decided to come as the full asshole.

'And he sort of herds me towards my room. Because he's a big guy, you know. Those muscles aren't all show. He's strong. And mostly I just can't be bothered dealing with this right now. The more he tells me he wants me, the less I want him to touch me.

'No, I tell him. Go away. Come back when you're sober.

'No, he goes, we should totally screw each other right now, right here. It would be so fucking hot. Only a drunk guy thinks that screwing a drunk guy might be hot. And by that point, he's cornered me by the bed. And I'm scared of him. I've never been scared of him before, but now? He's become more than a prick, he's become a prick with a purpose. And he stinks of alcohol and he's huge, red faced… he's terrifying.

'And my phone is somewhere else so I can't call anyone. I'm looking for something to hit him with but I've got nothing, just last night's underwear and some dumbfuck soft toys. Hit him with any of those and he'd mistake it for foreplay. So I draw myself up like this and I point to him like this. And I go: "Lance Parkinson, you're a monster. Swear to god, if you don't leave right now, everyone else will see it the way I do."

'And he grins, all drunk and lopsided like he's had a stroke. And he lurches forward anyway to try his luck. He gets one step closer and then... just like that, his eyes roll up into the back of his head like cherries in a fruit machine and he collapses on the bed.

'And then, he turns into a monster.'

Gil blinked.

'Five years ago,' Vicki said. 'Almost to the day.'

'Shit,' Gil said.

'Yes, that's pretty much what I said.' Her laugh sounded forced. 'Because of course you can imagine what I must have thought. There I was, staring at my hand like I just zapped him with something. Hell of a way to find out you're a witch, right? But first things first. I'm scared he's going to wake up, because now he looks *really* scary, you know what I mean? So I'm out of the room, and I barricade the door with the sofa.

'But that doesn't feel like it's enough. So I'm out of the flat and I'm running down the street. I don't know what to do. I don't know if I even believe it. Do I go to the police? Do I call an ambulance? What was I supposed to say? "Hello, I've just turned my boyfriend into a monster... I don't know what sort... Teeth, claws, tail? Can anyone help?"

'There was a laundrette down the road. An all-night laundrette-internet-café place. I'd sometimes go there after work if I was still buzzing. Go for a chat. Read a book. So I head there now, and there's a crowd on the street outside, staring in the big window at the front. And I join them and try and see what they're looking at.'

'Another werewolf.'

'Right. This hairy lump pitched forward with his head in one of the washing machines, halfway through emptying it. It would have been funny if it wasn't so... And then there are sirens, raised voices. Screams. And we can see the TVs on the wall on the back of the laundrette and the breaking news... And that was when I started to get an idea of how big it was. This was everywhere.

'And I still thought it was all my fault. This was all me? What if I was defending myself and I just overshot and... *this* happens. And there I was, staring at my hands, trying to imagine all the power that must have been backed up inside of me. All this time, something world-changing, just waiting for a release.'

'And was it?'

She laughed again, then raised her arm and pointed.

'Gil McKenzie, you are an animal. A monster.' She smiled, but again, there was a sadness there. 'No, see. Nothing. Coincidence. Nothing more. But for a few days I wasn't sure. I skipped work and I walked around the town terrified of what I'd do next, as though I might make a careless gesture and burn down a city block. Because it's frightening, isn't it? That sense that you're not quite in control of who you are. That sense that you might snap your fingers and people will get hurt.'

Across the courtyard, a blonde girl was dancing for the benefit of a thickset man with a shaved head and bulging eyes. The girl was much younger than he was, she wore a *Teen Wolf* T-shirt tied up under her midriff. The man at the bench was staring up at her, his expression somewhere between awe and horror.

'Do you know what really freaks me out about the whole thing?' Vicki said. 'If I'd had a better day that day, and Lance had turned up as he did, I might have gone "Sod it", and fucked him anyway. Can you imagine that? All those *were-*groupies desperate to screw an animal and I was this close to living their dream.'

She grinned at Gil.

'People are weird,' she said and downed the remains of her glass. 'Time?'

'Ten-past-twelve. Bar's still open. My round?'

'You're already drunk.'

'You're not drunk enough.'

She snorted.

'Go on then. One more, then we should pour you into a cab.'

'I'll walk. Can't afford a cab.'

'My treat. Get some crisps.'

There was a difference, he realised as he made his way to the bar, between being sober, but feeling a little bit drunk, and being drunk but feeling a little bit sober. Everything felt muffled to him, but there was a fraction of awareness which cut through his clouded senses like an open window on a winter's day.

He ordered two more drinks, another beer for him, another rum and Coke for Vicki and he could feel Warren studying him, trying to gauge his state.

'Near time for you to pay that tab, don't you think?' he said.

'Sure,' Gil said. 'Why not?'

The pub had emptied out a little, but there were new faces too, refugees from other venues which hadn't had their licences extended for the evening.

Somewhere behind him, a low voice pronounced his name, but it didn't feel as though it was for his benefit.

Ollie was there, standing in the middle of the room. He was dressed up for the night. Polished shoes, popped collar, bloodshot eyes. He'd clearly had a long night himself, and simply by looking at him, Gil felt more sober by comparison. He felt anger stir up as well, as though the drink had chipped something loose. At first, Gil assumed Ollie was alone, then he saw the shape of Troy near the door, Benny too. They were watching Ollie from a safe distance. They were on enemy turf and neither looked comfortable to be here.

'Look at this,' Ollie said. 'The working man.'

He reached out a hand and plucked at Gil's paint-spattered sweatshirt. 'Doesn't even bother getting dressed up for the evening, because this is you dressed up isn't it? You're the sort of stiff who puts on a tie when he wants to relax. And here you are, come to a bar, pretending to be someone who works for a living. Maybe pull a bit of skirt. Some idiot's idea of a bit of rough. "Look at my hands, ma! I got callouses on my hands!" Wanker.

'You know what you are? You're a fucking tourist. We all seen you going off in your suit to go to interviews every other week.' His voice switched to a public school falsetto: '"I'm too good for this place, I'm going to get me an office job like I deserve."'

Baleful, his expression was. It was serrated with resentment, glinting in the dull light of the bar.

He jabbed Gil's chest with his finger. Gil held the glasses steady, but took an involuntary step backwards. He felt as though the room was growing close and dark, as though Ollie had stolen the only light. He felt the flicker of fury brewing, and under his breath, he began to count its distance.

One. Two. Three.

'And you see all these other people in this room,' Ollie said, 'these fine, upstanding people? Tomorrow, they'll all turn into wolves. Sure. But wolves are fucking cool man. Not you. You're a dingo. A fucking *dingo*. You're going to spend the rest of your life licking your balls and humping the furniture.'

Gil breathed. Four. Five. Six. He breathed heavy and something caught making his breath sound like a low warning growl.

'And that's you,' Ollie was saying. 'Mummy and daddy must be so proud. Sweeping up after scum like me. All that money they spent on you and you're a fucking cleaner. You're literally picking up bitches in bars. You're a fucking dog.'

The last words were near-as spat, but Ollie didn't wait for a response. The triumphant look on his face was not for Gil but for the friends he turned back to, his arms raising, ready to accept their applause.

Gil saw storm clouds and they were beautiful.

'Fine.' He wasn't sure if he said it out loud but when he dropped the two glasses, they landed like punctuation.

He didn't drop them, he cast them down, so they shattered on the painted floor, their liquid contents achieving an impressive radius, which almost cleared the room; people leaped away from the beer and the glass, clearing an impromptu arena around him, a gap opened between him and Ollie, who turned in drunken surprise to stare at him with rheumy eyes.

Whatever the boy saw in Gil, it frightened him. All that confidence and bravado was flayed clean away with a quick stroke. Ollie looked scared and to Gil, the fear was narcotic.

Gil felt the eyes of the crowd turn first to him and then to Ollie and it was as though at that moment, everyone could see the boy as he did. They saw him as something small, insignificant, reeking with fear.

Gil could feel their hunger. They saw only the meat of him.

Gil saw the pub as a room full of hard sharp things, and Ollie was something soft and out of place. He felt a tide of something broiling inside of him, something that wanted to break that vegetable softness down and correct it, make it mineral.

He stepped forward, quick and deliberate and Ollie shrank back. Troy and Benny had fled, leaving him isolated and Gil saw him struggle in his pocket, bringing out something that glinted in the dull light. The knife looked smaller now; there was something toy-like and preposterous about it. Ollie wielded it too slow, straight armed, without confidence and Gil easily knocked it spinning across the floor.

It was almost disappointing. Gil could see how it would go from here and it was far too easy, almost unearned. He felt sorry for the boy; he felt sad for him. This was no way to be bested.

Ollie lurched to move, but again he was clumsy and again Gil was faster, he caught him with a hand on his neck, forcing him backwards against the wall. He balled up his other hand into a fist. With one punch, he knew he could drive straight through Ollie's face, through blood, through bone, all the way through the wall behind. He could feel that strength inside of him, he knew how to use it.

Ollie whimpered. He was just a kid after all.

Gil felt her looking at him. Even in the midst of such a personal storm, which had emptied his world of every other sound, every other sense, every other living thing, he felt her cutting through like a vivid splinter of blue sky, a trace of sun on the back of his neck, a flicker of heat that threatened to burn. He relaxed the hand on Ollie's throat and turned back to see Vicki spotlit in the crowd he'd forgotten was there. She was standing at the back of the room, her back against the wall. She wasn't looking at him; she was looking down to the side as though there was something of interest on the floor. But he was sure she'd been watching. He was certain he'd felt the weight of her look, the darkness of her reproof. He watched her avoid his eyes and slip away again, out of sight.

Time resumed, surprising him that it had slowed at all. The noise of the room was a roar. All eyes were on him, still high on a tension that for him had already slackened. Instead, he was overcome with a sense of vast, incomprehensible shame, so big and unwieldy he could barely comprehend the dimensions of it. The enormity of it set him close to tears.

He turned back to Ollie, his face bleached white and shining with sweat. Gil grabbed him in a rough and startled bear hug, before he blundered through the crowd and out of the door.

Vicki was standing by the curb, her telephone to her ear. The brief roar of the pub's interior made her glance around as Gil opened the door, but when she saw him there, she turned away again.

'Did your friend turn up?' Gil said. 'The one you were waiting for?'

Vicki pocketed her phone. 'Not really a friend. But yes. In that respect, they never disappoint.'

She turned back to him, and set her hand on his chest.

'Here's something I don't understand,' she said. 'Everyone's so concerned about the fact you all changed. The media, the government, all of you most especially. But no one asks why you changed back. You were given all that power, all that strength. And it was gone again before any of you could use it.' She leaned in close. 'Maybe, after all that, you were found wanting.'

A taxi pulled up at the kerb and Vicki kissed Gil gently on the cheek. When she turned away from him again, he was acutely aware of how cold the night had become.

'The guy we employed,' she said as she opened the taxi door. 'He came out of quarantine and fought his way back up the ladder. Went on courses, like I said.'

Gil stared at her blankly.

'The guy we hired is LPS,' she said.

'Bullshit.'

'No. He's nothing like Lance. Nothing like you. He's at home this evening. Got kids. One of them's LPS too. Apparently, he was really cute when he changed. Like a puppy.'

She ducked through the door and spoke to the driver.

Gil didn't hear what she said. Again there was a roaring in his ears that eclipsed everything else. The clouds were gathering again, the storm approaching. It was anger, he knew, but it wasn't aimed at her. It was directionless, arbitrary and if he could have changed there and then, he knew he would have. Oblivion. Violence. He would have welcomed it all. He closed his eyes and, clenching his fists, he strained every muscle he knew how to control as though he could have forced the monster out into the open, simply so he could have an excuse not to be there anymore, so he could absolve himself of anything it did. He willed himself to change, begged himself until he felt the tendons stretched and screaming in his neck, his teeth crack, his fingernails gouging his palms.

Five years ago, when he'd woken in the office, he'd found himself alone. His clothes were torn, his shoes had burst and he felt drunk and unsteady as he struggled to his feet. He'd barely thought about how strange his situation was; he felt so weary, so tired, he just wanted to go home. He saw others around the office, woozy and ragged, they moved like revenants, but they couldn't bring themselves to acknowledge each other.

He'd found his coat and stumbled outside to find an empty world which had changed irrevocably in the hours that had passed without him. He still wasn't sure how he found his way home, he only remembered it took longer than it ever had before and that everyone he passed backed away from him and gave him room. He'd heard sirens and later he wondered if they were because someone had reported seeing a van in the canal. Some sad and lonely workman, face serene and preserved behind glass.

When Gil opened his eyes, the taxi was still there outside The Volunteer. The door was still open and he stared at it for long enough to imagine it might have been an invitation after all. Long enough for him to wonder if he'd misjudged her opinion of him. Maybe she wanted him to come with her. For them to go home, to start something, anything, everything.

But he didn't move. The promise of the open door was such a delicate thing, he was loathe to risk breaking it with his own clumsy advance. Instead he watched as a hand reached out and pulled it shut with a snap. He watched, listless as the taxi moved away from the kerb.

He stayed until the bright, angry tail lights had receded into the dark like the eyes of something primal retreating into the night, then he pulled his hood up to counter the thin drizzle which had started to thicken the air.

There was one cigarette left in the pack. He teased it straight between his fingers and tried to light it, but the lighter failed to strike so he cast it unused into the gutter. The dull thud of an early hangover was making room for itself behind his eyes as he turned his back on the noise and music of The Volunteer and started, alone and heavy footed, on the long walk home.

Songs Like They Used to Play

In 1921, when he was nine years old, Tom Kavanagh walked into his sister Mary's bedroom at number 12 Westmorland Terrace and saw her kissing Peter Satchel from four doors down. Mary was six years older than her brother, but acted as though she was older still and whatever it was that was going on between her and Peter, it was an anachronism, because at the time, Peter was living in 1994.

Tom remembered how Mary had scowled at him, a stern and silent rebuke that Peter was too preoccupied to notice. He didn't even see the way she fluttered her hand at her little brother, shooing him out of the room with curt admonishment.

It was a memory, and although it wasn't recorded, there was every likelihood it really happened. As he'd got older, Tom found it harder and harder to tell. Some years earlier he had reached the conclusion that his memories fell into three categories: there were the things that happened, there were the things that had been recorded, and there were the things he invented to fill in the gaps.

On the crowded train up to York, he saw a young couple together in the vestibule space between the carriages and he admired the way everything else disappeared for them as they held each other close enough to only breathe in what the other had exhaled. It was 2012, and they were a good few years older than Mary had been in 1921, but the girl's hair was a similar strawberry-blonde and there was a similar sense that the boy knew less about what he was doing than he pretended. Enough, then, for the memory to come back, shoving its way into focus from the jumble of contextless imagery that had haunted Tom for the best part of his life. The memory was a bookmark his brain cross-referenced, and Mary was there again, her expression dark, her hands fluttering, her fury silent, but clear. Not for the first time, Tom questioned the memory's veracity. Had she and Peter really held each other like the couple on the train? Or had it been something smaller, something more innocent? Was it only a peck on the cheek, the recollection of which had become corrupted, which time had extrapolated into something more involved?

He caught himself staring too long at the couple on the train, and while they remained blind to his scrutiny, he looked away in embarrassment, turning his attention to the landscape rolling past the window. It was a late summer morning and in the passing fields, crops were being harvested. He watched fascinated as the bright modern machinery went about tasks that had otherwise remained unchanged for generations. A past augmented by the present rather than replaced by it.

With a clatter, the train plunged into a tunnel and his view was replaced by the dancing reflection of the rest of the carriage. The dimensions wrapped around vertiginously and in the glass, a young woman seated across the aisle caught his eye and looked away again blushing. He saw her lean forward and say something to the friend sitting opposite her and then both dissolved into fits of giggles, stealing glances at him, ripe with amusement.

The train rattled out of the tunnel and the countryside reasserted itself. Spots of rain struck the window and smeared into parallel diagonals. The rhythm settled back into the hypnotic *click-clack, click-clack* of the tracks and Tom closed his eyes, wishing the sound alone could lull him to the oblivion of sleep.

The house on Burton Stone Lane looked like it had been built in a less complicated time. It was located near the top end of a terrace of small Victorian houses, with a bay window by the front door and two smaller windows peeping out from the floor above. The cream-coloured rendering was cracked and the paint on the window frames was peeling. Across the road there was a pub with boarded up windows, and the whole street had a sense it had been left on pause.

Tom stood in the barren front yard and waited for his knock to be heard.

Beside him, a panel of the bay window was propped open a fraction, allowing the faint smell of tobacco and weed to drift across the front patio, the dampness of the afternoon's rainfall sharpening the odour into something barbed and unpleasant. The room's interior was masked by a plain grey-yellow net curtain, but Tom thought he could make out the shadow of someone sitting just inside.

He knocked on the door again and this time saw the figure turn and the curtains twitch as a hand reached up to part them for a moment. Before Tom could introduce himself, the shape had lurched to its feet and disappeared.

Tom took a step back, glancing behind him to make sure his escape route was clear.

It wasn't a licensed bed and breakfast. He'd found a website on the internet that let people rent out rooms in their homes peer-to-peer. It had the benefit of being a little bit cheaper and a little bit more anonymous, giving him the option to pay by cash and even indulge in a false name.

He'd trawled the site looking for accommodation in York and the house on Burton Stone Lane had surfaced when he'd sorted the results by price and proximity to the town centre. York was smaller than he was expecting, it had taken him only fifteen minutes to reach the address from the station, but the street still felt quiet and suburban.

There had been no movement since he'd seen the figure move away from the window, and he had the unpleasant sense that whoever it was, they had only moved out of sight and were now watching him from across the room. When he raised his hand to knock again, there were footsteps in the hall and the door opened, revealing a big man who had let himself go in his late middle age. The man was casually dressed, his jogging pants and T-shirt might have been used as pyjamas. His face and neck were evenly furred with white bristles, but he smiled down at Tom in the manner of someone both surprised and pleased to be disturbed.

'You must be Thomas,' he said, his accent soft and transatlantic. *American Yorkshire*, if there was any such thing.

Tom tried to remember which alias he had used. He often retained his first name for simplicity's sake, but his surname would vary: sometimes his mother's maiden name, sometimes something flippantly generic like Smith or Jones. Occasionally he even used Bobby's name, but that would have been asking for trouble here.

'You must be Max,' Tom said.

The man nodded with enthusiasm.

'Max MacConnell.' He stuck out a meaty hand, fingers splayed wide.

Tom took it, conscious that his own hand felt bony and delicate in comparison.

'A pleasure,' Max said, pumping his hand, his grin just a little too wide to be mistaken for sincere. He snatched his arm back and stood aside. 'Come in, come in,' he said. 'This is the house.'

The corridor was narrow and Tom's host was not slim, so what began as a polite gesture took on the connotations of an unsettling one as Tom was forced to squeeze both himself and his luggage past his host's ample belly.

The downstairs corridor was short and sparse. It showed signs of having been recently modified, with a thin layer of paint that didn't quite cover the seams in the newly built stud walls. To the left, there was one door standing closed and at the end, there was a second door built into an angled partition wall, which sloped across the space to meet the foot of the staircase, the banister rail of which had been meticulously boxed in.

'The rooms are upstairs,' Max said. 'Please. The very top floor, first door on your right.'

He pointed over Tom's shoulder, and again he just felt a little too close for Tom to feel comfortable.

The stairs switch-backed to a slim upstairs landing, with two doors off to the right, and a third at the end. The first door was open and when Tom hesitated outside it, Max edged past him to step inside, making his way to the window and opening the curtains wide.

'Bed. Wardrobe. Window.' He ticked off the room's inventory with a wagging finger. 'Bedside light and so on. The bathroom is at the end of the landing. We have another room next door but it's a bit noisy out the front. This is much nicer. You could say it's the *executive* suite.'

Tom blinked.

Max pulled a set of keys out of his pocket and, holding them by the fluffy keyring, handed them out for Tom to take.

'Small one's for the front door, big one's for the room. Just leave them on the bedside counter before you go tomorrow. Click the door behind you and we're all done.'

'Monday,' Tom said, taking the keys. 'I'm booked in for two nights.'

'Oh? Right you are.' He frowned. 'Are you here to study?'

'No,' he said. 'I'm just here to visit a friend.' He stumbled over the sentence; it felt as though there was something defeatist about it in retrospect.

'I could have sworn.' Max shook his head. 'Don't ever get old.' He fished in his other pocket for his wallet, and extracted a business card. 'That's my number if you lose the keys, and the WiFi password if you want that. We have the internet.'

He sounded quite proud of that, as though the internet was a wild animal he'd trapped and nurtured himself.

Tom reached out to take the card but Max seemed reluctant to let it go and they stood there awkwardly as though they were engaged in a genteel game of tug of war.

'Sorry,' Max said, letting go and stuffing his hands back in his pockets. He flushed and his smile flickered on and off. 'I'll leave you to it.' He retreated to the door.

Tom glanced at the back of the card. An unintelligible string of letters and numbers marked in ballpoint pen. He slid it into his wallet and looked up to see that Max was squinting at him from the doorway.

'Do I know you?' Max said. 'I didn't recognise your name, but I have to say you look awful familiar.'

Tom shook his head a fraction.

'I don't think so,' he said. 'No.'

Max's head cocked to the side. 'You not been on television or something? Maybe when you were younger?'

Tom laughed, perhaps too loud.

'I think I'd have remembered,' he said. He wondered if he sounded too desperate to be plausible.

Max pursed his lips and retreated onto the landing. His smile was sincere again, more so than it had been before. He looked as though the conversation saddened him for some reason.

'I understand,' he said. 'I absolutely understand.'

Tom had first been recognised in public sometime before the War. The 1930s had been and gone, but to the general public, it was a decade that had mostly been perceived as background noise. Once the family had settled back into the modern world, Mary allowed their parents to bribe her to take Tom off their hands for the day.

The Picture House cinema was in a part of town Tom was unfamiliar with and its ostentatious art deco façade struck him as being gloriously at odds with the neat suburban semis on either side.

It was the first time Tom had ever been to the cinema. His mother had always been just a little too busy, and never had any interest in films to pass on to her children, so she had never thought to take them. In later years, Tom would conclude that his father had few unscripted opinions of his own during that particular period of his marriage. He would only reiterate what his wife had already decreed, and so the idea of taking Tom or his sister to the movies would never have crossed his mind either.

Mary had been to the cinema before. Given their parents' attitudes, it had struck her as being a low-level act of rebellion; a chink in their carefully maintained reality, through which she could escape from time to time. Her first experience hadn't been in a cinema, but in the town hall where a live band had been brought in to accompany a screening of Buster Keaton's *Sherlock Jr*, projected at a skewed angle on the whitewashed back wall. She told Tom it had felt like a special sort of time travel, a window that had opened wide, letting her see through it to another world.

Tom's first experience was not magical in the same way. On the screen in the Picture House, a cowboy and a spaceman were sizing each other up in a boy's bedroom. The film acknowledged that neither character existed, but underlined the importance that their friendship *was* real. This seemed like a confusing moral to Tom.

It was a mid-afternoon screening and the cinema was almost empty. Mary lasted twenty minutes into the film before she leaned across to her brother and hissed an instruction to stay where he was. He nodded obediently and watched as she disappeared down the aisle and through the fire exit.

Tom had begun to feel frightened. It occurred to him that the film was like being trapped in someone else's memory, remodelled and polished into something bright and palatable. In it, things that would have been small in real life appeared too large on the screen and the sense of scale was disorienting enough that the cinema's auditorium, already enormous to him, felt even greater in its emptiness, certainly bigger than anywhere he'd ever lived himself. His sense of perspective skewed vertiginously and when he forced his attention from the bright colours on the screen, all he could see were rows and rows of empty chairs, lined up to obediently watch a film he couldn't concentrate on himself. When he squinted into the darkness, he saw there were little metal plates screwed to the chairs on the row in front of him. 'Susan Weaver,' 'Sebastian Boore,' 'Julian Peake.' A different name on each seat.

Why should the chairs need people's names?

'Be good,' Mary had told him before she'd left, 'and don't move.'

Logic abandoned him. He was being lectured on trust and friendship by a toy-box full of walking, talking automata after all. Was this what happened to children who weren't good? Were they turned into chairs at their local cinemas? Forced to watch endless, whimsical, brightly-coloured morality tales, collecting the leftover soda-stains and popcorn dust of the good little children who filled the matinee performances...

He glanced down at his lap, arrested with the inexplicable fantasy that his legs had taken on the same, bland upholstery as the neighbouring seats. He imagined his arms stiffening at his sides and the spike of pain as a neat little name plate was screwed into his spine—

He was screaming by the time he slammed through the double doors back into the foyer. The young woman who worked the concession stand stared at him in wide-eyed horror. When she glanced up at the door to see what film he'd come out of, her expression shifted to one of bewilderment instead.

She led him to the office and comforted him and fed him some custard creams and a glass of Ribena. And as they waited for Mary to come back, she told him that she knew who he was. She'd seen him in the 1930s, she said, it had been on the television, and she tuned in every week to see him because she thought he was so brave. As she spoke, Tom saw how she turned the ring on her finger, first one way then the other, a gesture so familiar, she was no longer aware she did it any more.

'It seemed,' she said to him, 'like a much simpler time, back then.'

Tom had arranged to meet Bobby in one of the café bars somewhere on Stonegate. In his last email Bobby had explained the street was touristy and tacky, but then went on imply it was as much as Tom deserved – he was a tourist after all.

It took less time than Tom was expecting to get to the town centre, and figuring he was early anyway, he let himself get lost in the knot of narrow medieval streets tangled around the Minster.

It was proving to be a pleasant afternoon. The morning's rain had passed, leaving the cobbles brightly glazed and there was a gratifying sharpness to the air. It was warm enough to slip his coat off and tuck it under his arm as he walked, and he tipped his head up to catch the shafts of sun cutting through the pale blue gaps between the timber-frame buildings. He lingered at the window of one of the chocolate shops and made a mental note to come back and buy something before he left.

If he left.

He sighed and on cue, a cloud passed overhead and the street felt altogether cooler and less welcome.

Betty's Cafe Tea Rooms on Stonegate had all the appearances of a tea shop that hadn't changed since the Edwardian era. It might have been true, but it was still part of a chain, which punctured some of its hard-won authenticity. The neat premises with the bulging glass windows were full of dainty tables and chairs, cake stands and bone china. Behind the counter, the staff wore pinstripe shirts, long brown aprons, and uniform expressions of tolerant boredom.

Bobby had already arrived. He was seated near the back of the café, leaning back in his chair, his newspaper open wide in front of him.

It had been six years since they'd last met, and even then, things hadn't ended properly between them. There had been that awkward meal together at Tom's flat the day Bobby had taken the train north. Bobby had kept checking his watch even though they had hours to spare. They'd walked to the station together and the whole thing hadn't felt real enough for Tom to see it clearly. In his mind, people didn't move to York to live, they moved to York for a weekend. To see the cathedral and the Viking Centre. It was a theme park, not a home.

He had a picture of the town patched together from clips he'd seen on television when he was small, and it made the news seem both more real and less at the same time. When he said goodbye to Bobby on the platform of King's Cross, an internal defence mechanism was already in control.

It wasn't a finished scene, it was a *take*. If it went wrong, they could just do it again until they got it right.

'Well, this is civil,' Bobby had said, and Tom wilfully overlooked the tone with which he'd said it.

'Isn't it?' he'd said, and even when they'd kissed, it had felt less definitive than a full stop.

The fallout had dragged on. There'd been a few weeks' grace period where Tom let himself believe he was missed, and then, with 200-odd miles separating them, Tom limped towards the conclusion that Bobby had already tried to make obvious. By email, by telephone, by late night Skype sessions, the stitches that had held them together stretched and loosened; the things unsaid coalesced and threatened to suffocate them both until finally, *mercifully*, realisation dawned.

Sometime later, Tom would come to consider his life as a series of very personal historical eras. There was the time after the show that he'd rather forget; there was the time when he was with Bobby which was vivid, frustrating, beautiful and stupid; and there was the time after Bobby, which had been mostly normal, mostly routine, mostly numb.

Bobby, he decided, had saved him from the pre-Bobby life, but left him ill-equipped for the post-Bobby one, and sometimes he considered fucking things up again, just so he would have an excuse for someone to step in and rescue him. But the Bobby sitting waiting for him in the café did not look like the sort to jump in after someone who was drowning. He looked like someone who would raise his paper and appear distracted as though he hadn't noticed him at all.

They hadn't seen each other in person since King's Cross, and so the Bobby who sat in the café came as something of a surprise. He'd always had height and confidence, but the years apart seemed to have given him licence to grow in both.

They were still friends online, by whatever definition that meant. It was a benefit of contemporary social media that they could remain in contact without having to actually communicate. It was a breach in their respective realities, a window to spy through, a platform to show off from. Tom had seen photographs of Bobby as the years had passed, fragmentary dispatches from his new life, smiling with strangers in unfamiliar landscapes. He would search them for evidence that Bobby's beauty had begun to fade, that his taste in men had succumbed to compromise, but while the Bobby sitting in the café was not quite the same Bobby he remembered, he had grown up as he had grown older. He had more poise, more polish; a smartly-chosen wardrobe on the same well-kept frame. The past six years had done Tom fewer favours. Barely thirty in real years, he looked at himself in the mirror and saw someone older. His hair had thinned and retreated, the blondness undercut with the threat of encroaching grey. He hung back a moment, feeling unkempt and unworthy. For some reason, he felt as though he had grown into something unaccountably seedy.

Bobby glanced up as Tom approached, he folded his newspaper and set it on the table, and while Tom recognised his smile and reciprocated with a tentative one of his own, he didn't believe in it any more.

The Second World War ran for four months because the hidden camera cop show was cancelled at short notice. The viewing figures for the 1930s had been more than respectable, and the 1940s had been commissioned almost immediately, but the new series was originally only scheduled to run for eight weeks and eventually be replaced by a new run of *CopCam* by early August.

CopCam was also in its third year by then. Focusing on the day-to-day activities of a police station in Islington, it was intended as an unapologetic propaganda piece for the Metropolitan Police Force. It was a bland corrective to recent news stories, intended to demonstrate how much of the police's work was dull, ordinary and pointedly uncontroversial.

Unfortunately, no one told Officer Kevin Blunt. With the camera crew granting him a bullish confidence, the thirty-six-year-old officer subjected an armed robbery suspect to a beating severe enough to break three ribs and cause permanent brain damage. The incident was caught on the cameras mounted in the interrogation room, which had always existed but which Blunt – having become used to the more obvious crew that had been following him around – forgot were there at all. The scene lasted for nearly twenty-four minutes without interruption. Such was the price of good television.

With the exception of edited footage shown on the national news, the scene was never officially aired, but the broadcaster reacted in the way television companies tend to do when caught in wrong sort of controversy. They cancelled the show with some fanfare then oversteered in a desperate attempt to appear unimpeachable.

Family Time was safe. Its first two series had attracted respectable audiences and decent press but more crucially, it was conceived as something educational, fulfilling a vital, if under-explored, aspect of the channel's remit. It was also a reality show, but its gimmick was more parochial, featuring a modern nuclear family living in a carefully contrived past, and went to great pains to detail a different decade each year. A house was dressed and furnished appropriately to resemble a time capsule and the family would move in, wear the period clothes, eat the period food and live their lives under the pretence they had travelled back in time. It had been done before, of course, but the scale of *Family Time*'s artifice was unprecedented.

The Kavanaghs were not the only family to apply for the first series; they won the role because both parents were historians of a sort. Penny Kavanagh had written three books about England's domestic history, and lectured on the subject at Kingston University. James Kavanagh on the other hand had written his thesis on the history of British public transport, and ran an online bulletin board calling out anachronisms in Hollywood movies.

The original plan had been to feature a different family each decade, but it soon transpired that the Kavanaghs possessed a certain quality that made the show watchable, even addictive. While Penny commentated on the events that shaped the period, and James observed the rise of popular culture first-hand with an infectious enthusiasm, most audiences found themselves fascinated by the children. Mary had a patient, world-weary air, quite at odds with her fifteen years, while Tom was young enough to simply accept his situation at face value. Of all the family members, he was the one who most convincingly seemed to have slipped back in time.

With the cancellation of *CopCam*, the production crew rallied to produce outlines and resources to cover a double-length run at short notice. Thankfully, the 1940s were rich in incident and, as one of the executives observed, *'Deep down, everyone loves a good war.'*

The 1940s series of *Family Time* was broadcast in the summer of 1996 and by its third week, it was averaging six million viewers. Midway through the run, an episode was broadcast live from the Anderson shelter that Tom had helped his father build in the back garden. The cramped, claustrophobic half-hour was rocked by a relentless simulated air raid. The doors were locked, the whole set vibrated, and a building across the road, purchased and prepared by the production company with only minor controversy, was demolished for effect.

It was gripping television, convincing enough as a spectacle to make a small number of people disproportionately angry. It was edited so well that arguments about the veracity and worth of the episode were fought bloodily in the following week's newspaper columns. The phone lines were jammed with messages of concern for the eleven-year-old boy who looked like he was enduring the real thing.

That was the recorded version. A concerned public appalled at the plight of Little Tommy, wide-eyed and silent, held tight in Mary's arms while she told him all the fairy tales she could remember by heart.

'Once upon a time, there was a boy who wanted to know where the shivers came from,' she said, and Tom had stared into the corner of the room, a little boy with a thousand yard stare, the stark green filter of the night vision cameras making his eyes bright, milky stars in the gloom.

It was a powerful scene, but Tom had other memories that may be less real. In one, the image breaks like old film reel, and the director comes in and squats down in front of him.

'We're going to try that one again,' he said. 'How scared can you look?'

Tom showed how he could look even more scared, he'd been practising over breakfast. His mouth gaped a little, and he raised his hand and sucked his thumb, something he hadn't been permitted to do for years but which came to him there and then, an inspired moment of improvisation. The director loved it. What was his name? Jack or John or Jules? The directors always insisted Tom called them by their first name but he never did remember them.

'Perfect,' the director said. 'Do that.'

And so they did it again. And again.

Was the shelter really in the garden or was it in a studio? Was it set up on pneumatics, shaking and rocking them in time with recorded sound of explosives? Technical staff in camouflage shorts and baseball caps winding cables in loops around their arms. Was the building across the road demolished in the same evening? Didn't Tom see them doing that as well? Standing next to the special effects supervisor and his little box of buttons, a pair of ear protectors wedged tight over his head, pinching the skin around his ears? When the building detonated and debris spewed across the street, why does his memory remember the unfiltered boom of it? Why does he remember it from a different perspective to the one in the recording?

This is something he had learned over time. Separate incidents don't form a narrative on their own. The one does not by default lead to the next, but this was television, so they could edit everything in post to make it look like they did.

The waitress at Betty's Tea Rooms recognised Tom when she delivered their coffees. She didn't say anything, but there was a splinter of confusion in the look she gave him, a sinking recognition, coupled with a panic that she couldn't quite remember where she had seen him before. Tom had been subjected to that look before, and as the years had passed since *Family Time*'s cancellation in 2000, the component of panic had grown as the component of recognition had dwindled.

'Another fan?' Bobby said after she had gone. When Tom looked uncomfortable, he laughed. 'She doesn't look old enough to even remember the show.'

'There are box sets,' Tom said. 'They keep reissuing it.'

Bobby whistled.

'Immortality, thy name is the box set binge.'

He raised his coffee cup in a solemn toast.

'I know my place,' Tom said.

'It must have dated terribly by now.'

'I think that was sort of the point.'

'You still look like him,' Bobby said after a while.

'I am him,' Tom said.

'No, I mean, you can still tell it's you.' Bobby set his cup on the table and leaned forward on folded arms. 'Some people age differently. You look like a little kid who got stretched.'

'And you've aged well too.'

'Don't knock it. I still get ID'd at bars.'

'Then you go to the wrong bars.'

Bobby grinned. It was a loaded expression and one Tom remembered well.

Tom had once decided that Bobby was the sort of person who dealt with his own vulnerability by diagnosing it in others. He'd once boasted to Tom how he had a gift for identifying a broken soul from a thousand paces. The first time they'd met, he said, Tom struck him as a man whose fractures spidered away from him like the roots of an enormous tree.

People often said things like that to Tom. He was fifteen when the show had concluded, and he found himself well known but with no discernible skills.

His mother convinced herself that a *real* life would be the best thing for him, particularly given what had happened to Mary (bless her soul wherever she was). Tom went back to school where he failed all his exams, except history, which he scraped through with an E. The papers enjoyed that, of course, and for a brief, perverse moment, Tom was pleased just to find himself with an audience.

Tom imagined his life as a transplant operation. The fictional world he'd lived in was being cut out of him and a weighty reality was being wired into the hole it had left behind. But transplants were dangerous, and Tom found himself living at one remove, convinced his body would rebel at any arbitrary moment, rejecting the reality he had been forced to accept.

When he turned eighteen, he fled his mother's house. He couldn't talk to her anymore. Everything she said felt like it was scripted, every look she gave him seemed to be followed by one for the benefit of an audience that was no longer watching them. When he moved out, he waited until she was gone for the day, because he knew she would cry and he knew he would imagine some sad library music to accompany her, and he wouldn't be able to deal with either.

Most people who met him told him they wanted to save him, and for a time he was happy for the attention. If they helped in some way, then so much the better, but it was never something he sought out with a purpose. And so from one to another, he drifted, spiralled, fell.

That's what he thought happened. Very little was recorded, very little he remembered himself.

When he met Bobby, and Bobby said he saw the cracks in him, Tom had a sense he saw the parts between them too. He saw the reality he had been given, leaking out into the world. Bobby's company not only granted Tom happiness, it gave him the luxury of letting the contentment grow stale.

'What brings you to York, Thomas,' Bobby said.

'I told you in the email.'

'Yes,' Bobby said. 'An interview. Bullshit, but whatever.'

'And I wanted to see you,' Tom said. 'It's been six years.'

Bobby whistled and picked up his cup again. There was only foam left; he drew circles in it with his coffee stirrer.

'Six years?' he said. 'So what, you're thirty now?'

Tom nodded. 'Same age as you were when you left.'

'You think queers migrate north when we turn thirty? Please.'

'Fuck off, Bobby.'

'You fuck off, I live here.'

Bobby set his coffee cup back on the table and crossed his arms.

'Listen,' he said. 'I was just surprised to hear from you. More so that you were finally coming up to visit. Six years ago I asked you to come up here with me and only now you show up.'

Tom looked down at the table.

'I know,' he said. 'I'm sorry.'

He could feel Bobby studying him.

'What did you think was going to happen here?' Bobby said. His tone wasn't unkind, but it was firm, no-nonsense in that way that Tom had come to miss, even though it had infuriated him when they'd been together.

Tom sighed.

'I thought we could have a drink. A chat,' he said. 'You could show me the sights, maybe take in a show. Then you'd see me to the station, and then I'd go home again.'

'Not forgetting the interview?'

'Not forgetting the interview.'

The café was starting to empty out, and the noise of the place – a friendly, boorish clattering of raised voices and crockery – had subsided as the tables had emptied. The waiting staff now had the time to engage in conversations of their own and Tom thought he caught the woman who had served him glance across at him as she talked.

'I thought you didn't do media interviews,' Bobby said.

Tom shook his head.

'It's some student thing,' he said. 'A psychology project, I think. Seemed like a good cause.'

Bobby raised his eyebrows.

'Are they paying you?'

'Something token, I think. A contribution towards transport costs, that sort of thing.'

Bobby snorted. 'So I was right,' he said, 'the interview is bullshit. Don't get me wrong, I'm flattered you should come so far on my account, but I wish you weren't so lousy about pretending otherwise.'

Tom could have retorted then. He could have said something about how he'd missed how narcissistic Bobby could be. How, if anything, he had come up to York and seen him again just because he wanted to reassure himself that their breakup had been a good thing after all.

But he didn't say that; he didn't want to cause a fuss. He didn't want Bobby to resent him and, deep down, it was still a cover story and one he didn't quite believe himself.

'So what about you,' he said instead. 'What are you doing? Still teaching?'

'I'm not being interviewed,' Bobby said. 'If we're going to do "the talk", I think I want something stronger than coffee. There's a bar around the corner, I'll get the first round in if you cover the tab here. They're more or less London prices, so you should be used to them.'

Tom fished out his wallet.

'Nice to see you haven't changed,' he said. When he slipped out his bank card, another fell out and landed on the table between them.

Bobby picked it up and looked at it, turning it over in his hands. 'Oh, Thomas,' he said. 'I had no idea this was your sort of thing.'

Tom frowned and reached for the card. Bobby held it out of reach.

'It's the WiFi password,' Tom said. 'The guy at the bed and breakfast I'm staying at gave it to me.'

Bobby was reading from the other side of the card with a smirk.

'Immortal Memories,' he read out loud. 'Classic songs from the Forties, Fifties and Sixties.' He grinned and passed the card back to Tom. 'Your vintage, I believe.'

Tom hadn't even looked at the back of the card. It was a glossy, but cheaply printed business card with over-decorated typography and one picture. It took a precious moment for Tom to recognise Max, and he realised he hadn't even registered his last name. Maximillian MacConnell, of all things, his landlord. The Max in the photograph was younger and slimmer than the one Tom had met. His jaw shaved close and clean, his sculpted hair glinting with Brylcreem. He looked dapper in his pristine tuxedo and if his matinee idol grin was anything to go by, he was more than aware of it.

During the 1950s, the episode that everyone remembered was the one in which Tom suffered from night terrors and told the nation his dreams.

The popularity of the previous series had seen Family Time recommissioned for another four month run, this time supported by considerable public interest, and the full weight of the broadcaster's publicity machine. There were features and profiles and interviews with the press. There was plenty of secrecy and speculation about what was planned for the family as they prepared to live their lives through a post-war Britain of ration books and bomb sites.

The set constructed for the series was astonishing. A warehouse district in South London had already been razed and he production crew set to work recreating a Blitz-scarred London suburb, with nearly six square miles of post-war terraced housing, a school and the skeleton of a church. During the live shows, the public were invited to dress up and serve as background extras, a proposition so popular that security was increased. To Tom, the set took on the aspect of a bizarre prison. One where people from the future were happy to queue for hours in the rain for a chance to get in, while he peered through the fences at the modern world beyond, and wondered if he might find the opportunity to escape.

One night Tom woke screaming and when no one answered his call – for reasons he wouldn't understand until some years later – he picked his way downstairs in the dark and found the friendly blinking light of the night vision camera mounted in the corner of the lounge. Standing underneath it, the twelve-year-old Tom addressed his audience directly as though they were the more attentive of his parents, the one who might offer him comfort or advice.

The show wasn't broadcast live that week, and when the producers found the footage during their morning trawl, it led to a debate about the anachronistic content of the dream, rather than the ethics of broadcasting such a strange and improvised monologue from a young boy in a clear state of distress.

In the end, the edited sequence took up the best part of episode eight. Later, when he saw the program as it was broadcast, Tom claimed he didn't remember telling his story, let alone the dream itself. Dreams aren't meant to be remembered, after all. They slip through the cracks of consciousness when more immediate experience elbows in to take their place.

Tom told the audience how in his dream, he found himself at an amusement park (he'd never been to an amusement park), and at the end of a lane of brightly-coloured fairground rides, he found himself standing outside the ghost train. It was a big ghost train, with a giant, painted façade showing a spindly black castle surrounded by a storm cloud of vampire bats, and lurking in the shadow of a dark forest full of ravenous eyes.

There was someone with him, his *friends* were with him (Tom didn't have any friends), and they all paid their money and took their seats. The ride started like you might expect a ghost train to begin: a slow and rickety rollercoaster through gaudy plywood sets, draped with cobwebs and thick with plastic spiders and bugs and broken pieces of bone, hanging on strings, sirens howling and shrieking around every corner.

But the longer it ran, the stranger it became. The sets felt more convincing, the lighting more naturalistic. The actors employed to jump out from darkened alcoves and surprise the riders no longer wore greasepaint, it was real scarred flesh stretched taut over real jagged bones.

As the background noises of the fairground began to recede, other noises took their place: a rumble of gears, a shriek of machinery, a roar of distant, violent industry.

The car moved faster and Tom understood that whoever had been there with him at the beginning of the ride had disappeared. He now rode alone, the track swerving at steeper angles and more precipitous drops until it broke out of the makeshift building entirely and ploughed into a vast, cracked plain. It was dark and hot, but somewhere ahead there was the dull red glow of something that looked as though it had been burning for a very long time.

Tom described all of this to the camera in a tone so matter of fact it could have been mistaken for deadpan. He explained how he was overcome with a very specific sense of fear and so he wrestled with the locking bar that had been designed to keep him safely seated for the duration of the ride. There was a trick to it, he saw. If you squeezed the discreetly positioned levers at each end, the mechanism could be retracted.

A blazing inferno filled the blackened horizon and Tom leapt from the carriage into the charcoal dust and let the car disappear into the flames unmanned.

Dreams don't always end where you expect them. This one went further. He didn't remember it all, but what he did remember was running back through the fairground and finding his mother there. Or maybe that was a different dream? Maybe it was the same one. How many dreams do twelve-year-old boys have in a night? How many do they remember?

Tom told the camera how he told his mother about the ghost train. She was calm and rational and believed everything he said. She told him to take her there so she could see it for herself, and so they went back together, hand-in-hand through the emptying fair.

The ghost train looked so ordinary from the outside, but his mother looked down at him and he knew she still believed him. She bought two tickets and they boarded the waiting car together.

'I can get us out before it's too late,' he told her as the locking back snapped into place, 'I know what to do.'

When she smiled in response, he felt a flush of pride. He'd never felt so grown up.

The ride worked in exactly the same way it had before. It started slow and normal and dull and then, by degrees, the artifice fell away until they were out in the dark plain, flying towards the distant inferno. His mother was sitting upright beside him; she looked attentive, analytical but also strangely unengaged.

Tom again felt that mounting sense of dread, steadily amassing until it threatened to crush them both. Desperately, he worked the locking bar in the same way he had done before, opening it wide and releasing them from its grip.

'We're free now,' he said, 'I've saved us. We can jump out and run back.'

But his mother turned to him, her expression passive.

'But I want to see what it does,' she said. 'I want to see what happens.'

And even though the bar had been lifted, she would not move. She looked forward, arms crossed, her expression analytical.

Tom told the camera how he had sat there beside her, impotent and desperately afraid, as the fires loomed closer and closer. He could have saved himself, he said, but how could he leave her there to burn alone?

His dream exorcised, the twelve-year-old boy turned away from the camera and went back to bed.

At half-one in the morning, Tom walked back to the bed and breakfast, alone but buoyant in mood. Initially, Bobby's behaviour had been as spiky as Tom had feared, but he'd mellowed as the evening progressed and they had left on better terms than Tom could have hoped, even going so far as to arrange to meet again the following afternoon.

The facts of the past five years had been pencilled in with minimal fuss. Bobby was in a relationship and it had been going strong for almost two years now. He said he was happy but he refused to go into further details.

His job was going well too. Yes, he still taught English and was better at it now than Tom would have foreseen, had he given it any thought. Bobby had boasted about how his GCSE class looked as though they would exceed expectations and his A-Level class would go some way to raising the regional average.

But news of both Bobby's relationship and career were delivered in such a brusque shorthand that Tom allowed himself to wonder how secure he was in either.

Tom's own relationship with Bobby had lasted just over two years, a short period when considered empirically, but Tom's perception of time had never operated in a conventional way. Instead, he considered their time together being roughly the same duration as two series of *Family Time*, by which measure, their relationship had lasted the best part of twenty highly compressed television years, repeated and syndicated. By comparison, the nearly-two years Bobby had spent with his new *someone-else* was short-lived and potentially breakable.

Time changed again once they'd separated. One year was one year as it was for everyone else. Perhaps that was one of the things Bobby had taught him, one of the things he would claim he rescued him from. It was true that the years he'd spent post-Bobby had a degree of stability the pre-Bobby years had lacked. Bobby's departure from London left him with a group of friends who bonded with their shared loss of Bobby's charisma, and Tom, standing on his own two feet by then, found he could move amongst them with more confidence than he had done before.

The previous Christmas, he'd visited his mother for the first time since he'd left home. They'd circled each other delicately and even when she nearly spoiled everything by suggesting how the meeting felt like a reunion episode, he bit his tongue and let the comment pass. Undaunted, they remained in touch over the intervening few months.

Was that why he had come up to York? He had achieved one success in reconstructing his past, perhaps he could achieve another?

As he turned onto Burton Stone Lane, Tom cautioned himself against hope. In all likelihood, nothing would come of it, but if he could ease even a handful of his concerns about the past then it would have been a journey worth taking. There was nothing to suggest that a future with Bobby was completely out of the question. It just wasn't something to count on. It wasn't something to expect.

He knew from bitter experience that hope could be toxic in the wrong circumstances. Just because he and Bobby had parted that evening with a smile, a hug, a kiss on the cheek, it was a shallow foundation on which to build an imaginary life together.

But still he had a grin on his face when he set his key in the lock; still he had a skip in his step as he crossed the threshold. He was so preoccupied, in fact, that he had reached the foot of the stairs before he heard the music at all.

At first, it sounded like a distant radio. A band of some sort, something vintage, heavy on the brass. The melody was that of a louche swing, something that should have been from the jazz age but which had been tamed and softened into something bland and safe like lift music.

A thread of amber light outlined the nearest of the two doors in the hallway, and he was certain the music came from behind it.

Immortal Memories, the card had read. He recalled the amusement he and Bobby had shared over the business card, that ridiculous photograph of Max.

The music sounded a little too insistent and a little too loud. It sounded like an invitation.

The evening's drink had granted Tom a confidence he didn't otherwise feel he deserved and it was perhaps this that made him first tap on the door, and then push it open.

He'd been expecting a suburban sitting room, and a dishevelled one at that. The sort of room where Max might lounge by the window smoking a joint while he waited for his guests to arrive.

The room the door actually opened into was rather more austere. The walls were trimmed with half-height dark wooden panelling and the wallpaper which covered the upper parts was a rich and swirling green. It was mostly empty except for a series of small occasional tables arranged with clusters of fat candles nestled in thickened pools of melted wax. In the far wall, a square archway was masked by a thick red velvet curtain. There was no one in the room, there was not even any sign of the bay window that Tom had seen from the outside, but the music still played, distant and half-heard. It sounded as though it was coming from behind somewhere far away on the other side of the curtain.

The fact the room was empty galvanised him to transgress further. He stepped across the uncovered wooden floorboards, and brushed his hands over the curtain pleats until he found a thin current of cool air that guided him to an opening.

Behind, there was a corridor. A long, wide passageway, panelled and papered on both sides in the same dark wood and green wallpaper as the entrance hall. It was lit by discreet fittings that looked like gaslights and it disappeared into the distance, curving gently to the right.

Tom was sober enough to appreciate its disorientating eccentricity. The house was part of a terraced street, and so the corridor must cut through the neighbouring houses for a purpose he couldn't imagine. He hadn't walked any further up the road, but he hadn't noticed anything out of the ordinary. Were all the houses on the street decoys? What of all their neat front gardens, their parked cars, their pot plants in the windows? He had a sudden sense that the entire street was part of the same elaborate and inexplicable deception; a paranoia that he was being set up for something cruel. Was Bobby part of it as well? How could any of this be real?

From the end of the corridor, the music persisted, clearer now it was unmuffled by the curtains. Tom glanced back, checking the corners of the room for evidence of concealed video cameras. On impulse, he performed a rather florid bow, a drunk and brazen *fuck you* to whoever might have been watching. Then he set off down the corridor to find out where the music was coming from.

During the 1960s, the family divided its time between houses in Carnaby Street and Liverpool, because someone high-up in the production team had heard from a contact-of-a-contact that Paul McCartney was a fan of the show and had expressed interest in getting involved in some capacity. This proved to be apocryphal, but the producers secured the rights to film in the Beatles Experience anyway, and booked a sound-alike, look-alike band to use in wide-shots.

The primary gimmick of the first half of the series was the gigs Mary attended each week. She and a Cavern-full of extras, whom the costume department had spent considerable time and effort working on, were filmed in a carefully dressed night-club set, dancing all night to recordings of bands from the era. The new material was then spliced with existing concert footage featuring the likes of Gerry and the Pacemakers and The Searchers. Cilla Black was one of the only acts to play herself.

One night, Mary confided to Tom that the recorded music hadn't worked for some technical reason, so someone stuck on a contemporary CD instead, and everyone danced to that instead.

'They'll add the right music in post and no one will notice,' she said. 'Maybe that's what we can take away from all of this. It doesn't matter what people hear, we all dance the same anyway.'

Mary was 19 that year, and the producers declared that having been lurking in the sidelines over the past few years, growing increasingly cynical about the entire enterprise, the sixties series was all hers. This meant she was the one who got to go out and do everything: nightclubs, shops, festivals and so on. It also meant the wardrobe department went to town using her as a mannequin to show off the breadth of the decade's fashions. There were rumours that in the dubious spirit of historical veracity, the producers were feeding her alcohol and drugs and setting up vast flower-power parties for her to attend. Tom didn't know how much of this was true. Nothing salacious made it to the final edit, but the tabloids were vicious regardless. Confident that *something* untoward had happened, they demanded the channel hand over the deleted material. By this point, of course, they'd already decided Mary was trouble: all those sarcastic asides to the camera as though she wasn't taking things seriously enough for the high standards they selectively upheld; all those raised eyebrows; all those sour expressions; all that disrespect. For the first few months of the show's Sixties run, Mary appeared on the cover of *The Sun* eighteen times, *The Star*, fifteen and *The Mail* and *The Express* ten a piece. Mostly the stories recycled the fictional narratives of the television show, treating them as factual gossip, carefully weighted to scandalise their readers.

The producers were delighted, the parents were nervous, and when she was alone with Tom, Mary was unsparing.

'It's a freak show now,' she said. 'Maybe it always was, but now? There's no history here. There isn't even any sense any more. There's just brightly-coloured pop culture and dumb nostalgia. It's bullshit.'

She wasn't the only one to hold the opinion. While the controversy kept the viewing figures buoyant throughout the run of the series, the broadsheet reactions were increasingly damming.

'A contrived fairground spectacle,' one commentator described it in *The Telegraph*, 'hamstrung by an increasing desperation to show us things we already know.'

'What began as an interesting social experiment has deteriorated into morbid sensationalism,' said another in *The Times*.

Close to the end of the series, during the feature length episode that afforded the producers yet another excuse to broadcast the 1966 World Cup match, Mary left. She packed up her bags with her new 1960s wardrobe and waited until she was sure the cameras were filming before she screamed at her parents for the best part of half an hour. The episode was supposed to have been about football, about England's win against Germany, but instead the game played on in the background, the cheers and commentary of the bottle-screened television repurposed with a grim irony for the fireworks centre stage.

Later, Mary found Tom and held him silently while he pleaded with her not to leave him on his own. And when the cameras stopped filming, she set him back down again and smiled as though the tears had never been there at all.

'Buck up, kiddo,' she said. 'It's only television.'

Late in the year, Tom received a letter from Mary. The postmark was from Quiberon in Brittany and the stamp showed a seabird in flight. She didn't include a forwarding address.

'Dear Tommy,' Mary's letter began. 'It's such a strange looking world from the outside, that when I say it's too easy to lose track of time, I wonder if you know what I mean. Remember when the production company flew us out to France that year for the Reality Television Festival in Cannes? It's like you've spent the best part of your life on one of those moving walkways at the airport, and then suddenly find yourself thrown off at the end. All of a sudden, I am mundane again. Time moves for me like it does for everyone else and for once in my life, I'm thankful for it.

'It's frightening in a way. Outside, everyone knows us. Everybody thinks they know us. But that's all bullshit. The version of me they think they know is, I hope, not the version of me you do.'

She signed off with her initials, and she punctuated them with a hasty X that looked stark and inadequate at the bottom of the page.

At the end of the corridor in the bed and breakfast on Burton Stone Lane, there was a nightclub. A second, red-velvet curtain concealed a second square archway, and behind it was a small auditorium. A windowless room that looked a little like something out of a 1920s gangster movie, right down to the miasma of tobacco smoke hanging just below the ceiling.

A few steps led down to a lacquered floor, where a number of small, round tables were arranged, each accompanied by wiry chairs. There were only a handful of people present, and they each sat in silence, nursing their drinks and smoking. A candle and an ash tray were set on each table, and all faced a stage set beneath a square proscenium arch in the far wall. The stage was arranged as though a performance was in hiatus: music stands were positioned in a semi-circle around old-fashioned microphone stands and behind each, Tom could see unattended musical instruments were propped, waiting. The band themselves were nowhere to be seen, but the music played on, the sound coming from a small old-fashioned gramophone, set on a stool at the front of the stage, its elegant amplifier horn aimed into the auditorium.

'Do you have a reservation?'

A woman stood beside him, dressed in a snug-fitting tuxedo. Her hair was a mass of bright blonde curls but her eyes were dark and her expression sour.

Tom grinned. He wanted to say something clever about the number of empty tables laid out, but he was starting to reconsider his earlier conviction that this was a hoax. It was simply far too elaborate to be anything other than real.

'I don't think so,' he said, hoping she might give him a clue.

The woman nodded.

'Follow me,' she said and started across the floor to an unoccupied table near the front.

Feeling extravagant, he ordered a glass of Talisker and the woman disappeared to the bar, returning with a tumbler on a tray.

'Cigarette?' The woman proffered an open case, cigarettes lined up like soldiers.

Tom hesitated.

'Isn't there a smoking ban?' he said.

'This is a private club,' the woman said.

Bobby had hated the smell of tobacco on him, but the idea struck Tom as oddly exhilarating. He took a cigarette from the proffered case, and leant forward while the woman lit it for him. It tasted harsh, but he swallowed his cough before he embarrassed himself.

'When does it start?' His eyes watered as he nodded at the stage.

The woman folded the case away and shot him a curious look.

'When everyone's here,' she said.

Tom waited. No one else arrived, and the gramophone continued to play unaccompanied.

As his eyes adjusted to the light in the room, he could make out the other clientele more clearly. At least three of the other tables were occupied. A couple sat at one; the man slouching in his chair, the woman's hand resting on his knee. They stared at the stage, unmoving. A man sat alone at another table, his face a ball of wrinkles that caught the shadows in the room and made him look gaunt and thin.

The third table was occupied by a tall woman whom Tom judged to be in her fifties or perhaps older. Dressed in a red blouse and a long black skirt, she was an elegant looking sort, a cigarette lodged in a holder and propped between her long fingers. Unlike the others, she turned to meet his eyes and smiled at him. Then, in a move that made Tom almost choke on his own cigarette, she stood up and walked across the floor to his table, pulling up a chair and sitting down.

'I've not seen you here before,' she said.

Tom leant back a little, wary of the attention.

'First time,' he said.

'Well,' the woman smiled again, her teeth bright under the haze of lights, 'let's make it memorable enough that you come back.'

She summoned the waitress to the table and ordered more drinks, choosing a more expensive single malt than Tom would have chosen himself. The waitress opened her cigarette case again, but the woman in the red dress waved her away, producing a pack of her own from her handbag and offering one to Tom.

'I shouldn't,' Tom said.

The woman rolled her eyes.

'I'm not asking if you should,' she said.

Tom shrugged and took a cigarette.

'It feels a bit strange,' he said, borrowing her lighter rather than letting her light up for him. 'What with the ban—'

The woman snorted. She pushed a new cigarette into her holder and leaned in as Tom reached across to light her.

'This is how things used to be,' she said, leaning back again. 'This is how things should be. There was a time when we didn't need to be nursed like babies. A time when we were treated like adults. And sure, smoking might be bad for you – hell, so much in this world is bad for you they can't ban all of it. Back then, we had a choice. We all had a choice.'

She smiled and extended a hand, long bony fingers bunched together like a shark fin.

'Joan,' she said.

'Tom.'

Her grip was solid. Her skin warm and dry like parcel paper. She turned his hand over, tracing her thumb over the roots of his fingers as though she was looking for evidence of a ring.

'A pleasure,' she said.

Tom extricated his hand and set it on his lap, out of reach.

'I'm here with someone,' he said.

Joan smirked.

'Aren't we all, honey? Aren't we all?'

She took the lighter off him and relit her cigarette, taking another drag.

Tom nodded to the stage.

'So who are we waiting for?' he said. He tried to be offhand about it, faintly embarrassed his ignorance would be exposed. But Joan didn't seem concerned; in fact her smile became dreamy at the thought.

'A great man,' she said. 'A great *artist*.'

She looked at him, her eyebrow arched.

'You listen to music?' she said.

He nodded.

'No,' she said, 'I mean do you *listen* to *music*? I'm not talking about your dance music, your rap, your drum and bass. I'm not talking about your modern rock or hip hop or whatever the noise of the moment calls itself. I mean real music. Music with a melody, songs with a purpose. Twin tools to get themselves inside of you and remake you bone-by-bone, every time you hear it.'

Tom smiled. 'I like music just fine,' he said.

'You *like* music?' she said. 'Have you heard of Nadine Burr?'

Tom shook his head.

'Louis Mendoza?'

'No.'

'Jackson Prentiss? Dewey Lanchester? Louise Aristoe?'

'No, sorry.'

'Maximillian MacConnell?'

'The landlord?'

Joan stared at him in disbelief, then laughed.

'Landlord?' she said. 'Oh, child. What have you done with your life?'

She shook her head and closed her eyes.

'When I was eight years old,' she said, 'I went to visit my uncle in Barnsley. My papa had just run off, and my mam was shopping us around looking for a place to hole up until things righted themselves. Now, Uncle Larry had himself no kids, no woman, not even a dog. But he did have a new record player and we spent the evening sitting around it working our way through this little snakeskin travelling case where he kept his records. And amongst them, he had this dusty vinyl LP. It had a plain paper sleeve, no picture. *Nadine Burr Sings By Heart*. My god, I had never heard anything like it. My *god*, I never believed in magic until that moment right there.'

Her eyes still closed, her head swayed as though she could hear it still.

'There was a group of them, I found out. Same label: *Immortal Memories*. Same thing, same magic. Nadine, Jackson, Max, and the others. They did things... their music... Back then, apparently, they used to play together. Can you imagine it? More than one, together! Oh, but you have to hear it yourself and then you'll understand.'

Her eyes opened and when she looked at him, her expression was weighed down with sadness.

'Only I'm guessing you never have,' she said. 'And I believe you. They're not easy to find now. Out of print. Most of the records were lost and they flat-out refused to let their work be demeaned by all this new technology. CDs! *Digi*-tal! As if some mass produced junk could do something so... individual, so personal, any justice at all. Music isn't ones and zeroes. Music is contours in a groove. Everyone else has been had, mark my words.'

Her hand reached out and took his again, her grip remarkably strong.

'But he's here. Maximillian MacConnell is here. And he will sing for us. In this room! Live! Can you imagine such a thing? Can you imagine how lucky we are?'

Her eyes were wide and wild and something about her expression made him glance across the room at the other tables. He saw something similar in each of the patrons: a hungry anticipation as they stared at the empty stage.

'Listen!' she said.

She closed her eyes and her head tipped back as though she was in ecstasy. She swayed a little, her mouth open in a wide, joyous smile.

'Listen,' she said again, and she started to sing along wordlessly, tapping her thin thumb against the meat of his hand.

But the music she sang, the beat she described was different to the reedy music coming from the record player on the stage. Hers was something more expansive, something richer, its rhythms complex and strange. Hers was something that brought her both tears and joy and it was clear then that she was listening to something that he could not hear himself.

Unsettled, he withdrew his hand from hers. Her eyes flicked open and her expression slackened to one of disappointment. Tom took the opportunity to push himself to his feet.

'I think I'd better go,' he said. 'I don't really think this is my kind of thing.'

'I guess it was before your time,' she said.

'You'd be surprised,' Tom said.

She didn't say anything else. He lingered there awkward for a moment, but had nothing else to say. She let him walk away, her attention captured again by the stage.

Walking away proved more challenging than Tom expected. He felt absurdly drunk, more so than he had any reason to be. The fog of smoke seemed to thicken, while the floor felt soft underfoot and the room pitched like it was on a cruise ship. He grabbed a chair for support and it felt too light, too papery to hold anyone, so he dropped it, letting it clatter loudly as though he'd misjudged it.

The music from the gramophone player lifted in volume, and for a moment, he imagined it was pursuing him, trying to cut him off before he could make his escape. The waitress was nowhere to be seen, so he left a handful of notes on the bar and when he reached the doorway, he imagined the fresh air outside and it drove him onwards and through the curtain.

In the corridor, he lifted the curtain once more to see that clientele hadn't moved since he'd arrived. Joan, still sitting at the table he had left, stared at the stage, smoking in silence, a tense expression on her face.

He let the fabric fall and backtracked up the corridor a few paces. He felt nauseous; unsettled in a way he hadn't done since he'd been a child, overcome with a sense of heavy and appalling expectation that something terrible was going to happen. It was an inexplicable feeling, one that should have driven him away at a run, but nevertheless, he stopped to collect himself, as though he could face down his panic and prove it foolish.

A cool, sobering current of air distracted him further, a thin draft that he traced to a discreet doorway set into the panelling of the corridor which he had overlooked on his way in. He glanced up the corridor to confirm he was alone, then pushed the door open.

The room was a small antechamber, lit by the blue-grey haze of a bank of monochrome monitors stacked in a grid on the far wall. The setup was resolutely non-contemporary, a matrix of old, hooded cathode ray tubes, controlled with physical dials and throw switches. Even compared with the studied decor of the club he had just left, they still appeared dated and anachronistic.

Tom hadn't seen any cameras in the club, but it was clear there must have been at least one trained on each of the tables, as well as others recording the stage and a couple on the bar. He could see the shape of Joan, degraded to a crowd of white noise sitting at the table. From his privileged perspective, she seemed less detailed and more desperate.

In the middle of the room stood Max, his back to the door. He was staring at the screens, his shoulders were hunched, his arms slack at his sides, his legs apart as though bracing himself for impact. He wore nothing except for his wristwatch, and the light from the screens made his pale flesh glow with a flickering grey halo. He didn't move, he didn't speak, and if he knew Tom was there, he made no obvious indication. He just stared at the monitors as though he was waiting for something very specific to occur.

Tom stepped backwards, pulling the door closed behind him. He backed down the corridor until the door was out of sight, and only then did he start to run.

Two things happened in the 1970s that set *Family Time* on its final, fatal course. The first was that Mary, having not returned home during the course of the following six months, was replaced by an actress. Jessica Pilcrow was 21 and took the role of cousin Janey whom everyone pretended had come to stay in the family house for reasons no one bothered to fully imagine. Susan was blonder and slimmer than Mary had ever been, and while the tabloids continued to take an interest, it was mostly expressed in archive pictures of her previous performance work, not all of which was suitable for a family audience.

The second event followed a pay dispute with the crew, inadvertently mirroring the episodes dealing with the General Strike of the late Seventies. After one particular round of negotiations broke down, one of the technical staff leaked the news that throughout the past two series, Tom's mother had refused to stay in the same house as her husband, and spent each night in a hotel instead. She'd split up with him during the 1940s after discovering he'd had a brief affair with a young ARP warden in the partially constructed Anderson shelter.

James Kavanagh had done this before. Penny was his second wife, although she didn't know that until their wedding had been planned. Marriage number one hadn't lasted long, and there'd been no kids to stretch it further. In a sense, James was simply trying to rewrite his own history in a more favourable light, but that too had failed, even if Penny was happy to hide that fact from the viewing public.

As one newspaper put it, the family was now as fake as the history the series purported to follow.

More crucially, it was the first Tom had heard of the split. Both his parents had come to act towards him as they did in front of the cameras and it was only with the benefit of hindsight that he realised they rarely seemed to be in the same room at the same time. Whatever happened between them was strictly off-camera, it wasn't recorded, and therefore perhaps it didn't really happen at all. He imagined the world off-screen as a void, a green room where his parents sat silently apart waiting for their next cues.

As their son, he came to the conclusion that he was just another audience for their performances. Like the show itself, they had started as professional and diligent historians, but success had made them a cabaret. It was the first time in his life that he would feel like he was a prop in someone else's carefully constructed fiction. It would not be the last.

Near the end of the series, he received another letter from Mary, this time with a postmark from Seville.

'Dear Tommy,' she wrote. 'They're showing *Family Time* here in Spain. They're a series or two behind and we've all been dubbed so I sound like I have a little girl's voice, and you sound like a fifty-year-old man. I don't know if anyone recognises me. I can't even tell if anyone takes it seriously.

Why would they care, over here? Seeing it from this side, it feels so English and trivial.

'Occasionally, I'll see an English newspaper and there's so much about it in there that anyone would think it was real. The world outside doesn't care anymore. It's not about what you say, it's about what they hear. I don't think anyone wants the real any more. The fantasy of the happy family persevering over the years, the illusion of staying strong together. That's all they're interested in and it's all nonsense.

'It's funny to think how much I miss it sometimes.

'But then I wonder what I think I'm missing. Because everything has changed since I've been away, just as I've changed. Sometimes I wonder if you miss me and I hate myself that I sound so arrogant to want something like that. Sometimes I wonder if, given that I've been away so long, I'm still the person you miss at all.'

Bobby almost spat out his coffee.

'He was naked?' he said.

'As a baby.'

'What was he doing? Jacking off to the televisions?'

'They were monitors, and no, he was just standing there.'

Bobby sat back and shook his head.

'That's insane. You still stayed the night there?' Bobby said.

'Well I doubt I'd have been welcome at yours,' Tom said. 'I put a chair under the door and barely slept, but yes, I stayed all night. Kept expecting to hear music drifting through. Expecting to wake up and see Max at the end of the bed with a microphone, but no, it was almost completely silent.'

They were back in the same café on Stonegate. Same table, same drinks arranged on it. Bobby was even wearing the same blazer he'd worn the day before and for a distracting moment Tom wondered if it was still the same day after all.

'I would have spent the night on the street rather than stay there,' Bobby said. 'What sort of music was it, anyway?'

Tom shrugged.

'I don't know,' he said. 'It didn't really even start properly. There was a record playing and it sounded... I don't know? Some sort of smooth jazz I suppose. The last thing I can imagine with a cult behind it.'

Bobby blanched and shook his head at the horror of it all.

'Two words which should never, ever go together,' he said, 'are smooth and jazz. I'm amazed you got out alive.'

Tom was about to say he almost didn't. It would have been a lie, of course. As he'd passed the lounge door on the way out that morning, it had looked so ordinary in the plain light of day that he wasn't sure how much of the evening he should attribute to drink and exhaustion. But now he was enjoying himself and he realised he was dangerously close to elaborating the story with details that almost certainly didn't happen. Another invented memory. Another story for the book. He was saved from making a fool of himself by the gentle sound of someone clearing their throat behind him.

He turned around to see the waitress, the same one who appeared to have recognised him the day before. She was young and pretty, high cheekbones and a dark bob of hair, cut through with a streak of pink. When he looked at her and smiled as best as he was capable, her cheeks flushed to match her hair and her eyes darted away in embarrassment.

'I'm so sorry,' she said. 'It's just that I thought I recognised you yesterday but I wasn't sure and my friends said I should ask, and...'

She gestured over her shoulder to where two other waitresses were waiting for her by the counter. When he caught them watching, they spun away and doubled over, their laughter strangulated.

'Are you Tommy?' she said. 'Little Tommy from *Family Time*?'

Tom smiled. He could feel Bobby brewing impatiently opposite him, desperate to interject something, to take control.

'I was,' Tom said. 'I am.'

She ducked a little, a gleeful motion like her knees had just given away.

'Oh,' she said. 'Oh, I used to love that program when I was little. We used to watch it together, all of us. Every week. Don't tell anyone, but I so wanted to grow up to be like Mary.'

'Thank you,' said Tom. 'I'm glad it meant something to you.'

Her eyes rolled, confidence blooming.

'Meant something?' she said. 'It was so special. That program was my childhood, really it was.'

Tom's smile was genuine, but inside he quavered. He was used to the hyperbole of those with something they needed, although it didn't usually blossom so quickly.

'Thank you,' he said again. 'What's your name?'

'Kerry.' She flustered for her notepad and pen. 'Can I… can I get your autograph? Please?'

Just an autograph. He could deal with that. But then Bobby spoke up, his eagerness irrepressible.

'Why don't I take a picture?' he said. 'You got a phone? I can take a picture of the two of you, how does that sound?'

'Bobby.' Tommy took the notepad and scrawled a simple note, pushing it back to Kerry with a little too much force.

'Oh my god. That would be amazing,' Kerry said to Bobby, the analogue appeal of the autograph already forgotten. She fiddled in her pocket for her phone, unlocked it and passed it across the table.

The episode that followed was the sort Tom would have worked hard to avoid had he the choice. Attention begets attention; stand in a street and stare into the middle distance and strangers will join you as though there really is something to see. Bobby was noisy, he played the dumb photographer, forcing Tom to stand and smile and look as though he was enjoying himself. He wrestled with the technology and clownishly let it fail him. He gathered the other waitresses over, they introduced themselves as Sharon and Chloe. Chloe had never even heard of *Family Time*, but Sharon had sat through a few episodes once and proclaimed it both 'cute' and 'kind of old'.

Tom felt them cluster around him like limpets. He felt the eyes of the café centre on him. They looked to see what the commotion was, then their gaze lingered while they judged it for its worth. Some ignored him, others, he saw working their phones, a few discreet photos from the other side of the café, while others were busy working at typing something on their touch screens. Tom felt himself rising to panic. The situation bred a paranoia that he was the subject of a thousand texts, emails and status updates—

And then it was over. Only minutes had passed and Tom hadn't snapped, he hadn't screamed, he hadn't succumbed to the need to fight his way free, but he did feel exposed and humiliated. He could barely speak, but no one really noticed because Bobby was doing all the talking and of course that just made things worse.

He was using that deceptive, gentle tone again, the one he always had used when he was giving instructions. Tom shook his head, clearing the spell of it.

'We should go somewhere else,' he said once they were alone again.

'Nonsense,' Bobby said. 'It would look rude now.' He grinned. 'You never used to be so embarrassed by the attention. I remember you hammering on the bar at Saviours, shouting, "Don't you know who I am?"'

There were parts of Tom's life between the show's cancellation and the present that he couldn't account for, but he knew he would never do something like that and he said so.

'Well, you were pretty drunk.' Bobby smiled at him fondly. 'You were quite the lost little boy when I found you. Unanchored, all adrift.'

Tom shook his head again, a denial this time.

'And you were always scouting around for a new project,' he said. 'Someone to fix. Someone to control. If we're going to bring up memories, I remember you holding court in Grenadine's, boasting about how you fucked the kid from *Family Time*. It was like I wasn't even there.'

'You were a good investment,' Bobby said. 'Even now, that line never gets old. You have no idea how often you've got me laid.'

'Jesus, Bobby.'

'Oh, relax. I'm just teasing you.' Bobby sat back in his chair. 'You always were far too sensitive. You're all grown up, Tommy. You're not a little kid crying through a pretend air raid anymore.'

Tom stared at the table. His coffee cup empty, pushed aside. A slick of undissolved sugar crystals smearing its sides.

'You always knew how to get to me,' he said.

'You always let me.'

They lapsed into silence. Eventually, Bobby said, 'Should I even ask about that interview?' and Tom laughed.

'I cancelled,' he said. 'After last night, I just… you were right. It was bullshit. I came here because I wanted to see you.'

Again silence fell, just as heavy, but warmer by a fraction. Again Bobby broke it. This time by taking out his wallet from his jacket pocket and summoning Kerry to bring the bill. She beamed and smiled and did as she was told. Everyone always did what Bobby told them to.

'So we're going to go out,' Bobby said when she was gone. His tone was precise and confident, as though he were trying to win over a class. 'We're going to get a little drunk. Not too much, but a little. And then…'

He trailed off, grinning.

'And then?' Tom said.

Bobby removed a business card from his wallet and set it on the table between them. *Immortal Memories*, it read, and there was Max MacConnell looking as though he was about to burst into song.

Bobby tapped the card with his fingertip.

'And then we're going to take in a show,' he said.

In the real world, the year 2000 arrived and for the briefest moment, the television-viewing public looked forward and not back. *Family Time* was cancelled eight weeks into its proposed twenty-four week run illustrating the 1980s. Already the right-wing press were fired up, anticipating how the series would lay into Thatcher's stance during the Falklands War, or deliver some unspecified socialist propaganda while recreating the miner's strike or even the poll tax riots. It never got that far; the viewing figures diminished week-on-week until the series was ultimately replaced by a run of repeats of a popular American sitcom.

By the time *Family Time* was cancelled, Tom was the same age Mary had been when it first started. Perhaps if the series had continued, he would have done the things she had done. Maybe they would have hired a new little kid for him to take care of. He could have been the older kid, the respected one. He was pretty sure none of that ever happened.

In the intervening years, Tom imagined he was living in subsequent series that would never be aired. The time-travel conceit had long been abandoned and so the subjects were now much more down to earth, the audience just *loved* things that were down to earth. Here's Little Tommy trying to fit in at the new school. Here's Little Tommy failing his exams. Here's Little Tommy being photographed by the press tonguing a guy called Jim outside a pub in Shoreditch. These scenes don't form a narrative on their own. The one does not by default lead to the next, but this is television, so we can edit in post to make it look like they do.

The audience roars with laughter, the music swells. When we're done, there won't be a dry eye in the house.

During a charity fundraising telethon the year after the show was cancelled, the cast of *Family Time* were reunited once more to star in a sketch purporting to be a clip from the unmade 1990s series. In the sketch, the family sat together on a sofa, doing nothing but watching episodes of *Family Time* on the television. The following day, the *Telegraph*'s television critic remarked that it was the most historically accurate and relevant the show had ever been.

'A few days ago,' Mary wrote in her final letter, 'I met Peter again. Do you remember Peter? Peter Satchel. He lived down the way from us in 1994. He didn't recognise me at first. I can't blame him for that, I've done as much as I can to make myself someone new, but despite that, I don't think I've changed as much as I thought.

'He's married now. Has a few kids, and I realised his wife was somewhere in the bar with him, and maybe he did recognise me after all. So it wasn't that he didn't know me. It was that he *did*, but he was embarrassed to admit it, because of course all his wife saw of me was what they showed of me on the TV. Remember that? Mary the bully. Mary the slut. Mary the bad sister. I saw the look of panic on his face. As though his wife might see him talking to this awful woman who had grown up from the baddest of seeds, the girl in the too-short skirts with loose morals, whom the newspapers wrote acres of gossip about back in the day, and still would if they could be bothered to find her.

'And so he backed away from me, and I let him, because the funny thing was, I understood. Because although I had seen him look at me with fear, I hadn't seen so much else which surrounded that fear. I didn't know him. So how could I judge him without knowing everything?

'Let me see if I can think of an example, and given that Peter is involved, let's make it about him. Do you remember that time when you were small and you walked into my room and found me with Peter? You came in, you saw us there and you left again, the door slamming behind you. You saw the cut that day. That tiny moment of me embarrassed, and Pete being clumsy. That's how stories work, they tell you enough to make you care in the right way and for the most part they don't bother you with everything else because it's unnecessary.

'But you never saw the whole take, you never the raw footage, the rehearsals, the improvisation sessions. Even you didn't really ever see me as I was. You didn't see Peter and me doing homework together, you didn't see us laughing when we got something wrong, you didn't see him being stupid, you didn't see us being kids.

'And that's it, isn't it? It's no one's fault that we can't be attentive all the hours of the day. Your memories of someone are never enough to know them entirely and so, in the end, the things we miss were never real at all.

'Isn't it strange to think as we go about our lives, how much context is lost in the final edit.'

By the time they reached the house on Barton Stone Lane, Tom was almost convinced that he had imagined the whole thing. He could see Bobby looking up and down the street, his expression aloof and critical but he remained silent, reserving his scorn for when they were inside.

Never bring a witness to the site of a miracle.

Tom unfastened the lock and stepped inside, Bobby followed and they stood together in the narrow hallway.

'This is it?' Bobby said.

Tom nodded.

'Dump,' Bobby said.

Tom put a finger to his lips and although Bobby fell silent, his expression remained arch.

The house stood poised. There was no sound. The two men were silent for a good few minutes before Bobby gestured to the staircase.

'Your room up there?' he said.

Tom nodded and Bobby pushed ahead to the foot of the stairs.

'Well I could probably squeeze in a pity-fuck, but I'm working tomorrow so I can't stay long.'

'Bobby.'

'Oh for heaven's sake, Tom—' He broke off, distracted by something.

'Alright,' Tom said, embarrassed. 'I'm sorry, just drop it.'

Bobby's hand came up to silence him.

'You hear that?' He pushed his way back past Tom again, and stopped by the door in the hallway, ducking his head to listen closer. Then, without knocking, he pushed the door open before Tom could say anything.

Only then did Tom hear the music. It was the same as it had been the previous night, the same loose, lazy riff that sounded to Tom like the sort of thing that might be piped into a supermarket.

'Son of a bitch,' Bobby said and he disappeared through the doorway.

Tom waited a moment longer before following. A distance had grown in him since his experiences the previous night. Alone, he had tried to rationalise it, with Bobby he had tried to make light of it. Now, with every indication that it had happened as he remembered, he finally recalled how afraid he had been when he fled.

The front room looked much the same as it had the previous night and its bland uncanniness felt more unsettling now that it was familiar to him. Dreams were not built to be remembered, let alone reconstructed in every detail.

The red-velvet curtain was still settling where Bobby had passed through, a sigh of heavy fabric that set the candles chuckling on their wicks.

'Bobby,' Tom said.

He pushed through to find the corridor was empty, but he could still hear the music and accompanying it, he could hear the snap of Bobby's footsteps, delineating their own rhythm into the distance.

'Bobby.' Tom spoke louder this time.

He hurried onwards, but the corridor swerved ahead keeping Bobby just out of sight beyond the turn. Only his footsteps served to indicate he was there at all as Tom jogged after him.

Did the corridor feel longer than it had before? Had it sloped downhill like this the last time?

When the end came in sight, the second red-velvet curtain shifted with another trace of movement indicating someone had just passed through.

Tom stopped before it, overcome with the same sense he'd felt once before: a nauseous, overwhelming weight that gathered deep inside of him, a vertiginous horror that to step through the curtains would be like blindly stepping off a precipice. Alarmed, he turned away, his hand snatching at the wall to steady himself. Its cool solidity was both reassuring and anything but. When he had regained some control of his breathing, he glanced up to where he had previously seen the antechamber door. The outline of its shape was masked by the lines of the wood panelling, but even closed, Tom had a distinct feeling that someone was watching him.

He straightened and exhaled, dressing himself in a desperate confidence that didn't fit before he pushed his way through the curtain and into the nightclub.

The stage was still empty, the barmaid still looked morose, but there were more people in the club than there had been the night before. A new couple on the table near the front, another man leaned against the bar, two women sat together at the far side of the room. Bobby was seated alone.

Tom made his way through the tables, passing Joan as he did so. She nodded at him as he passed, then turned her attention back to the gramophone on the stage.

Tom pulled up a chair beside Bobby and sat down.

Bobby pushed a glass towards him.

'Got you something warm,' he said. He looked around and grinned. 'I have to hand it to you, I've lived here for five years and I didn't even know this place existed. You always could find some crazy shit. I missed that.'

'Bobby,' Tom said. 'I think we should leave.'

Bobby laughed. It sounded too loud, too big.

'Are you kidding? We've only just got here.'

'I'm serious. We should just go.' Tom looked up, searching the folds in the moulded plaster ceiling where a camera might be hidden. 'This place...' But he trailed off; he didn't know what he was feeling. He couldn't imagine the words that would make Bobby understand.

The music from the gramophone warbled on, a jaunty, lightweight tune. It sounded so fey and inappropriate. Remorseless, it picked at Tom's nerves.

'So you've met this guy?' Bobby said after a while.

'Just the once.'

'And he's going to sing here this evening?'

'I don't know.'

Restless, Tom turned in his chair and looked back at the entrance, gauging an escape route. He remembered how difficult it had been for him to leave before, it had felt as though the room had a gravitational weight that needed to be overcome.

Beside him, Bobby whistled. 'If this record is anything to go by,' he said, 'this guy has the most extraordinary voice. Honestly, Tom, I've really never heard anything like it.'

His tone was wistful; it yearned for something Tom had no way of understanding. And it was that, more than the fact there was no voice on the recording which made Tom turn back to him, afraid of what he might see.

Bobby was staring at the empty stage, his expression a stiffened mask of rapt attention.

'Bobby,' Tom said again. 'Please can we go? It'll be hard, they won't want us to leave, but we can. I did it before and I can show you how. Bobby, please.'

A moment passed before Bobby turned back to him. But when he did, Tom saw how his eyes were wide and wild, greedy with anticipation.

'I don't want to go yet,' he said.

He turned his attention back to the stage, but he reached out his hand blindly and Tom caught and held it. It felt dry and warm, already fragile to the touch.

I don't hear anything, Tom wanted to say, but he remained silent and stared obediently at the gramophone player on the stage. The injustice of it brought him close to tears, and he heard Bobby make a shushing noise beside him. An idle, sympathetic tone like a busy parent might make to an impatient child.

'You know, I never really had any time for nostalgia,' Bobby said, 'and that alone puts you on the back foot in this country. The present is built on the ruins of the past, and my *God*, are they some flaky foundations to work with. Tea with the vicar, bobbies on bicycles, cricket on the green and the village clock striking the hour? Was that really the best it's ever been?'

He sighed.

'We get a lot of stag parties in York,' he said. 'I've got double glazing, but you still hear them out there screaming at each other. You know what I hear most? "Two world wars and one world cup." And they're still talking about the fucking Empire, like that was ever a good idea. But that's all we've got in the world now. We're this little island rotting into itself, feeding off our sordid little past, lying to ourselves that it was something to be proud of. I see it in the classroom too. All these bright young kids with their lives ahead of them... all distracted, all looking the wrong way...'

He fell silent for a moment, his eyes closed.

'But then you hear something like this and somehow... Somehow it all makes more sense. Like it's an anchor, a safety line. Something beautiful to hold on to. A promise that if the world could have been this good once, there's hope for us yet. My *God*, would you listen to it, Tommy? Are you listening to this? Tell me you're listening to this?'

'Bobby, please,' Tom said, but beside him, Bobby shook his head without turning around.

'I want to see what it does,' he said. 'I want to see what happens.'

Sometimes it only takes a single word to make the temperature fall. Sometimes it only takes a moment of clarity to reframe the world.

It was all Tom needed to leave. Even sparing a final glance at Bobby, it alarmed him how much easier it was than he expected. He realised then that he didn't want to hear whatever it was Bobby heard, the thought of it repulsed him, and his haste was driven by a sudden paranoia that if he were to stay much longer, then he too might fall under its spell.

He let go of Bobby's hand and it fell from him, as good as lifeless. He didn't even hear it strike the table. He kicked his own chair away so he could stand. It skittered off across the floor behind him but he ignored the chaos of it as he fled for the curtains.

This time, he felt no resistance. He didn't feel drunk, the floor didn't pitch and the music didn't reach out for him as he could have sworn it had done before. He wasn't wanted anymore, and he had no problem with that at all.

In the corridor, he saw the antechamber door was open a little, and in the long, dark gap it exposed, the figure of Max McConnell stood, bathed in a thin blue light. Max was watching him, but the expression he wore was a desperate one, a plea for patience, for understanding, for help.

Tom didn't stop, he didn't even slow down. He walked down the corridor, he walked down the road, he walked as far away as he could. It was so easy this time, and when he understood why, it was so obvious he laughed loud enough to surprise himself, then laughed again because he had caught himself so thoroughly off-guard.

Ahead of him, the horizon was beautiful, vivid with dancing ribbons of red and gold. He felt giddy, he felt free. He spread his arms wide and bellowed into the dark.

'I'm Tommy Kavanagh,' he shouted. 'I'm little *fucking* Tommy, and it's my time now!'

Such a stupid, shallow thing to say, but the night ignored him. It always had been polite in its way.

Tom grinned so wide his cheeks ached. Unafraid, he walked onwards into the burning red. The trick of it was not to look back.

The Last Meal He Ate Before She Killed Him

At eight o'clock sharp, three men from the Company arrived for a meal in the room where the widow had murdered the General.

Neat and prim in the northern suburbs of the City, the house looked much the same as any of the others on the terrace. It must have looked homely to those ignorant of its history but the guards on the doorstep were a clue to the contrary, as was the constant parade of visitors: tourists, pilgrims, closet revolutionaries who choked the street six times a day.

Inside, changes had been made since the night of the murder, but they were mostly cosmetic. The wallpaper was no longer authentic, but the pictures mounted on it were as they used to be. Here were the widow's sons, here the widow's husband, once a loyal military man himself, frozen at a point twelve years earlier; a silent reminder the future was on hold.

The portrait of The Autocrat, proud and dominant on the far wall, was new. It looked too big for the room, which was appropriate because it was well understood the character of The Autocrat was expansive and would not be contained.

It was such a small room for so big a crime, Dominik thought as one of the house staff took his hat and his overcoat and pointed him through the door, which was flanked with a pair of government guards.

The dense, rich smell of the lounge struck him first. Too warm and close to be comfortable; it was sweet and airless.

The stained carpet was frayed at the edges and, with the heavy curtains drawn tight, the room looked like one which had been forced to brightness like an overexposed photograph.

It reminded Dominik of the set of a stage play which Maria had insisted on seeing when they had only been in the City for a few weeks. A cramped tableau framed a domestic melodrama. Dominik had watched, bored and unengaged whilst Maria was rapt. In the crowded theatre, the little gasps which greeted each turn in the story were hers alone. During the interval, he had warned her that people might have considered them unsophisticated, provincial. She watched the second act in silence, and when the play had finished, she did not join the applause.

Behind him, Administrator Zeitler blustered with amused impatience.

'Come come,' he said, 'there will be others waiting.'

He steered Dominik into the lounge and Lukas followed. A year or two younger than Dominik's twenty-three years, Lukas was also the more confident of the two clerks. His slim frame at ease in his light summer suit, while Dominik felt clumsy and ape-like by comparison.

On Lukas' first day in the office, Dominik had been tasked to show him how the filing racks were ordered. He'd watched as Lukas worked the files, long-fingered and agile, as though he were playing a piano concerto. Dominik had looked at his own hands with their square palms and stubby fingers, then folded them out of sight behind his back.

'Farmer's hands,' his father would describe them, with a degree of pride which Dominik had never understood. He remembered witnessing the farms to the south of the village being repossessed by the State. What need had The Autocrat of people with farmer's hands, he had thought as he watched the buses of grey, sad faces being swept towards the City.

In the middle of the lounge, a pair of square Formica dining tables had been arranged, each covered in clear plastic and surrounded by four kitchen chairs. The table settings were basic: stocky tumblers, paper napkins, cutlery embossed with the insignia of The Autocrat.

Zeitler settled himself between the arms of the chair at the far end of the room. He invited the younger men to occupy the places on either side.

'Usually when I come here,' he said, 'I try and bring seven colleagues so we can have the whole place to ourselves, but I'm afraid this evening, we shall have company. *Non-Company* company.'

He smirked and Lukas laughed too easy in response.

Administrator Zeitler was a big man, both in size and temperament. His face was bunched close in the middle of a head which seemed to have outgrown it, and a thick comb of a moustache served to compensate for his polished pate. His eccentric devotion to The Widow's House was a source of amusement amongst Dominik's peers at the Company. The Wall of Heroes in the Civic Square and the Long Gallery in the Law Courts were more colourful diversions but when his invitation had arrived, Dominik had been moved because he was sure it was the first time the Administrator had noticed him at all.

Zeitler stuck a finger under his collar to loosen his tie, then sneezed abruptly.

Both Dominik and Lukas rushed to provide him with a handkerchief.

'At ease,' Zeitler said, producing one of his own. 'Tail end of a head cold. My apologies. Never taken a day off in my life and I'm not going to start now.'

He blew his nose then folded the handkerchief away.

'Where were we?' he said. 'You, Dominik is it? How long have you been with the Company?'

'Two years, sir, but only as a filing clerk.'

'There's no such thing as being *only* a filing clerk,' Zeitler said. 'Be proud of your role. The Company certainly is and that, my friends, is why they permit me to indulge our staff every now and then.'

Dominik inclined his head.

'Thank you, Administrator.'

'Don't thank me, thank the benevolence of the State.' Zeitler sat back in his chair and rolled his shoulders as though he could extricate a knot from them. 'The Government prefers civilians to take an interest in their country.'

Lukas cleared his throat.

'I have known about the Company's reputation since I was very young,' he said. 'It is an honour to have an opportunity to work there.'

Zeitler beamed at him.

'I understand your uncle is Julian Gortat?' he said. 'A formidable man.'

Dominik stared at the surface of the table. How had he not known that before? In the main lobby of the Company, a portrait of Chief Administrator Gortat filled the wall opposite the grand front doors. Painted in dark, portentous oils, 'formidable' was too benign a word to describe the eyes which Dominik sometimes felt on him when he was still streets away.

He looked up to see Lukas' smile was a thin one.

'He is,' Lukas said. 'But I must stress again, that I am here strictly on my own merits.'

'I should hope so.' Zeitler sounded amused. 'My current assistant has just accepted the role of Deputy Head Administrator for the Department of Information. He has assured me – *assured me* – that the fact his wife's father works there has absolutely nothing to do with it.'

Was that a joke, Dominik wondered? Would he look better to Administrator Zeitler if he laughed?

Instead, it was Lukas who spoke up.

'If you'll forgive me asking,' he said, 'does this mean you will soon be recruiting for the role of Assistant Administrator?'

Zeitler laughed, delighted at the younger man's audacity. Dominik felt a pit open somewhere inside of him. He cursed himself for not speaking first.

'Well, of course we shall have to see,' Zeitler said. 'If we are, I'm sure we shall consider all avenues. Fathers, mothers, daughters, sons.'

He looked thoughtful, then glanced at Dominik.

'Did I hear you have children?'

'Next month,' Dominik said. 'God willing.'

He sensed Zeitler was trying to change the subject and wished he had more to say. In their apartment in the City, Maria was alone except for the child that grew inside her, and although she talked and sang to it as though it were born already, Dominik knew fine well it was no company at all.

Zeitler unfolded the paper napkin, flapping it open like a bullfighter with a cape.

'You have my sympathies and my congratulations,' he said, tucking the napkin under his collar. 'I have two girls and a boy. And when the first of them was born, it was as though the world I had once known had been held to a ransom I am still unable to pay.'

He looked rueful.

'But they are precious things, children. You fill them up with your hopes and fears and you send them out into the world as though such thoughts will sustain them. But they are their own souls and ours is but one influence upon them. It is sobering indeed to see how willing they are to open themselves to others.'

He was interrupted by the arrival of a pair of elderly women, arm-in-arm. They wore expensive silk scarves and felt hats. They had the same amusement in their eyes as they nodded and smiled at the three men from the Company. They took seats at the other table then each unfolded a fan and talked quietly as they waited.

A short while later a young couple entered the room and, with bashful smiles to the room at large, took seats at the women's table. Both were dressed smartly and spoke quietly, leaning in close to murmur in the other's ear.

Zeitler checked his watch.

'The Widow's House is always full,' he said. 'I have been here more than most, and I have never seen an empty seat. Have either of you been before?'

Dominik shook his head. 'No sir,' he said.

Lukas looked uncomfortable.

'My father thought it unnecessary to bring me,' he said. He was about to say more, when the door opened one more time and an older gentleman came in.

The man picked his way to the table where Dominik, Lukas and Zeitler were sitting. The pencil line of ribbons along the top pocket of his jacket confirmed the military status his bearing implied.

'Good evening,' he said, nodding to the room.

'Good evening, Colonel.' Zeitler's voice boomed. He stood with a swiftness Dominik found surprising. 'It is an honour.'

The other diners hurried to their feet, none wishing to be the last to stand, but the Colonel waved them down.

'Please,' he said. 'I am here only to observe the formalities of this terrible place. I am here as you are, no more.'

Dominik sat back on the chair with relief. The uncomfortable heat made him itch. Already he had sweated through the seat of his trousers, and his woollen waistcoat felt unpleasant and tight around his chest and armpits. He eyed the carafe of water on the table and wondered when it would be considered acceptable to pour himself a glass.

When the widow stepped into the room, the low level of conversation snapped to an expectant stillness.

Dominik had seen her picture before of course, the photograph taken before her trial; a stark, unsparing portrait, head and shoulders against a white-tiled wall. The picture was black and white, the contrast so high, the shadows around her cheekbones pooled into voids which made her look wasted and skeletal.

The woman who entered the room was dressed as she had been the day, twelve years ago, when she had murdered the General. A tarnished silver locket hung on a chain and nestled at her breast. She must have been well into her fifties, but she wore her age with a grace that Dominik could not help but find admirable.

She tilted her head slowly so she was looking first at the strangers in her lounge, and then through them. Twelve years of defiance and regret concentrated and etched like cracks and shadows around her eyes.

'Welcome to my house, General Subosky,' she said. 'You honour me with your company.'

Her voice was clear but her inflection was lifeless.

The diners murmured their own responses:

'Murderer.'

'Whore.'

Unsure what he should add, Dominik was thankful his vague, indecisive murmur was eclipsed by the sharp voice of one of the elderly women, who spoke with such venom that spittle flecked across the room like punctuation.

'Traitorous bitch,' she said.

The widow lowered her eyes again and turned back through the kitchen door. She returned with a pair of large decanters – one square, one round – both filled with a colourless spirit. Working from the sideboard at the back of the room, she poured eight glasses and passed them amongst the diners without hurry.

Once she had returned to the kitchen, the Colonel pushed himself to his feet and lifted his glass.

'Before we eat,' he said, 'I would like to invite you all to join me in a toast.'

When everyone was standing, the Colonel turned to face the portrait on the far wall and raised his glass. He spoke clearly and proudly.

'To The Autocrat,' he said.

At the door, the guards snapped to attention as though they would have joined him in the toast had they been armed with glasses rather than assault rifles.

'The Autocrat!' the diners said.

Dominik sipped the drink. Plum schnapps. The widow had served it to the General before he died. It tasted strong enough to mask anything that might be added to it; a sweetness which coated the inside of his mouth with a thick, sugary film. It threaded a current of heat down his throat, making his forehead bead with sweat. Its aftertaste was cheap and chemical.

He grimaced on reflex then, conscious that this reaction might betray inexperience, he stole a glance at Lukas to see if he had been observed. The younger man was not paying attention; he was setting his own glass on the table, watching the Colonel with care.

The kitchen door opened again and the widow came, carrying a tray burdened with eight ceramic soup-bowls. Dominik could see her brow lined with concentration; the tray looked heavy and awkwardly balanced. He could see red trails edging down the side of the bowls as they pitched and yawed.

'Borscht,' Zeitler said, watching the widow as she worked. 'The first course she gave the General when he visited. A paltry meal for such a great man. They say it was her late husband's favourite food. He was from the country; he had simple tastes.'

The Last Meal He Ate Before She Killed Him

The widow set the tray on the sideboard, then served them each in turn.

Dominik looked down at the bowl in front of him. A pale blue ceramic well, filled half way with a thick, maroon liquid. A dark, greasy parabola stained the side where the soup had slopped in transit. The surface was spotted with discs of pale yellow oil and there was an acrid odour which made him recoil.

Borscht had been a favourite of his father's as well. Dominik would sometimes prepare the family recipe for Maria. Richly spiced, it tasted as it smelled: warm and comforting. Maria said it could dispel a winter's day and for a moment, make it spring. It occurred to him he hadn't cooked for her in a while and he wondered if the sentiment would still hold true in the City, away from the line of the mountains, and the sweeping fields of wheat and maize that surrounded the village.

He waited until the widow had finished serving before picking up his spoon. He tasted the soup and found it lukewarm. It lolled around his tongue; a thick, grainy texture and a taste of sweetened, undercooked beetroot which made him gag. As he swallowed, a sharper sense of over-boiled cabbage and sour milk chased it uninvited.

He poured himself a glass of water and drank it all.

'Is there any salt?' he heard one of the elderly ladies say from the other table.

'The General didn't have any salt,' her companion said.

The Colonel cleared his throat.

'I understand you work for the Company,' he said.

Dominik looked up in time to see Lukas flinch.

'We are proud to represent the Company, sir.' Zeitler's smile was expansive. 'I hold a tombola every few weeks and this time, the names of these two lucky gentlemen came up. The Company lets me bring them here. Such a treat for them!'

'And a lesson,' the Colonel observed.

'The Widow's House is a lesson to us all,' Lukas said.

The Colonel ignored him and Dominik saw Lukas look down at his bowl, his cheeks almost as rosy as the traces of the soup he had left behind.

'You seen any combat, Administrator?' the Colonel said.

Zeitler leaned back in his chair and smiled with good humour.

'Not as such, Colonel,' he said. 'I was attached to the Hussars for my National Service, but never out in the field.'

The Colonel's head bobbed.

'There's no shame in it,' he said. 'The Monarchy has long since fallen, and there are other things that must be achieved for the State to prosper. A good friend of mine once told me that we all have battles to fight and those involving pencils and paperwork are no less important than those involving saltpetre and steel.'

He studied them each in turn.

'Do you know who told me that?' He nodded to the portrait of The Autocrat before anyone had time to answer. 'He has a remarkable sense of humour.'

Lukas looked astonished. Zeitler beamed.

'I say this not as idle flattery,' the Colonel said. 'Your company is one of the most loyal to the State. Thus, we are all part of the great machine, small cogs and big. We all work to drive the same glorious purpose.'

He nodded thoughtfully. Zeitler cleared his throat.

'Thank you,' he said, a thin edge to his voice which Dominik had not heard before. 'Humbly, we thank you very much.'

The Last Meal He Ate Before She Killed Him

The Colonel frowned.

'Oh, nonsense, nonsense.' He pushed the soup around with his spoon. 'Is it considered poor etiquette to leave most of this?'

'The General ate all of his,' Lukas said, his bowl already empty and clean.

The Colonel shook his head in wonder.

'He was a braver man than I,' he said.

On the other table, the young woman sat staring at the spoon in her hand. The bowl before her was untouched.

'Is it true,' she said loud enough for the whole room to hear, 'that someone is poisoned each year at The Widow's House?'

In the seat beside her, the young man spluttered into his spoon and red spots of soup speckled across the table.

'The widow is a convicted poisoner,' The Colonel said, his tone level. He swallowed a spoonful of the soup as though it was an act of defiance.

One of the elderly women spoke up:

'Once in a while,' she said, 'someone takes ill; on rarer occasions they say some have died. But that is part of the risk of coming here and we all know it. It's part of the thrill, young lady. *Part of the thrill.*'

Her companion put her hand on her arm in an expression of solidarity.

'If it is any consolation at all,' Zeitler said, 'I have been here many times and to the best of my knowledge, I have not been poisoned.'

'Perhaps you're immune,' the young woman said.

Zeitler laughed heartily and scraped his bowl clean.

'When you leave,' the Colonel said, dabbing the corners of his mouth with his napkin, 'you can say you survived her. You can say the enemies of The Autocrat have no power over you and that is a powerful thing because of what she represents.'

He smiled but his expression was cool.

'But have no fear,' he said. 'It was the schnapps she poisoned The General with, not the borscht, so please relax and enjoy your meal.'

He raised his glass in a mock toast, then drank defiantly.

The main course was chicken. Thighs and wings, boiled almost dry because on the night the General died, the widow was waiting for her husband to come home with her sons. Her husband never came home; the food was spoiled. It was dark when the General arrived instead, and without question or judgement, he had eaten what was given to him.

The chicken was served with a round scoop of mashed potato and five green beans arranged at the side; the whole plate swam in a thin layer of greenish water which discoloured everything else.

Once all the plates had been set, the widow walked around with the square decanter and topped up the glasses.

Dominik picked at his plate. The beans were stringy, out of season. But at least they weren't from cans like most of the produce in the City. He thought of his mother's garden and in his memory, everything seemed so fresh he doubted the truth of it.

'Lukas here,' Zeitler addressed the Colonel. 'His father is in the army. Is that right, Lukas?'

The young man blushed again.

'My brothers, too,' he said.

The Colonel studied him.

'What's your name, boy?'

'Lukas Bresco.'

'Your father is Lieutenant Karel Bresco?'

'He is.'

The Colonel nodded.

'I know of him,' he said. He shovelled a forkful of beans into his mouth and chewed, looking Lukas up and down.

'You don't look like him,' he said.

Lukas shook his head.

'My brothers do.'

Dominik finished his course, realising with some embarrassment how hungry he must have looked. He set his knife and fork on the plate and looked about him, squinting at the family pictures on the wall opposite.

'Her husband,' Zeitler said.

'I'm sorry?'

'The man in the middle. The one in the uniform? That's Emilia Cusco's husband, the *widow's* husband. Rudolf Cusco.'

The man in the picture was wearing the dress uniform of the Hussars. He looked into the room, serious but unflinching.

'And the picture beside it,' Zeitler said, pointing with his fork, 'those are their children, Anton and Stefan. Ten and fifteen when The General was killed.'

'Murdered,' the Colonel said.

'Murdered,' Zeitler agreed.

Unlike their father, the boys were not posed. They were sitting on a sled under a royal blue sky. Their faces were blurred in excitement, as though the camera was incapable of capturing the energy of them with any fidelity.

'What happened to them?' Dominik asked.

'The man was a traitor,' the Colonel said, 'and he died that way.'

The General was dead before he could eat dessert, so none was served to the diners of The Widow's House. Instead, once the dishes had been cleared from the main course, Emilia Cusco returned with a tureen of hot custard and, without ceremony, she poured it on the carpet.

Hemlock poisoning takes its time. After the vomiting and the pain, the body shuts down piece by piece. Wide awake but unable to move, it was said The General was forced to watch as the widow played blacklisted music. She taunted him with her nudity and performed depraved sexual acts in front of him.

He died of respiratory failure just before midnight.

The diners in The Widow's House watched in silence as Emilia Cusco drew spirals on the floor around them. They said nothing, and no music was played.

Once the widow had left the room, Dominik stood and excused himself. A door in the lobby led to the back of the house; a small sign mounted on it gave directions to the bathroom. He stepped awkwardly around the two armed guards who stared through him as though he wasn't there.

Behind the door, there was a short corridor. To his left, another door was propped open an inch and inside, Dominik could see the kitchen. It looked large and industrial, extended considerably from its original, suburban dimensions to cater for the number of visitors the Widow attracted. He could see a member of the house staff, a nightstick tucked in the belt of her uniform. She was standing with folded arms, and turned when she felt Dominik's eyes upon her, her expression sour. Without a word, she reached across and pushed the door closed.

In the bathroom, Dominik ran the taps and doused his face, feeling so hot he would not have been surprised to see the water turn to steam. In the mirror, his face looked red, blotchy, his hair was slick with sweat.

He shrugged off his jacket and hung it on the hook on the back of the door; he unbuttoned his waistcoat and loosened his tie. He breathed out fully; his breath clouded the mirror and slowly dispersed.

He wondered what Zeitler must think of him. Fool, probably. Bumpkin. Idiot.

He looked more critically at the face in the mirror. He looked like all of those things. Worse, he looked like his father. A face and physique better suited to overalls than a businessman's suit.

He had shaved thoroughly that morning, but a day's growth now stained his cheeks and jaw with a burred shadow. He thought of Lukas, so polished, so fresh-faced and effortless, it sickened him.

Before he had left for work that morning, he had said goodbye to Maria as he always did.

'I don't want you going to that place this evening,' she had said. 'That poor sad woman.'

'That poor sad woman killed a General,' he said, stooping to check his tie in the mirror on the dressing table.

Maria just watched him from the bed; sitting on the covers, legs splayed, holding the largeness of her belly as though it were a medicine ball on her lap. Her silence felt like a reproach.

'I can't not go,' he said. 'It would be considered rude, ungrateful or, worse, an insult. And we don't want to be seen insulting anyone, least of all the Administrator.'

She looked troubled. She had been the one to see the arrest of the couple from apartment 411 after all. She had told him how she'd pinned herself in the corner of the landing as the soldiers had bundled them past. *A nice couple*, she would tell him for days afterwards. *My God, the looks on their faces. Such a nice couple.*

He smiled at her and hoped he looked encouraging.

'Besides, it'll be good for us,' he promised. 'I can talk to the Administrator. You know there's rumour of a vacancy opening for his assistant. I've worked there for two years now. He knows I'm reliable. Think of it! A bigger salary, a bigger apartment.'

She had smiled at that.

'That would be nice,' she said, but he knew she didn't believe he would say anything, and she was right. It wasn't something he could do. He could try, but he would stall. He would stutter and say the wrong thing. She had seen it in him so many times, but still she smiled at him with encouragement, as though this time he might be capable of succeeding.

In the bathroom of The Widow's House, Dominik scowled at the cowardice of his reflection. He would be condemned to an endless life on the ground floor of the Company and Lukas would soar. And it would be his own damned fault because he couldn't say what needed to be said.

'No,' he said. 'Not today.'

He refastened his tie and buttoned his waistcoat. He pulled his jacket back on and stepped into the corridor.

The door to the kitchen was open again, and in the narrow shaft it exposed, he saw a movement which struck him as misplaced. A large, grey shape ducked out of the way. It was too quick and abstract to identify, but there was something about it that was familiar to him.

The door to the lobby was also open a crack and Dominik could see the guard there facing away from him, engaged in an animated discussion with the same member of the house staff he had seen in the kitchen earlier.

Dominik was about to return to the lounge when he heard the sound of a muffled sneeze from the kitchen and the question of the grey shape resolved itself in his mind. He hung there, indecisive, then gathered himself and pushed the kitchen door wide.

He heard Zeitler swear before he saw him. The big man was standing at the back of the room beside a barred door, a handkerchief held over his face. On the other side of the room, the Widow Emilia Cusco was standing motionless. She stared at Dominik, her face blank. In her hands, she held a pair of brown paper files, the shape and shade of which were familiar to Dominik after two years as a clerk. Instinct led his eye to the department code stencilled in the top corner. Partially hidden under her hand, it was clear enough to read: PNL. *Personnel.*

Zeitler cast a quick look at the widow, then marched towards Dominik, an accusatory finger outstretched before him.

'You!' His voice was a clenched, furious whisper.

Dominik ducked away from him. He had witnessed the Administrator's anger only a few times and that was from a distance. To be the focus of it terrified him, but the sense that he wasn't the only one in the room to be afraid gave him strength.

'What's happening here?' Surprise made him sound more confident. He stared at the documents in the widow's hands. 'What is she doing with those?'

Zeitler scowled, steering Dominik away from the door and motioning for him to be quiet.

'Nothing you need concern yourself with,' he said, glancing back as the door swung silently to.

The widow moved the files from one hand to another. The movement jogged loose a few pages and they sailed free, drifting across the floor. Some came to a halt on the tiles, another slid beneath the counter, one settled to rest under the toe of Dominik's highly-polished shoe.

He looked down and two versions of himself stared back. A distorted reflection in the leather and a photograph on the page.

'That's my personnel file,' he said, wondering why he needed to say something so clear and obvious out loud.

Zeitler stepped forward and snatched the papers off the ground. He grunted with impatience as he rooted around for the page lost beneath the counter.

'I think that's perfectly clear,' he said, standing and dusting himself down. He thrust the papers back towards the widow, who took them and teased them back into the folder.

'And you,' Zeitler said, 'will now promise me – *promise me* – that you'll keep what you have seen here to yourself.'

He emphasised his words with arm movements so fierce, Dominik almost laughed.

'But this is infraction,' he said. 'This is treason.'

The words came out hoarse as though he did not feel fully qualified to pronounce so loaded a sentence.

Zeitler prodded a finger at him.

'Do you know how many times she has to do this? Six times a day, seven days a week. This is her punishment for killing the man who murdered her husband. This is her penance for killing the man whose followers still hold her children hostage. Her children!'

Frustrated, he gestured to the kitchen as a whole.

'All because she said "no" to him. That was her treachery and this is her reward. This… this *charade*.'

'Please,' the widow said. Zeitler glanced back at her, his face anguished.

'I can't save her,' he said. 'I wish I could. But her sons? There may be hope for her sons. Anton. Stefan.'

He spoke their names with reverence, searching Dominik's reaction for a trace that his meaning would be understood.

'The children of traitors were once imprisoned or executed,' he said. 'Now, they're simply fed back into the machine. What better punishment for a traitor than to know their own children will be raised by patriots? They're conditioned, made to forget. They're placed in families who will raise them as zealots. They're set to work in Government-sanctioned workplaces. One day, Dominik, they will come through my door and I will bring them here, as I bring everyone here—'

He broke off.

'And until then, she is forced to stay here,' he said. 'Every day, they do this to her and she—'

The widow silenced him with a gentle hand on his shoulder.

'I have become used to others telling my story for me,' she said to Dominik. 'Some mean well, others do not. None speak for me.'

She passed Dominik the folders and he took them without thinking. There were two of them. His name was on one, Lukas' was on the other.

'Sometimes,' she said, 'I wonder if I said everything I needed to say twelve years ago in that room over there. I said it so loud and so clear, and yet people still misunderstand.'

She stepped toward him.

'Where are you from?' she said.

He told her without thinking and when he said the name of the village its memory flared brightly and then died. She nodded.

'I know it.'

She took his free hand and held it as though she were a palm reader. She traced the shape of his wedding ring with the tip of her finger.

'A wife?'

'Yes.'

'Children?'

He nodded. It was almost true.

She glanced at Zeitler and shook her head, a sad gesture which looked as though it had become over-familiar to her. Then she turned away from them and picked up a tin bucket, sloshing with suds and water. The door flapped shut behind her as she disappeared into the lounge.

Zeitler snatched the files out of Dominik's hands. He scowled as he opened his waistcoat and jammed them underneath it. His fat fingers clumsy as he refastened the buttons.

Dominik watched, silent and appalled.

'I want the promotion,' he said.

'What promotion?'

'The Assistant Administrator role. I won't tell anyone what I've seen here. I want the promotion. I have bills. A child. I need this more than Lukas does.'

Zeitler scoffed. He straightened his jacket.

'You're not qualified. You're a filing clerk for pity's sake.'

'Then I'm sorry.'

He marched back to the door. As he pulled it open, he felt Zeitler's hand on his collar. The big man's face was red, his cheeks glistened.

'Alright,' Zeitler said. 'It's yours. Congratulations.'

Music started up in the lounge: a scratched vinyl recording of the national anthem. Dominik could hear the diners singing along. He could hear the two elderly women warbling and the deep bass of the Colonel. He could pick out Lukas' voice from the rest, high, competitive, and defiant.

Zeitler looked to the door and when he spoke, his voice was quiet.

'They're humiliating her,' he said. 'They force her to her knees and they stand above her. Sometimes they spit on her. Sometimes they kick her.'

When he turned back, Dominik saw that when he wasn't smiling, Zeitler's face lost its structure. His moustaches drooped unhappily, and his jowls hung resigned.

'I only wanted to give her hope. A little hope to keep her strong.'

'You think I might be her son?' Dominik said. The words sounded blunt, unruly. But as he spoke them, he found himself desperately wishing it to be true.

Zeitler shook his head, eyes downcast.

'You?' he said. 'No. Lukas? Maybe, but I couldn't bring him on his own. Safety in numbers, that sort of thing.'

He glanced up at Dominik and met his eyes.

'I'm sorry,' he said. 'We'll be missed if we stay much longer. Bribing the house staff will only pay so far, but this is important: how does your wife like the City?'

'My wife?'

'She's from the same village as you. You've said so before. You were childhood sweethearts? Something like that.'

Dominik didn't remember such a conversation. Certainly not with Zeitler; the man had barely acknowledged him before. He glanced around the room as though someone might be listening.

'She misses home,' he said and the Administrator smiled.

'So take her home,' Zeitler said. 'Leave now. Take the cab, pick her up and leave the City. Whatever you think you're going to achieve by doing this, you will fall harder if you stay.'

He laughed but there was no humour in it.

'This is a city where you can be convicted of treason by not raising your glass to toast The Autocrat; how long do you think you'll last as a blackmailer? How long will you last as an accessory to treason?'

'You've done alright.'

Zeitler shook his head.

'Go home. Go back to your village and take your wife. Raise your children amongst the wheat fields and meadows; teach them to play in the mountains. I'm giving you a way out, Dominik. You'd be a fool not to take it.'

Dominik shook his head.

'The promotion,' he said. 'I need the promotion.'

Zeitler looked down, his eyes screwed tight. He let out a long breath, as though the fight in him was escaping. When he looked up again, his expression was overcast with a weary resignation.

He nodded.

'You'll have to announce it,' Dominik said.

'I will.'

'Outside. To everyone here.'

Zeitler looked at him sadly.

'You have my word,' he said.

Dominik was the first back to the lounge. One of the house staff was serving coffee to the diners. The widow was on her hands and knees, scrubbing the dessert from the carpet. No one paid attention to her, and she did not acknowledge him as he passed.

When Zeitler returned to the table shortly afterwards, he sat, beaming as though the conversation in the kitchen had not taken place. He turned to smile at one of the elderly women, who fluttered her hands over her face because his attention made her blush.

Dominik tried to make eye contact, but Zeitler's gaze ducked and weaved out of his way until, fearing their deal would be ignored, Dominik stood and raised his glass of schnapps.

'I would like to propose a toast.' His voice was clearer and steadier than he had ever known it. 'To Administrator Zeitler, who has just this moment promoted me to the role of his assistant.'

The silence which landed across the room was uneven.

Lukas blinked in surprise then stumbled to his feet. He snatched his glass from the table and raised it smartly. He looked at Dominik not with resentment, certainly not with surprise, but with respect, as though he believed the promotion was well earned.

One by one, the other diners stood and raised their glasses, and all the while, Zeitler remained in his seat, looking up at Dominik with a wry expression.

'The Administrator Zeitler,' Dominik said and his words were echoed throughout the room. Dominik swallowed the contents of his glass. The clear liquid burned down his throat as though it was coursing its way through the core of him, scorching everything in its path. He felt himself turn pink as he slammed the glass on the table.

Zeitler's smile broadened. He inclined his head.

'My dear boy,' he said. 'You flatter me.'

He took his time to stand, picking up his own glass as he did so.

'While everyone is on their feet, I have a toast of my own.' His tone was calm, friendly. He turned to look at the widow standing in the corner.

'Mrs Cusco,' he said. 'If you would be so kind, would you refill the glass of my new assistant? He appears to have finished what was given to him.'

His dead-eyed smile sent a cold white spike of tension down the back of Dominik's neck.

'Mr Administrator,' he said. 'Please, don't trouble yourself—'

'Nonsense,' Zeitler said. 'It's bad luck to toast with an empty glass.'

Dominik felt the widow at his side. He saw with unexpected clarity she was holding the round decanter and not the square one.

It doesn't mean anything, he told himself. But when he turned away, the look on Zeitler's face caught him like a trap.

As the widow filled his glass, Dominik's hand began to shake. The widow reached out to steady it and in the oppressive warmth of the room, her skin was cold and dry. The coolness of her filled his hand and climbed his arm to his heart.

He could feel her eyes on him, but he could not bring himself to meet them.

'Administrator Zeitler,' he said. 'I can't. Really. I have to work this evening, my head should be clear—'

I have a wife, he thought. *I have a child.*

He knew he was babbling and Zeitler roared with laughter.

'Drink more,' he said, 'and you will be capable of drinking more. Think more and you will be capable of thinking clearer. You're young, you have much to learn. But the choice is yours. You are your own man.'

Zeitler raised his glass.

'To The Autocrat,' he said.

In Dominik's stomach, the General's last meal curdled and froze.

The other diners raised their glasses.

'The Autocrat,' they said and the guards clicked their heels to underline the sentiment.

Dominik stood motionless, his glass heavy in his hand.

He felt the faces in the room turn towards him with an intent that was almost mechanical. He felt the eyes of the guards, heavy upon him as though they had seen him for the first time.

He exhaled a breath and it sounded like a sigh.

At the far end of the room, he could see Emilia Cusco turn away and face the portraits on the wall. He thought of Maria alone in their apartment. He thought of the way she ran through the meadows outside the village when they had been young, the dandelion heads filling the air about her with sparkling seeds. He thought of the child they would have together: a son, a daughter, a clear and focused confluence of everything he dreamed and everything he feared. For some reason, the thought gave him hope.

'The Autocrat,' he said.

He raised his glass and drank to success.

The Bridge

When we first visited the house, there was a model in the attic. The whole town in miniature, clustered under the eaves of the roof and lit by forty-watt bulbs. The river snaked through it as it did the real thing, only this river was plate glass and papier-mâché; it was dotted with tiny wooden boats with cocktail-stick masts and onion-skin sails.

It was the work of Mr Bryce, the house's previous owner. The agent was unable to hide the pity in her voice as she told us. She looked at the model as though it were the symptom of something unspeakable.

'Mr Bryce was a widower,' she said. 'He was childless, all alone.'

She shook her head.

'The poor man,' she said.

I was not yet familiar enough with the town to see how accurate the model was, but I could appreciate details of it: the filigree weathervane on the town hall, the cluttered window displays in the high-street shops.

The agent said: 'We can get rid of it. The house-clearing boys were sentimental; they didn't have the heart to throw it out.'

She cast me a suspicious look as though I might suffer from a comparable affliction.

Louise was not looking at the model, she was looking at the room and I could see her gauging its possibilities.

'We can deal with it,' I said before she could answer. 'When the time comes.'

'His wife died,' Louise said.

The model was built in a broad square ring. To get to the middle, you had to crouch low, avoiding hanging cables and endless boxes of tools and off-cuts of timber.

We stood in the middle, our new town surrounding us.

'It was either an accident or a suicide,' Louise said. 'No one really knew.'

It was the first time Louise had seen it since we had moved. We were still living out of crates and boxes and there was too much else to do. But the model fascinated me. I found myself spending my spare time drinking in the details of every tiny room in every tiny building.

'He must have missed her so very much.'

Louise had come upstairs to find me; she said I was spending more time with it than with her. She told me it would make her jealous. She told her friends I was seeing a model behind her back.

I'd guided her to the middle and thrown the switch so the town lit up and constellations of lights reflected in the glass water. I showed her the details I had only recently found: a woman ironed a shirt in her kitchen; a man in a vest watched a blank-screened television; a woman stood on the bridge, gazing downwards at her reflection.

'Listen,' Louise said. She took my hand and pressed it to her abdomen. 'It's kicking.'

The house had more character than space. A compact knot of misshapen rooms propped on a rise overlooking the town, it had a potential we could not yet afford and so we arranged our belongings to mask the spaces Mr Bryce had left behind. The ghosts of his furniture furrowed the carpets, the shadows of his pictures discoloured the walls.

For one room, we decided, we would make an exception.

'The attic?' Louise said.

I shook my head.

'The model's in the attic,' I said.

There was a smaller room which overlooked the back garden. It wasn't perfect but it was practical. When we peeled off the wallpaper, there was another layer underneath: teddy bears and balloons; dark mould scattered like buckshot.

'I thought they didn't have children,' I said.

Louise ran her hands over the design, the paper whispering under her fingertips.

'They didn't,' she said.

We stripped it down and repainted the walls left exposed. In a stubborn silence, we claimed the room as our own.

Later in the evening, I watched as Louise collected the wallpaper that had fallen. She gathered the fragments. She folded them and bagged them. She looked only at her hands until she was done.

That night, Louise went to bed early without a word. I waited until she was asleep before I made my way upstairs barefoot and quiet, like someone with something to hide.

A woman looked at herself in a mirror, her hands flat against her thighs. A man stood at an attic window, his palms pressed against the glass, his tiny features a mask of shock. The streets were thinly populated: men and women walked alone, missing one another at every turn.

A raft spider picked its way down the high street like a B-movie monster. I shooed it away, and it took off, scuttling over the rooftops and down to the waterfront. Its jagged movement was so alien in the silent town that eviction did not seem enough. I cornered it and flattened it against the glass river, smearing it across the surface with a violence that struck me as childish; snapping one of the boats from its mooring as I tried to restore the perfect tranquillity of the scene.

The man in the model shop examined the boat, his eyeglass kept in place with a scowl. It was a small, cave-like shop with enough stock for a larger one; colourful boxes stacked high against every wall.

'You fixing it or selling it?' the man said. He turned the piece over in his hands, his fingernails gnawed to fat ellipses.

'We've only just moved in,' I said.

The man looked up at me through his eyeglass.

'The town,' he said. 'The model.'

I told him I was mending it. Just a part of it. Something I had noticed was broken.

'Broken,' he said.

He sold me a box with a picture of a smiling boy with 1950s hair on the front and parental advice on the back. Inside were plastic tools and six thumbnail-sized paint pots from signal red to moonlight blue.

He gave me his card.

'In case you change your mind,' he said.

I was more familiar with the model than the real town. On my way home, I took a wrong turn and lost my way in a tangle of new red-brick terraces that had no counterpart in the town I knew. The model was a moment, polished and refined, while the town that inspired it had moved on.

When I regained my bearings, I found the streets crowded

with Saturday shoppers. A group of kids rushed past with an enormous kite, their faces bright with excitement.

On impulse, I bought myself an ice-cream and stopped on the bridge, leaning on the balustrade to look up the river to the rise of the hill. I found our street, its neat regiment of copper beech trees made toy-like themselves by the distance. The road turned upon itself, winding downhill to where the Church of St Catherine stood in the crook of the river.

It was a stocky, boldly puritan building that drew attention to itself, but it took me by surprise as though I had never seen it before.

That night as I lay awake, I listened to the town beneath us and imagined the one above. I closed my eyes and tried to fit the one to the other, but the model was silent by its nature, trapped and preserved in a frozen frame. I pictured myself drifting through its streets towards the river; the painted hardboard walls reared up around me. The inhabitants I passed were statues, arrested mid-motion. Their faces waxen and indistinct, their backs were to the water, walking away. The silence grew dense and oppressive like the shadow of a storm cloud. I opened my eyes like I was coming up for air.

The bedroom curtains were carelessly closed and a seam of moonlight divided the room. By the bedside clock it was nearly two and I could tell by the sound of Louise's breathing that she was also still awake.

I thought about Mr Bryce. I thought of him working in the attic, hunched over his intricate work. I thought of him alone in a silent house, how as his miniature town grew around him, the real one diverged and took its own course.

Beside me, Louise stirred.

'What are you thinking about?' I said.

I heard her turn her head towards me. I stared up at the still unfamiliar ceiling. Cobwebs clung to the naked light-fitting. They cast grey shadows like cracks.

'You know what I'm thinking about,' she said.

The man from the model shop came to take the town away. It had been built in sections and came apart with only minor damage which the man promised he could repair. Jumbled in the back of his van, it looked like an earthquake had struck. Great tectonic plates overlapped each other but the townsfolk carried on as though nothing had happened.

The man slapped the dust off his hands, a job well done.

'You know he never let me see it?' he said. 'I sold him everything he used to build the bloody thing, but I never so much as stepped through that door until today.'

He shook his head, as the estate agent had shaken hers.

I asked him about the church.

'That's the least of it,' the man said. 'If you knew anything about the town, you wouldn't recognise it from what he did. He told me about it once. Church, hospital, police, he said. None of them were there for him when things got bad, so he didn't build any of them.'

Even without his eyeglass, his expression was pointed.

'Is that why you want rid of it?' he said.

'No.' I shook my head. 'Of course not.'

The man slammed the roller door down and the van bounced on its suspension.

'We'll take good care of it,' he said.

Louise picked a rich ochre and the following weekend, we

The Bridge

started painting the attic. Louise wore one of my old work shirts. We'd both got bigger since I last wore it and it barely stretched to cover her.

Between coats, we sat on the floor of the empty room and shared a pot of coffee. The window was open and a cool breeze made the bare light-bulb swing in circles.

'It's such a beautiful room,' Louise said.

She was right, of course. The model had shrunken and diminished it. In its absence, the room felt airy and pleasant.

Louise told me about the furniture she wanted and how she would arrange it. She told me about a picture she had seen which would look just right on the far wall. I let her talk and pushed myself to my feet to look out of the window.

In a small crack between the wooden floorboards and the wall, something caught my eye and I crouched to retrieve it. It was a figurine from the model, shaken loose and forgotten during the move: the woman from the bridge, posture bent to consider the water beneath her. Shorn of context and alone in the palm of my hand she looked stooped and sad.

'What is it?' Louise said, standing up carefully and stretching. Her hands pressed against her kidneys.

I slipped the figurine into my pocket.

'It's nothing,' I said. 'It's rubbish.'

She joined me at the window and I put my arm around her. The town spread beneath us, hugging the banks of the river, warmed and golden in the early evening sun. It was vivid and alive with a distant buzz of day-to-day activity.

Louise tilted her head, resting it on my shoulder.

'You can see the bridge from here,' she said.

The End of Hope Street

Number Five

The Potterton house became unlivable at a quarter past three on Saturday afternoon. Lewis Potterton had been sitting in the lounge reading the business section of the *Daily Telegraph* when he first saw the symptoms, but when he got to the hallway to call his wife and daughter, he saw they were already hurrying downstairs, his wife Lydia fresh from the shower and still wrapped in a towel.

They hesitated, surprised at how, in a moment of bemused concordance, everyone else's actions had mirrored their own. No one spoke, but then no one needed to. It was true that there had been frictions between them over the past few months; Lewis' work had demanded too-long hours of him, Lydia appeared helpless under threat of redundancy, and Monica had felt ignored by the both of them. But standing there together in the hallway, there was an unshakable sense that the connection between them ran deeper and stronger than any of them had previously anticipated. In that one, precious moment, they were still and hyper aware, listening to the sounds of the house settling, sounds that only the previous day had been normal and reassuring.

Then, as one, they made for the front door and let themselves out, hiding their haste from one another until they were safely together on the front lawn where they stopped and looked back at the house that Lydia and Lewis had lived in since they had married fifteen years earlier, the house that Monica had known all of her life.

It was a bright sunny afternoon, and Lewis was struck by all the times he had woken in the night, fretting about what he should rescue in the event of a fire: the laptop, the accounts, the family photographs. He'd had a plan for them once, but he knew now that the most important parts of his life were there with him. His wife, his twelve-year-old daughter, his health so he could take care of them. Everything else was as good as gone now, locked and lost inside the house they would never enter again, and at that moment he really didn't care anymore.

It was the Feltons who took the family in. They lived two doors down at number seven and on that particular afternoon, Una Felton had been putting the recycling out early, which she did every weekend. She saw the Pottertons standing together on their front lawn. She saw how the father (Louis? Larry?) stood with his arms around his wife and daughter, she saw how all three of them stared at the house they had lived in, and she recognised the look of sadness and pride in their expressions.

She'd been unhappy when the couple had first moved to Hope Street. How long had that been now? She remembered them driving up to view the property in that ridiculous red sports car. He had a pony tail then and she tottered on heels across the lawn. Hidden behind the net curtain in the lounge at number seven, Una had listened to their unguarded enthusiasm and assumed the worst. They were young, she'd thought. They were loud and vulgar. Maybe they'd come armed with the means to lower the tone and the price of the neighbourhood.

With hindsight, it had been a rather un-Christian assessment but when she saw them looking so lost in their front garden, her heart went out to them completely. How could it not? The wife (Linda?) was only wearing a towel – the poor thing – but all three of them looked vulnerable. They were a *nice* family, she decided. And she decided that she'd always thought so.

She unpeeled her gardening gloves and joined them on the lawn, looking up at the new veneer of darkness their house wore.

'Oh good heavens,' she said, her sincerity genuine. 'Come with me, let's keep you warm. Let's see what we can do.'

They exchanged glances with each other before they followed her, and they saw in each other the same feeling of being lost they felt themselves. They joined hands and followed Una back up the path to the pavement and along the road, past the untidy lawn of number six to the pristine one at number seven.

In the lounge, sitting on his favourite armchair, Alasdair Felton looked up from his newspaper, surprised to see his wife bringing guests back into the house without having organised a concerted campaign to make it look a fraction tidier than it already was. Una ignored him – she often did when she had something more pressing on her mind – so he watched and smiled as she fussed around, her frown of concern masking an irrepressible enthusiasm for her newfound purpose.

'Let me see if I can find you something to wear,' Una Felton said to Lydia, looking her up and down. 'My daughter, Suzie, still has clothes here. They're old, she hasn't been home in so long. But she's a big girl, too. Healthy.' She disappeared upstairs, leaving the family slightly shell-shocked.

Lewis Potterton noticed Alasdair sitting, watching them and nodded to him in wordless acknowledgement. He still held his wife by one hand, his daughter by the other, but in his expression, Alasdair saw a man who was *being* held. A look of weightless panic behind his eyes, grounded only by those around him.

Alasdair nodded back. His smile, he hoped, was an encouraging one. He pushed himself to his feet.

'I was going to make some tea,' he said. 'I'll use the large teapot.'

He went to the kitchen and filled the kettle, still oblivious of the purpose behind the Potterton's visit. He knew his part was to simply act as host for as long as it took.

It took longer than anyone anticipated. The Pottertons squeezed into the Feltons' spare room, the neat little loft conversion Una had thought to use as an art room, had she ever found the time. There were other rooms, bigger ones, but the closeness of the space under the eaves felt more important to them. They unfolded the futon and spread out an inflatable mattress so they could all stay together.

In the master bedroom on the floor below, Alasdair Felton sat down beside his wife, who looked tired but flushed with the day's charity. She had reclothed them all and put the washing machine on. She had fed them and kept them warm, and now, although tired, she seemed to hum with a bristling energy he remembered from Suzie's childhood. He took her hand and he smiled at her like he hadn't done for years.

'What a beautiful thing you are,' he said.

Number Eight

The second house to become unlivable was number eight. Milton Bream had not been home since his divorce from Jemima had *finally* reached its conclusion at the magistrates' court earlier in the week. When he pulled up in front of the house, he knew it was the only thing he had left in the world and for a precious, fleeting moment, he felt as though all the screaming and shouting and tears and grief had been worth it after all.

His lawyers had spoken to Jemima's lawyers and, after much back and forth, they had agreed that, despite everything, she should be free to go home 'one last time' to pick up her belongings. Brimbley, his solicitor, had advised Milton he should go home first and put away anything of value, but Milton wasn't interested. He just wanted the whole thing over and done with and he wasn't sure he would want to keep anything that Jemima had set her sights on anyway. He knew from experience how her glassy-eyed desire had the power to corrupt anything in its path.

Standing outside the front door for the first time in just under a year, Milton was under no illusion that there would be anything of value left behind. Certainly not his collection of first edition *Harry Potter* books he had diligently collected and shrink-wrapped for posterity. Certainly not the binders of first-day covers his uncle had left him in his will. Certainly not those gold and ivory cufflinks his grandfather had worn when he got married.

Jemima knew where all the treasure was in the house; he imagined her with pirate maps, digging through the attic detritus in her quest to exhume it all. He imagined too how that dipshit Welsh oaf, Barri-with-an-i, would have been waiting with his van in the drive, rubbing his fat steak-like hands in drooling anticipation of a wealth beyond his meagre, stunted dreams.

It was something of a surprise, therefore, to see the curtains still hung in the margins of the lounge windows, and when

Milton squinted through the glass, he could make out the obsidian slab of the plasma TV still mounted on the wall above the fireplace, and the glittering stack of his precious hi-fi neatly embedded on the shelves.

Maybe they didn't have the tools to take them down? He wouldn't have put it past them to act on spite alone and break everything instead.

With a sigh, he set his key to the lock and only then did he stop, sensing a thick pressure on his chest, a heat behind the ears. He had been so preoccupied with Jemima he almost hadn't noticed the house had become unlivable in his absence. The irony of this was not lost on him. Thinking of Jemima at the wrong time had led to his first divorce after all; thinking of Jemima had been what had driven him to go home that lunchtime to find her in bed with Barri-with-an-i, who she hadn't seen since they'd been at school together in Swansea, and for whom she'd always harboured feelings – even though his middle-aged form was somewhat less athletic than the one she'd lost her virginity to all those years before.

And now, thinking of Jemima had almost made him walk blindly into an unlivable house. He barked a laugh, an ugly sound even to him, and backed away down the path, staring up at the dead façade in front of him. So hard fought for, so easily lost. He sat on the edge of the rockery and cried for the first time since he was eight years old.

Milton Bream was rescued from his doorstep by Penny Moon from number nine. Like Una Felton, she took him home and took care of him, and like the Potterton family, Milton accepted her charity with a grace and humility that was new to him, but which he found fitted him well.

Penny Moon was nearly ten years Milton's junior but knew exactly what it was like to lose someone you loved to another. She had moved into Hope Street six years earlier to care for her father after a stroke had rendered him housebound. She had set up a bedroom downstairs where the lounge used to be, opening the curtains wide each morning so her father could see the birds feeding in his beloved garden.

While he slept during the day, Penny had worked hard, making the upstairs rooms of number nine into the apartment she had once thought to have bought with Gary. She pictured a lounge, a bedroom, and spaces for all her books and the paintings she imagined she might one day buy. She made the upstairs rooms into a little box for herself, a nest with four walls and a door she could use to shut herself in. It was a long way away from her friends in London, but they had been Gary's friends too and she simply didn't trust them any more. All their concern and advice seemed more for his benefit than hers, so she stopped replying to their messages and answering their calls. Another door left to shut on its own.

After her father died, she inherited the house but remained upstairs. The rooms downstairs felt both too dark and too bright at the same time. The barbed smell of her father's final, humiliating hours lingered in the dark patches on the ceiling, in the gaps in the wallpaper, the scuff marks on the floor. She sat upstairs alone in the bedroom she had made a lounge, the curtains closed so she couldn't see the garden her father had spent his life tending, and which had grown wild and unkempt without him.

When Milton moved in, he knew nothing of her history and, in those early days, he didn't think to ask. When she showed him her father's room, he didn't see the history of it, scribbled into the walls and the furniture. He just saw a sanctuary, illuminated by the sort of diligent love he had no experience of himself.

He followed Penny, docile and silent as she led him to the kitchen and made him a bowl of soup and still-warm soda bread, the same meal her father used to make her when she had been a child.

Number Eleven

Less than a week after Milton Bream's house became unlivable, the same happened to the house at number eleven.

This house was owned by Marlon Swick, and he lived there with his partner of eight years, Julia Prin. It was another Saturday and they had spent the afternoon at his mother's house in Barnstaple. She spent the whole time they were there talking about children. She'd always wanted grandchildren she'd said, and she'd said it with one of those pointed expressions which was probably supposed to be subtle, but failed.

She'd given up on the two of them getting married by that point, and while both Marlon and Julia had tried to explain to her how they both very much wanted children too, their own subtlety was missed entirely.

And so, while Julia patiently washed the dishes after lunch, Marlon's mother stood close behind her.

'Tick tock,' she said, a benign twinkle in her voice. 'Tick tock.'

They excused themselves from the evening meal which Marlon's mother had lovingly prepared. Marlon lied to her, faking a phone call and explaining something had happened back home which they absolutely had to attend to, and he had looked away while his mother cried. He would call her later on. He always did find it easier to deal with her over the phone.

She shouted at them a little, she screamed a little more. Everyone was miserable by the time they finally left.

On the way home, they stopped at a country pub and ordered the most enormous meal they could afford: three courses, artisan bread, a jug of wine which Julia was too upset to enjoy.

Marlon ran a small office cleaning company from a pair of stacked Portakabins on the south side of Midholme. Business had been slowing since he'd lost out on a few contracts over the last few years, but his mother's influence had left him well versed in the tactic of allaying sadness with food, no matter what the cost.

Back in the car, he turned to Julia and smiled at her in the most encouraging way he knew how.

'When we get home,' he said, 'we should go to the Oak and get drunk like teenagers. We should absolutely make fools of ourselves.'

Julia laughed, but Marlon knew she would probably rather just go to bed and forget the afternoon happened at all.

Unlike Milton Bream's experience, Marlon and Julia knew something was wrong with Hope Street as soon as they turned off the Brenthwaite Road. The whole street felt darker than it should have been, and for a brief moment of intense clarity, Marlon saw how there were three nodes along its length where the night was most clenched and dangerous. One was the Potterton house, one was the Bream house and one was their own.

'Oh, baby,' he said.

Julia was asleep on the passenger seat beside him. He parked by the kerb and arranged a coat over her to keep her warm, then sat back beside her, watching the house until dawn.

Daniel Dormer lived in number twelve with his wife Kelly and their six-year-old son who, to Kelly's consternation, he had insisted be named after his father, Hilary.

On the morning after Marlon and Julia's house became unlivable, he walked out his front door to greet the morning, as had become his custom of late, and saw his neighbours asleep in their car.

Daniel Dormer had very strong views regarding neighbourhood aesthetics. The cars on Hope Street should, he believed, be parked in the driveways provided, or better still, in the garages provided. He'd heard somewhere that Julia was an artist of some sort and that she and Marlon had converted their garage into a studio. To Daniel, this seemed like a terrible waste of time, more so given that his neighbours' ageing and tatty Volvo estate was just the sort of vehicle that suburban garages had been invented to conceal.

He tapped on the driver's side window, clearing his throat as he mentally prepared himself to make a speech, a speech that would be both reasonable, concise and fair. Churchillian, if you will.

Marlon rolled down the window and nodded at him. Before Daniel could utter a word, Marlon pointed past him to number eleven, which still looked dark in the early morning sun.

'The house has gone wrong,' he said. 'We can't go home.'

Daniel had heard about the Potterton house, of course. He'd also heard about Milton Bream. But his own house at number twelve was the closest to the junction with the Brenthwaite Road, and Daniel had little reason to traverse Hope Street to its far end, so he'd never actually seen how the houses could change so utterly.

Seeing the shadows that overcast number eleven, he was stuck with a stark and inexplicable sense of horror. Objectively, the house looked little different; its window frames were still in need of repainting and the lawn was rough and overgrown. But there was something else about the house which felt wrong to him, a deep almost-imperceptible vibration that made his blood worry, and his bones scrape inside of him.

Daniel Dormer did not intend to take Marlon and Julia into his family's home. It was a decision he made too soon and with too little thought. Even as they stepped over his threshold, looking and acting as humble and docile as the others in the street who had been taken in by their neighbours, Daniel felt a sudden panic that he was doing the wrong thing, a nagging sense that they were infected by the same careless toxicity which had made their home unlivable: an infection they might carry with them, an infection they might spread to the military orderliness of number twelve. The others in the street had been hosting the homeless for weeks now, months. He wondered how he would ever get rid of the couple now they had moved in.

Despite the fact that Kelly Dormer was delighted by her husband's decision to invite the couple into their home, despite the fact that Hilary was excited to have visitors he could show off his toys to, Marlon Swick and Julia Prin only stayed one night at number twelve Hope Street.

As they lay awake in the spare bedroom – a pristinely ordered room that had been barely used – Julia stared at the shadows of the thin curtains which streaked the ceiling and made it marble.

'Perhaps our luck is a limited resource,' she said, 'and so far, we've invested it all in one part of our lives and not another. We've been so lucky living here on Hope Street, but that's gone now. So perhaps the luck will work on something else now? Maybe we'll be lucky where we've been unlucky before?'

And she turned to him and traced her hand over his chest and down his abdomen.

They made love in a stranger's house that night. They were slow and careful and as silent as they could be, surrounded by floral wallpaper, lace and perfume. Every feeling was bitten back, friction dulled, movement muted.

And on the other side of the wall, while his wife slept beside him with an eye-mask over her face, Daniel Dormer listened hard, hearing every distended breath. He smiled to himself greedily because, good neighbours that they were, Marlon and Julia had given him an excuse to become himself again.

The following morning, Marlon and Julia were asked to leave number twelve and find their own accommodation elsewhere. Daniel told them this without malice, acting simply as though his offer to host them had only ever been for one night.

Marlon didn't want to make a scene, Julia looked as though she was preoccupied by other concerns. Outside, they stood by the car, listening to Kelly Dormer raising her voice for the first time in her marriage, saying things she would later regret, because regret was easier to manage, easier to accommodate.

Julia took Marlon's hand.

'I want to go home,' she said. And Marlon nodded, as though deep down part of him wanted the very same thing.

They ignored the darkness of number eleven, seeing only the sunlight in each other. Marlon unlocked the door and they kissed on the threshold, a long, deep and beautiful kiss. Julia took Marlon's hand and guided it down to her abdomen.

'Lucky,' she said.

'Lucky,' he agreed and opened the door.

Together, they stepped inside. Together, they fell. Together, they died in the unlivable house, their feet splayed across the doorstep. To the casual observer, they looked peaceful and content, a couple who loved each other very much, holding each other until the end.

Some Valuable Context

Hope Street was a line of neat detached houses situated nearly halfway between the town of Midholme to the south and the village of Brenthwaite to the north. It lay with its back to the outer seam of St Crispin Woods, and faced sixteen acres of farmland, sloping downhill before it, separating the line of houses from the Brenton Road Estate on the northern edge of Midholme.

Geographically and psychologically, Hope Street was neither part of the town to the south (except for administrative purposes) nor part of the village to the north (except for the few who patronised St Joseph's church). It was its own little world, a holloway between the wood and the field, between the town and the countryside.

There were twelve detached houses built side by side with neat apex roofs and ruddy red tiles. Each had originally been constructed to an identical design in the late 1960s, with the expectation that the farmland would ultimately be sold to developers and the road, cheaply procured at the time, would find itself at the vanguard of the town. Nearly fifty years later, the farmland, still mired in complex negotiations, continued to cycle wheat and rape seed, while Hope Street had gone from cheap and isolated to exclusive and private, the individual houses evolving independently to reflect the change. Each now diverged from its original schema in its own particular and distinct manner: number three had a new front porch; numbers six, eight and twelve had loft conversions; most now had conservatories of various sizes and designs; and number four had a new double garage and a swimming pool.

From midway across the field, the line of twelve pointed roofs looked like a row of filed teeth bordering the woodland. From the top floor of the number 16 bus as it swooped up the hill every twenty minutes towards Brenthwaite, they looked like a large picket fence that had been subsumed by the surrounding farmland.

From ground-level, the street was quiet and pleasant, curving gently to the west and out of sight from the Brenthwaite road. The tarmac had seen better days, but the pot holes were easy to avoid if you knew where they were and many an estate agent had mistaken them for character. And while the low stone wall that separated the road from the fields had collapsed in a number of places, there was something about it which connected deeply to the middle class investor. It was neither completely urban nor completely rural. It was both, and it was neither, and when the wind picked at the trees of St Crispin Wood and made them roar, it sounded as though it could have been the sea.

The Residents' Committee

The community of Hope Street prided themselves in their strength and their support. Together, they considered themselves a text-book example of how people could work together, even if individually they were less idealistic, and certainly less confident in the motives of their neighbours.

The residents' committee met on the first Thursday of every month, cycling through the houses from number one to number twelve, from January through to December. It was a neat system and a consistent one. Every January, Bryn Purbrick hosted the meeting in his open plan lounge, which his partner Howard would redecorate each year to an agreed theme, and every December, Daniel Dormer would use the opportunity to host his annual Christmas-tree party, in which the residents would be invited to help decorate the family tree, while drinking sherry and eating Kelly's mince pies.

Attendance at the meeting was certainly not compulsory, but several years earlier, Carla Bretton had taken it upon herself to record non-attendance in her little Moleskine notebook, arguing that those who paid more attention to local affairs should rightfully have more say. On the morning Marlon and Julia died, she pored over her findings to try and determine a correlation between the houses which had become unlivable and the residents who had the poorest attendance record at the monthly meetings. She was disappointed to find there was none at all.

Over the past few years there had been only few major incidents that the committee had been required to address. There had been a handful of planning applications, but few were contentious and most were modest in scope, each being passed with the minimum of attention. A council proposal to build a new recycling depot opposite the Hope Street turn-off was successfully petitioned against, as was the council's decision to remove the Hope Street bus stop, even though none of the residents of Hope Street used the bus which sped past twelve times a day.

Crime was also low. There had been a brief spate of burglaries some six years earlier, but nothing since the Neighbourhood Watch initiative had been instigated. There was a half-way house on the Brenton Road Estate, and one of its residents occasionally found their way into the cul-de-sac, but on the whole it was a quiet and peaceful little street; one the authorities rarely needed to venture into, let alone trouble.

Perhaps this was why nobody moved the bodies of Marlon and Julia when they died. A vague sense of unreality made the incident look perversely gauche in the neatly-trimmed street. It was something people struggled to engage with, it felt too unlikely to be genuinely tragic. The other reason was easier to explain: nobody dared. The house was unlivable after all, and the bodies proved it to anyone who would look.

Milton Bream got the closest. He was frustrated that no one thought to try and move the bodies. It was disrespectful, it was unkind. Marlon's foot had fallen across the threshold, so he imagined it might be possible to reach it and pull them both free from the house that had ended them. A small crowd gathered to watch him edge up the driveway of number eleven as though it were a steepening hill, his arm outstretched as though he might draw the couple towards him with some telekinetic will.

Later, he told Penny Moon how he'd felt a dense pressure growing heavy in his chest the closer he got to the house. It felt as though he was pushing himself through successive curtains of something viscous and suffocating. He said he saw how Marlon's body had landed. Not on Julia's, but beside it, his arm draped around her waist as though he were still holding her to him and would continue to do so.

It felt like desecration, he said, justifying his retreat without admitting to the fear which had driven him away; and Penny reached across to him in the bed they now shared and slid her own arm over his. He took it and held it too tight. Over the past few nights, he'd been subjected to the same nightmare. That he'd looked through the window of number eight and seen Jemima inside, lying across the sofa in the same way that she used to when she watched that dancing programme on Saturday nights, but also very much not in the same way at all. In his dream, her head lolled too far to the side, her mouth hung rudely agape, and her legs were splayed and awkward. He'd rapped on the glass until his knuckles had split and the glass had smeared red so he couldn't see her at all.

On this occasion, the authorities did arrive but they didn't stay long. They'd seen this sort of thing before, they said and they milled around the garden of number eleven from a safe distance then went on their way again, leaving only a stern admonishment that no one else go near the affected houses. They promised that they'd be back to build a barrier of some sort, but they never did.

'It's probably happening all over,' someone said, but no one really thought to find out.

A week later, Una Felton planted a small Anne Harkness rose in the front garden of number eleven. Years before she had planted the same variety in her back garden at number seven. Suzie had chosen it from the display at Hawsham's Nurseries like she was picking her favourite colour from a paint catalogue. They had planted it together, a pleasant afternoon made more so with hindsight, and to Una it represented a connection lost, the promise of potential left cruelly unexplored. She hoped its beautiful, apricot colours would have pleased Julia, and how that in turn would have pleased Marlon. Despite Alasdair's concern, she planted it as close to the house as she dared. It didn't block the view. Its scent was too subtle to mask the smell of the bodies as they turned, but it was a gesture, and sometimes that was all that was possible, sometimes that was enough.

When she got home and washed the dirt off her hands in the utility room sink, she turned to Alasdair who was standing watching her from the doorway, and to Lewis and Lydia who were waiting behind him.

'I think someone needs to do something,' she said, her tone underlining how she didn't trust anyone else to do so on her behalf.

The first emergency meeting of the Hope Street residents' committee was called for the following weekend. The Feltons had hosted the meeting only the previous month, but Milton's house was now unlivable and so they volunteered, given the strangeness of the circumstances, to host it again. The feeling that things had changed irrevocably was impossible to ignore, but there was still a sense amongst some that in calling the meeting without consultation, and by calling a second meeting at her own house, Una had done something vulgar and untoward.

As such, the faces that greeted her in the living room at number seven were not, she judged, entirely receptive to what she had to say. She centred herself and began.

'People are losing their homes,' she said. 'People are dying. We have a responsibility to act. We have a duty to help.'

She outlined her hypothesis that other houses in the street would become unlivable, that other families would become homeless; that others might die.

'We have to watch out for one another,' she said. 'The only way we can get through this is to do what we do best. To *watch* our neighbours, to *notice* when something looks wrong. To open our doors when their own becomes closed to them.'

The faces that looked back at her were blank, denting her confidence enough to make her falter.

'We can't stand by,' she said. 'We simply can't.'

Her neighbours – those who had lost their homes and those who had not – looked at her impassively. There was no agreement, no argument. No one had anything to say in reply to her.

She wanted to tell them how she and Alasdair had started to work on the house so more people could stay. They'd cleared out the dining room, they'd emptied Suzie's room, even the lounge could accommodate a family should the need arise. She wanted to tell them how Alasdair had been working in the shed at the bottom of the garden, making box-bed frames and futons to a design Una had found on the internet. But she didn't tell them that. The faces that looked up at her reminded me of the children she used to teach before she'd retired, the same looks of insolent defiance she remembered when she took the whole class to task for whatever minor infraction.

She sighed.

'Also, I made biscuits,' she said instead.

To this at least, there was a murmur of appreciation.

'Oh, thank god for that,' Daniel Dormer said. Una Felton's biscuits were legendary, after all.

Number Two

The next few months passed by without further incident and it felt for a time as though the crisis may have passed by entirely. Certainly it didn't look as though the houses already affected might revert to normal again, but there didn't seem to be any signs that the problem would continue. Over the course of the next three committee meetings, Una's passionate concern seemed increasingly hyperbolic. The consensus of the other residents of the street was that what occurred already had been tragic, but it was time to move on, to look forward.

Despite this, the November meeting of the Hope Street residents' committee took place at number two Hope Street, and the jarring disorder of this was more than enough to make the residents feel uncomfortable; a stark reminder that there were fewer houses in the street than there used to be.

But Daniel Dormer was adamant.

'It was like a storm,' he said, sitting comfortably in the high wing-backed armchair Carla Bretton's husband used to favour. 'It passed over us, it took its toll. It's gone now.'

He smiled at Kelly, sitting beside him on one of the folding dining chairs.

'It certainly seems that way,' she said.

Carla Bretton leaned across Kelly to top up Daniel's cup of tea from her Portmeirion teapot. She nodded in vigorous agreement.

'I made up a chart for the whole street during the last week,' she said, 'and it says we're home free. The stars never lie. They say the weather will be good for the next few months too.'

Una didn't say anything. She'd humoured Carla's 'gifts' in the past, allowing her to make one of her star charts for Suzie after she moved out. It was all nonsense of course: Carla didn't foresee how Suzie would drop out of her economics degree. She didn't foresee the pregnancy or the termination, and she certainly didn't predict how she would chase some square-jawed surfer halfway across the world to move in with him in some beach hut in Sydney. Of course she didn't. And of course, Una hadn't believed a word of it at the time either; she'd invited Carla over as a courtesy. She was being neighbourly, she was being nice. Considering her argument with the committee, perhaps it was ironic that she could now see how niceness was a weakness that could be perceived as a trap. How typical that by being accommodating more than twenty years ago she should risk exposing herself as a hypocrite in the present.

She cleared her throat.

'This isn't about how things are now,' she said, 'this is about what might happen in the future. It's household insurance. If you had a power cut and spent the night in darkness, you would buy candles the next day so you won't be caught out a second time. All I'm arguing is that we offer the same compassion to others as we might hope to receive ourselves.

We each put a candle in reserve for each other should we need it.'

She looked around the room sternly.

'Because you can never tell when it will happen again,' she said.

Carla cleared her throat to say something. Her expression was one Una had seen before: part persecuted, part condescending. It was the expression she wore when someone quoted science at her, the expression she wore before she launched into a defence of the gift she claimed to have inherited from her grandmother.

On this occasion, Lydia Potterton got there first.

'I think we should all leave,' she said. 'I think we should all leave right now.'

She was staring up at the corner of the room where Carla's fuchsia-striped wallpaper met the moulded coving which ran the circumference of the ceiling. There was nothing there to see, but there was an unshakeable sense that there would be. The sense that, under scrutiny, the paint would darken and peel and the wallpaper would bubble and blacken.

Milton Bream was on his feet first.

'I'm sorry,' he said, bundling for the door, Penny Moon close on his heels. The remaining residents heard the front door open and slam shut before they thought to do anything themselves, they heard footsteps diminish on the garden path.

It was like something out of a cartoon, Una thought. That coyote running out over the edge of a cliff. And he's doing fine until he notices how casually he's breaking the laws of physics. He only falls when he realises that he should. The safety of ignorance before understanding, the precious calm before the fall.

The calm in number two Hope Street lasted all of fifteen seconds before the panic muscled in and took its place. In the very same moment, everyone was on their feet. A moment later and everyone was at the lounge door. The houses in Hope Street were built during a time where smaller doorways were preferable because it meant the rooms would be easier to keep warm, and so the crowd quickly bottle-necked, frustration and fear flaring like wildfire.

Una and Alasdair were near the back of the crowd, seated by the window. Una had found herself unable to overcome her habit of stepping aside to let others go before her. She glanced up at the corner of the room and, while it had not changed in any visible manner, she felt the threat of it had intensified, like a magnifying glass focusing the late autumn sunlight.

'If everyone just goes one at a time,' someone said. It sounded like Bryn, his voice far too reedy to carry any weight or credence, no matter how good the advice was. Everyone was pushing towards the door. Whenever they relaxed just a moment to consider the logic of the situation, someone else pushed from behind and that only made them redouble their efforts.

The fear was animal. The smell of it seeped into the room, made it dense and primal.

Una heard the door clatter open as the neighbours fought to free themselves, popping out into the hallway like champagne corks. She heard their footsteps faltering on the path outside.

She felt Alasdair's hand in hers and felt his own impatience coiled up tight within it.

'We're going to be too late,' he said. He looked behind him at the window. Then he kissed Una on the cheek and stepped across the room to examine it closer.

The window was locked. Alasdair recognised the residents' committee approved window fasteners bolted to the levers on both opening panes; they were the same model he had himself and he had a key for them somewhere, probably at home in the glass jar where he and Una kept such domestic ephemera. Instead he picked up the dining chair that Kelly Dormer had been sitting on, and thrust it legs first towards the glass. It took a few attempts before the glass gave way, more with a creak and a crack than with a satisfying shatter.

'That's my window!' Carla Bretton squeaked from the front garden, apparently having been one of the first to escape from the house. Alasdair ignored her. He hammered away the remaining shards of glass with a broken chair-leg, and tore down the curtain to cushion the jagged teeth they left behind in the frames.

'You can't break my window!' Carla said. 'When this is all over I'll have to fix it. You're paying for it, Alasdair Felton. I tell you *right now*, you're paying for it all. Otherwise my lawyers will hear of this, you mark my words.'

She hovered on the other side, her hands flapping. Behind her, the crowd of residents watched from a safe distance.

'And those are my best curtains,' Carla said. 'You have no respect for other people's property. Those were my mother's curtains. She had them made after she got married and I kept them as a reminder of her. Those are precious things. You can't treat them like that.'

'Carla,' Alasdair said, 'please step out of the way so my wife can get out of your house.'

But a polite request was not enough to move Carla.

'This is an outrage,' she said and she started pulling the curtain away, her little fists grasping the fabric and ripping it over the remains of the broken glass.

Alasdair shot a glance to his wife, then to the door which remained blocked by the dwindling jumble of remaining residents.

'One moment, dear,' he said. He vaulted out of the window with a deftness that belied his years, then took Carla by the shoulder and gently guided her away from the window. She was still arguing, still flapping her arms as Penny Moon stepped in with an apologetic expression to lead her away.

Una approached the window and smiled. She set her hands on the ledge, made soft by the curtain, and watched as Alasdair hurried back across the garden to help her.

'What a wonderful thing you are,' she said.

And then the house became unlivable and she died.

After the Meeting

Five people were left in number two Hope Street when it became unlivable after November's residents' meeting. Alasdair had seen Una fall at the window as though she had simply been taken by a swoon like one of the characters from the Regency romances she had a weakness for. Elsewhere, Cyril Styx, the large gentleman from number three, had got stuck in the living room door and his wife Brenda had been tugging at his arm from the other side. He'd spent more time complaining that she was hurting him than appreciating how she was trying to help. Both died where they stood, both had tears in their eyes. Bryn's partner Howard had been on the toilet upstairs when everything went wrong. He had eaten something the day before which had disagreed with him and as a result he missed most of the stampede because, when he realised what was happening, he was determined to make himself presentable and avoid showing either himself or Bryn up. The final resident to die was Lewis Potterton, who had been waiting behind to help both Cyril Styx through the door or Una through the window, whichever opportunity came first.

Alasdair had stared at empty window where Una had fallen. He could hear Lydia Potterton screaming behind him, but he felt numb and disconnected because there was nothing else he could do other than find a way to come to terms with the hole that had opened up in his world. If he had pushed Cara out the way, he could have helped Una immediately. If only he hadn't been so patient and polite, his wife would have been standing there with him. He shook the thought out of his head. There was no time for such speculation, the street wasn't done with them yet. It occurred to him that he'd left his watch on the small table beside the sofa in Carla Bretton's front room. It had started to worry at him of late, his wrist coming out in a rash where the leather of the strap rubbed against the softening folds of his skin. But Una had given it to him the Christmas after they married and in some ways it reassured him that she was there looking after it for him.

He retreated back up the path and put his hand on Lydia Potterton's shoulder.

'Let's go home,' he said, emphasising the word home in a way that made it sound as inclusive as Una would have wanted. Lydia nodded. She would be strong for her daughter, but there would be time for that later. For now she was unashamed to be led.

They walked a few steps up the path before Alasdair turned back.

'Carla,' he said. 'There's room at ours should you need it.'

Carla was standing on her lawn, staring at her broken house. For the first time in her life, she didn't know what to do, or what to say.

Number Four and Number Six

Three more weeks passed before two further houses on the street became unlivable, and when they turned, they did so within hours of each other. At number four, Judy Khamen woke in the night, untroubled by dreams. Lying alone in her dark bedroom with only the memory of the woman she had once loved keeping the bed warm beside her, she felt a knot of cold panic ripen inside of her and for a moment, she wondered if Francesca had come back while she'd been asleep. If she turned her head just a little, taking her eyes off the ceiling and looking at the pillow beside her, she imagined she would see Francesca there, her hair a comb of richer shadows spilling down the back of her neck to pool on the silk sheets.

Judy was a personal injury lawyer and only the previous week she had been delivering a series of presentations to a handful of financial companies in Midholme, detailing her own company's position on the merits of liabilities insurance. Francesca had been a liability and Judy had known that when she first met her. She'd heard people describe how someone's smile could be *wicked*, but she'd never seen such a thing until she'd met Francesca. And there it was: a shard of something mischievous in her eye that widened into something beautiful and dangerous when she smiled.

Judy was already in a relationship at the time. Marjorie was an older woman and they'd fallen in together by one of those happy accidents where people who fit together find themselves in the right place at the right time. She was a pleasant soul. Homely. They'd been together for the best part of three years, and while their definition of 'best part' didn't quite align (for Judy it was duration, for Marjorie it was quality), Judy was content.

Francesca didn't give a fuck.

Weeks later when they met again, Judy recounted how her world had since fallen apart now that Francesca was in its orbit. She told how Marjorie had fled. She told Francesca the things Marjorie had said to her, how her face had looked ruined, painted bright with anger and tears. She told Francesca how everything now felt hollow and empty.

Francesca looked at her pointedly.

'I will break your heart,' she had said.

Judy weighed up the risks, then bet everything she had, starting with a kiss.

Lying alone in her bed at number four Hope Street, watching the darkness clot around her, she considered staying where she was and letting the dying house take her with it. It had been months since she'd last seen Francesca and everything she owned now felt brittle and grey, whether the house was liveable or otherwise. Why should she save herself? What was left to be saved?

But she pushed herself up and out of bed anyway. Sitting on the edge for a moment, her toes arched down to the bare floorboards. She allowed herself the luxury of time to wake up. If the house took her, then so be it. She was in no rush. She took her time finding some clothes to wear, a warm coat, a few paperbacks, some boots. Her hand passed over a locket that Marjorie had given her one Christmas, but she left it where it lay on the dresser. She found her phone and her wallet instead, she found the phone charger and put everything into a canvas bag, one of the ones she had picked up at a conference a few years earlier. She trudged down the stairs, the wallpaper curling and blackening behind her as she laid her hand on the door handle and turned it.

Just over an hour after Judy Khamen locked the door of number four behind her for the very last time, Brandon Vine, who was renting the house at number six, woke briefly in his bed in a similar state of distress.

In his barely awakened state, it didn't occur to him that his panic was anything to do with the house at all. He attributed his fear to the usual things that woke him up in the night: the upcoming round of redundancies at the consultancy firm he'd been working at for the past seven years; the fact that he was ill-prepared to complete his tax assessment this year; the sheer volume of grey in his beard; the nagging sense that there might be a lump on one of his balls; the sinking pit of knowing that he had now been single for four years, seven months, and three days.

These were familiar fears, each of which had woken him periodically in the past. And on this occasion, as on any other when they had troubled him, he stomped out of his bedroom and crossed the hall to the bathroom where he dosed himself with the homeopathic anxiety medication his mother had sworn by.

Back in bed, he fretted briefly that his failure to believe in homeopathy would render the tablets redundant, but this worry didn't stop him from falling back asleep again, and for the first time since he'd been a child, he snored.

The expression of sheer contentment on his face when he died might have been read as evidence that he knew his concerns would never bother him again.

An Invitation

As Christmas approached, there were only three houses left in Hope Street that had not yet become unlivable. They stood out like pools of bright sunlight punctuating an otherwise unpromising day. The residents who had outlived their home's decline remained in the street, clustered together, their shared survival granting them a collective experience more profound than any number of residents' committees or contrived community events. For the first time, they recognised how they were all *alive*, how they were all *human*, how they were all still *there*. For the first time, they recognised how important the simple commonalities were between them. They were precious hand- and footholds in each other that they each clung to desperately.

Alasdair Felton was still at number seven and he had taken it upon himself to continue Una's charity as she would have herself, were she still there. If this was her legacy, he was grateful for it. The house would have been empty without her, unlivable in its own very particular and equally dangerous way. Instead, he busied himself with the needs of his guests, considering ways to break the house further into tiny domestic polities which could accommodate more refugees should the need arise.

Lydia Potterton and Monica still lived in the small spare room in the attic and they filled the space Lewis left with a memory of him which gave him a greater stature than he could have ever filled in life. Downstairs, Carla Bretton had claimed a curtained-off section of the lounge, and made herself a nest of scatter cushions and blankets in one of the box beds Alasdair had constructed. The result had an appearance part Bedouin tent, part Scottish bothy, and part child's den. There was something transitory about it which appealed to her, and in a peculiar way, she felt as though she had finally become the eccentric gypsy seer she had always imagined herself to be.

Bryn Purbrick had moved into Suzie's old room, which hadn't been redecorated properly since the mid-1990s because Una had desperately hoped she would come home one day, and because she was terrified she would leave again if the room hadn't been exactly as she'd left it. One wall was still covered with a collage of curling clippings from the *NME* and *Melody Maker*, *Rolling Stone* and *Select*. The kohl-rimmed eyes of minor starlets peeked out between demo reviews and interviews with musicians; heavy on supercilious snark and wretched word-play. When Bryn woke in panic during the night, when his simple dreams would be invaded by the more nightmarish truth that Howard had died, he would calm himself by picking his way through the clippings with a torch. He didn't really know what any of it meant, he didn't know who any of these people were, but in a curious way it grounded him, it kept him whole.

At number nine, Penny Moon now hosted Milton Bream in her own room, and Judy Khamen in her father's. Stephen and Deirdre Spiller and their three kids had also moved in from number ten. They had missed much of the previous activity on the street; they'd been in Portland for the past six months, where Deirdre had been working on a project and Stephen had been failing to write a novel. They returned to find their home had become unlivable while they were away. Penny Moon had already left a note in their driveway, wrapped in plastic and set in place with a hefty pebble.

'There's a room for you all at ours,' it said.

'You're not alone,' it said.

And so the Spillers had moved into Penny Moon's upstairs lounge, and being of similar dimensions to the condo they had shared for the past six months, it felt more like home to them than the house they would never enter again.

Throughout all of this, the Dormer family at number twelve remained on their own.

'We simply haven't got the room,' Daniel said when Alasdair brought up the subject one afternoon. He'd come round to invite the family to a Christmas meal with the other residents. It had been Monica's idea. She'd raised it over breakfast one morning the previous week, idly trying to imagine how Christmas might work now that everyone was in different places. She worded things delicately so as not to upset her mother.

'This place is too small for us really,' Daniel said. He spread his arms to encompass the lounge. 'And Hilary suffers from terrible claustrophobia. It's a family thing. My father was exactly the same.'

Hilary ducked behind his mother's legs, his eyes downcast.

Alasdair nodded.

'I understand,' he said. 'I really do.'

He didn't mention that all the houses in the street were built to the same design, and that while many had subsequently acquired alterations of some description, none were quite so large as the extension which stretched out into what had once been the Dormer's back garden. Thirty square metres of additional lounge space on the downstairs, two more bedrooms up top.

Alasdair inclined his head and made his move. At the door, Daniel watched him walk down the path.

'I don't know why they stay,' he said.

Alasdair stopped and turned back. He looked at Daniel a moment, trying to see the same hand- and footholds on him which were so clear and apparent in everyone else on the street. But the man was smooth and soft, like a curl of butter on a warm day.

'It's their home,' Alasdair said. 'Why should they leave?'

'It's not their home anymore.' Daniel looked imperious in the doorway. Part sentry, part bouncer. 'Circumstance might be unkind, but there's nothing anyone can do when it gets in your way. It's a message. We should listen. We *all* should listen. It started with the Pottertons. Maybe it's still happening *because* they stayed.'

Alasdair shook his head slowly.

'No,' he said. 'I don't believe that at all.'

Daniel remained unmoved.

'Well, it's something to consider.' He plunged his hands deep into his pockets and looked up at the threads of cloud crawling across the grey of the sky. 'And if it's true,' he said, 'perhaps your wife's compassion has put everyone at risk. If the Pottertons had been sent packing when their house went wrong, who knows how many people would still be alive?'

When he looked down again, his smile was stiff and straight.

'Christmas dinner will be at two,' Alasdair said. 'You're all welcome. Bring a bottle if you can spare one.'

Number Nine

Late on Christmas Eve, Penny Moon's house became unlivable. Judy Khamen noticed the signs first. It was nearly nine o'clock and she was in the back garden with a cigarette. She found herself strangely content with her new life. She had always liked Penny, but even Milton was less of a dick than she had assumed. She liked the closeness of the situation. The warmth, the tolerance, the fact you had to lean into the wall to let people past in the morning. If it was not the companionship she had wept for, perhaps it was the companionship she had needed.

With her back to the house, she felt a growing warmth at the nape of her neck which had no business being there so late in the year.

The others were still in the house, watching a DVD in the front room; a stand-up comedy routine that Judy had seen before. The volume was turned up high, and she could hear the din of distant laughter, echoed by intermittent barks of amusement from Milton and Stephen, yaps from the kids. When she tried the back door she realised it had locked behind her. Penny didn't have enough keys to go round, so the doors were kept on latches and sometimes they slipped. Sometimes they locked themselves when they were closed too forcefully. Sometimes.

Judy hammered on the glass but no one came. She knocked louder and shouted herself hoarse, but the tinny roar of laughter from the television turned mocking and cruel. She searched the garden for something to wield at one of the windows, perhaps even to break it if she could, but Penny's garden was wild and untended, filled only with limp knotty grasses and soft muddy hollows.

There was no footpath through to the front of the house, so Judy took a different approach. She jogged up the garden as far as it went and clambered over the wall to the garden next door. Milton Bream's house glowered at her with black and empty windows, but its toxicity had yet to consume the garden as well so Judy passed through it unharmed.

Over the next wall, in the garden of number seven, Judy found Bryn Purbrick playing Swingball with Monica Potterton. Both were wearing head torches, making the ball flit in and out of the skittering light as though it was a planet ducking in and out of eclipse. She hurried past them into the kitchen where Alasdair and Carla were dressing the turkey.

'Penny's house is going,' she said, breathless. 'Penny's house is near as gone.'

What happened next happened briskly and without discussion. Just as all those months earlier, the Potterton family knew to leave their house as one, the new and expanded Felton household understood how they needed to act. The meal was abandoned, the house was emptied and everyone hurried up the street to Penny Moon's house.

Nobody on Hope Street died on Christmas Eve. The Felton household ran shouting and waving and the Moon household didn't need any other cue to understand their situation. This was a matter beyond language. This was a matter beyond explanation. They fled the house at number nine without further hesitation or thought. They ran down the path into the arms of their waiting neighbours, looking back only to see how the house they lived in had dimmed and diminished, retreating into a darkness considerably deeper than the one the evening had painted for it.

Alasdair looked down the road to see there were lights on

in the Dormer house, but no one came out to see what the commotion was, no curtain twitched to suggest they were watching, no figures lingered in the doorway. He turned away, his inexplicable sadness moderated only a little by the adrenaline-laced energy of the crowd.

'What do we do now?' someone said, and someone else laughed darkly.

'It's Christmas,' Alasdair said. There was something miraculous in the air after all.

'That's tomorrow,' Monica said, but as she spoke the first flakes of the season's snow began to fall.

Alasdair shook his head.

'Why wait?' he said.

An Early Christmas Party

The Christmas party at number seven Hope Street lasted from the evening of Christmas Eve to the afternoon of Boxing Day.

There were now twelve guests staying in the house at number seven, and with a little imagination, Alasdair found room for them all, packing them into the corners of his house as though he was capable of tucking them away safely; as though he was strategising some inexplicable game of hide and seek with whatever darkness it was that pursued them from door-to-door.

Instinctively, his guests understood all too well that if time was not on their side, they should – for the first time in their lives – do the things they wanted to do, when they wanted to. There was an inescapable sense that their lives had shifted into a higher gear. They could see their future written in the shadows of the empty houses on the street and they knew there was little sense in sitting back and waiting for it to catch up with them.

There would be a Christmas that year in Hope Street, no matter what happened, no matter what it represented. It would be both spiritual and secular, and in its own peculiar way, it would be an act of rebellion. Because even joy and companionship could be subversive under the right conditions.

Without fuss or argument, on the night of Christmas Eve, they broke into work details and set about preparing their ultimate celebration.

Alasdair and Lydia worked in the kitchen, finishing what they had started with the turkey, and deciding they would serve it when it was ready to be eaten, not when it was traditionally acceptable to eat.

Stephen Spiller took Milton Bream and Carla Bretton, and the three drove out to a late opening garage in his four-wheel drive Mitsubishi, where they bought as much wine, beer, whiskey, and fruit juice as they could afford.

The young man behind the counter – the peak on his company baseball cap skewed to four-o'clock – whistled as he packed the bags.

'Must be a hell of a party,' he said, glancing with deadpan bemusement to the clock above the door.

On any other day, Milton would have said something in response. Something like 'You have no idea,' or 'More likely, heaven.' But that evening, it didn't feel right. Small talk meant words wasted, and at that moment they felt like such a precious resource, the thought of wasting them on someone else – someone who wasn't Penny Moon – frightened him. He paid up, and smiled a thank-you, then the three of them left in silence.

Judy and Penny took the head torches and followed the directions they'd been given to Bryn and Howard's allotment. The snow continued to fall around them, but it was too heavy and damp to settle in a satisfactory way. But the way the night speckled ahead of them reminded Penny of a documentary she had seen about a village somewhere in North America that had been destroyed by a volcano. There it had been ashes which had fallen, settling into a blue-grey snowscape that painted the abandoned streets and houses with a melancholic palette which was beautiful in its way; the once-bustling streets and squares condemned to a gentle peace.

The two women emptied the allotment of everything they could find. They ignored the cold and the damp, digging briskly, without discussion. They carried the goods back across the field in bulging carrier bags, their faces flushed with a pride so warm it kept the winter well at bay.

Deirdre Spiller had a friend who worked as part of the tech crew for a local theatre. She harried him over the telephone until he arrived with a sound system and lighting in the back of his van.

'This will cost you a fortune,' he said, having been talked into accepting her bank card with her PIN number written on a slip of paper.

'What other time will I have to spend it?' she said.

Monica and the three Spiller kids searched the attic for decorations and found, amongst other things, a crate of spray cans including festive reds and greens and golds. To begin with they were cautious with them, spraying the boughs of oak and pine and the chains of ivy Bryn had cut for them, but Alasdair saw what they were doing and squatted beside them.

'Think bigger,' he said. He took one of the cans of gold and, across the kitchen wall, drew a lopsided festive star that glittered brightly as it dripped and dried. The look the children exchanged when he handed the can back to them was one of the most beautiful things he had ever seen.

Dinner was served at five in the morning and there was more of it than most of those who attended the party had ever seen. It kept coming, on plates and pans and in Tupperware boxes. Everyone had seconds. Most had thirds. It seemed perversely rude to leave anything behind.

There was music too. There was light and movement, spilling from the windows of the house all through the night. There were no immediate neighbours to worry about; almost all the neighbours were there after all.

The Spillers danced in the front garden, their children chasing around them with coloured torches. The snow turned to rain but nobody cared.

There was singing, dancing, stories and jokes. As the morning subsided into afternoon, everyone clustered together in the lounge because no one wanted to be alone.

Carla Bretton presented the new chart she had been working on for the street. It was a large piece of blank paper, taped together from a dozen sheets. She spread it out over the floor of the lounge and passed pens around the group so that everyone could write or draw their own future.

They slept where they sat. They woke, they ate. They slept again.

Two o'clock came and went, but the Dormers didn't appear.

The evening fell again, the day had moved so swiftly, the sun racing through the sky as though it was in a hurry to be done. The second night was more subdued, but the residents of number seven remained together throughout.

Number Seven

On the morning of Boxing Day, Alasdair was the first to leave the musty nest of the house in more than twenty-four hours. There had been snow during the night, not much, but enough to dust the tarmac of Hope Street, coating the fields opposite. They glittered as though they had been painted with precious stones. He crossed the road to get a closer look, and for the first time in years, he was struck by the modest beauty of the place where he lived.

He had a smile on his face as he walked down the road to the Dormers' house and slotted a card through the door. The Spiller kids had made it themselves. It had been signed by everyone.

When he got back to number seven, he saw at once how the house had become silent and dark in his brief absence as though the Christmas celebrations had reached their apex point, and plunged downwards into an irreversible night. The stereo was still playing. That party album of Suzie's that one of the kids had found. It was jolly and insistent.

He steeled himself, suddenly feeling the morning's cold he had brusquely dismissed only moments earlier. Then he took the path towards the door.

He was surprised to find himself feeling betrayed, and he was disappointed he should imagine such a thing. He was disappointed too, when he stopped well short of the front door, his hand outstretched and impotent. He could feel the weight of the darkness that occupied the house and he remembered how Una had planted the rose bush outside Marlon Swick's house. How had she got so much closer to the house than he could now?

If everyone else had gone, why should he be the one to be left behind? It was a problem with a very simple solution: he just needed to go home and join everyone. But at that moment, he knew he wasn't brave enough to follow them so baldly. A fear gripped him, compounding both his isolation and the weight of the darkness. He stepped back and back and back under its influence, cursing himself as a coward, cursing the street for leaving him so alone.

From the upstairs window of number twelve Hope Street, Kelly Dormer saw Alasdair approach up the front path for the second time that morning, and she saw her husband step out to intercept him before he reached the door. She didn't hear what they said to each other. The double glazing installed throughout the house had been expensive for a reason. All she heard was the hum of the boiler, the soft breathing of Hilary as he clung to her knees. He seemed so frightened of everything these days. Her hand reached down to touch his hair, a simple act of communion that comforted them both.

When she had first met Daniel, she had thought him to be a quiet, gentle little man. The fourth child of five, he had the look of someone who had been left behind. Back then, the friends they knew had thought of her as the confident one. Back then, she would lead him by the hand, and he would follow after her, a smile on his face as she taught him the way. They had rented a little flat together in Midholme in the early days, a little one bed place above the chemists on Aston Street. Stained carpets, threadbare curtains, but warm and welcome and *theirs*. Good fortune got in the way as good fortune sometimes does. Unexpectedly, they had come into some money when his father had died – complications and conditions in the will gave Daniel unexpected favour, even as his brothers and sisters disowned him. They bought the house at number twelve. It wasn't so far from the town, but as the years passed, it felt as though it were drifting further and further away. Daniel didn't mind. It had never occurred to Kelly how her husband might have considered ownership to be a kind of victory.

Outside, she saw he was doing all the talking, while Alasdair Felton simply watched him. Alasdair's posture was slouched in resignation and his expression was a sad one. He shook his head at something, then nodded at something else. Then, he glanced up at the window where Kelly stood and smiled briefly to acknowledge her before he turned away.

She watched him walk across the road, not looking one way or the other. When he reached the low brick wall, he climbed over it, bouncing to his feet in the field beyond as though his agility had surprised them both. She saw him brush the dusting of snow off his jeans and jacket and she stayed watching as he set off across the field, painted white, a diminishing figure, a scarecrow, a stick man.

Downstairs, the front door slammed, and she felt the heat of her husband's fury rising, theatrical, to fill the hall.

'The cheek of it,' he was saying to an audience he could only imagine hung on every word. 'The absolute cheek of it.' Then he stopped, his abrupt silence leaving space for the muted *dunk-dunk-dunk* rhythm of an insistent bass line delivered by distant hi-fi speakers.

'And they've left the music on!' he said, the pitch of his voice rising to a point. 'Can you believe this? They've left the fucking music on.'

Kelly closed her eyes. It helped, in a way.

Number Twelve

Three days later, Daniel Dormer woke to find his wife and son had left during the night. They'd taken the Saab, his mother-in-law's jewellery box, and the first edition of *Brave New World* which they'd found in a second-hand bookshop in Frome during their honeymoon. Kelly had left a note on the kitchen table – four pages, double sided – in which she laid out exactly why she was not coming back. He read only the first page before consigning the rest to the fire in the living room.

It didn't make any sense to him. Number twelve was the only house left on Hope Street. He had been right all along. He had done the right thing. He had acted in an exemplary manner and he had absolutely nothing to be ashamed about.

So why was there now this hole in his house where his family had once been? It felt inexplicable. It felt unfair.

It was too early to open a beer but he did so anyway, sitting in his armchair in the lounge, the thin rhythm of the sound system from number seven tapping into focus whenever he allowed himself silence. It seemed to him that the same ten or twelve tracks were cycling over and over. Awful music. Cheap. *Poppy*. How the power hadn't been cut off yet he didn't know. He'd made enough phone calls. Left enough messages. *Good God*, it was grating.

He stared up at the corner of the ceiling.

This was how it started, he thought. In corners. In clefts. In alcoves where the shadows conspired and bred like spiderwebs. As he stared into the corner of the room, he imagined how the darkness might creep across the contours of the ceiling tiles, snaking across the room like tangles of long black hair.

The thought alarmed him. He leapt to his feet and edged closer, searching for evidence that his home had been compromised. He pulled the foot stool across the floor and climbed onto it so he could peer closer, but he felt nothing. There was nothing there at all.

As the days passed, his paranoia grew. He moved restlessly from room to room, searching for signs, brushing his fingers across the walls and floors, inspecting his home's infrastructure, looking for anything that might demonstrate to him how it was destined to fail.

There was a picture in the dining room that Kelly had loved, but which he had never warmed to. In it, a woman sat alone in a cluttered country kitchen, her head turned slightly to look out of the painting, her expression a little arch as though she had only just realised she had been seen, caught in the act of something impossible to prove. He didn't know the artist, he'd never asked. But on that particular afternoon, he was struck with the idea that the kitchen in the painting was starting to become unlivable in the same ways as the houses on Hope Street.

There was nothing to support this hypothesis. The painting hadn't changed in any meaningful way; the colours were still vivid and bright. But Daniel's fear was irrational and untamed, he only needed to see the picture from a slightly different perspective to assume it had become the breach he had been looking for. He took it with both hands and tore it from the wall, throwing it to the floor.

Staring at the discoloured rectangle it left behind, his fear was compounded as it dawned on him just how little of his house he could actually see, and the realisation made him stagger backwards, inadvertently stamping on the glass frame and making it splinter under his heel.

Over the next few days, he worked his way through every room, clearing each of furniture, pictures, carpets, light fittings, as though the corruption could breed in the spaces they had occupied. Out went the computers, the accounts, the family photographs. Out went the flat-screen television, the hi-fi, his wife's paperbacks, his son's toys. Out went everything with gaps and nooks and spaces where shadows could be smuggled in.

He stacked everything in the front garden, the pile teetering dangerously until it spilled into the road. He didn't care. He had too much work to do. He emptied cupboards in the kitchen, he tipped out the drawers. He retrieved his Makita drill from the shed and pulled down the internal doors. He tore up the carpets and fought them through the doorway. He hacked away at the laminate, exposing the real wooden floorboards beneath. They looked bald and dusty, unused to being seen. He bought paint – white paint – and worked through every room, every wall, leaving them as bright and blinding as he could. He surprised himself when he started to sing along to the hum of the music from number seven. He'd heard the songs so often now, he knew all the words. They would see. His wife, his son. When they came back, they would see. Layer after layer after layer, he painted, as though he might ward off the darkness by making the whole house shine.

Acknowledgements

That this book exists a second time is something of a surprise. Thank you Gary Budden dusting it off, thank you enormously to Angela Slatter for an introduction and thank you to Luke Bird for the gorgeous cover.

From the previous version, my debts remain largely the same. Thank you Gary Budden -- again, George Sandison, Dion Winton-Polak and everyone at the much missed Unsung Stories.

Enormous gratitude to Andy Cox, Simon Strantzas, Michael Kelly and all the editors who have supported my work over the past few years.

"Passion Play" and "Dogsbody" were first published in Black Static #38 (2014) & #54 (2016), TTA Press; "Two Brothers" was first published in *Aickman's Heirs* edited by Simon Strantzas (2015) Undertow Publications; "Breadcrumbs", "Her First Harvest" and "The End of Hope Street" were first published in Interzone #264 (2016), #258 (2015) & #266 (2016), TTA Press.

Thank you Nina Allan, Nathan Ballingrud, John Clute, John Costello, Ellen Datlow, Samuel R. Delany, Geetanjali Dighe, David Edison, Fabio Fernandes, Alia Formoy, Neil Gaiman, Jennifer Giesbrecht, Neile Graham, Elizabeth Hand, Sarah Hickingbottom, Joe Hill, Catriona Hopton, James Hoskins, Les Howle, Nicole Idar, Alex Kane, Margo Lanagan, Vicki Lloyd, Usman T. Malik, Liam Meilleur, Shannon Peavey, Bob Pomfret, Nick Salestrom, Kelly Sandoval, Alix Sky Solano, Michael Taylor, Paul Tremblay, Hugo Xiong, Neon Yang, E. Lily Yu and Helena Bell who personally kicked almost all of these stories until they stopped squeaking.

Finally, thank you to Helen Marshall for the world.

About the author

Malcolm Devlin is the author of *And Then I Woke Up* (2022), *Engines Beneath Us* (2019) and the collections *You Will Grow Into Them* (2017) and *Unexpected Places to Fall From* (2021). His short fiction has been published in *Interzone*, *Black Static* and *Shadows and Tall Trees*. He currently lives in Brisbane, Australia.

Influx Press is an independent publisher based in London, committed to publishing innovative and challenging literature from across the UK and beyond.

www.influxpress.com
@Influxpress